Where was she?

The question pounde[illegible]
with a throbbing pain. And it was really a ridiculous question. She knew she was at the Palazzo di Medici, in Venice. She was a guest there, of course. A guest of the old contessa—and of Marcus di Medici. Marcus . . .

She opened her eyes slowly, cautiously. The first thing she saw was her own hand, lying beside her face on the silk-covered pillow. For some reason her long fingers appeared very delicate. Even her nails, with their polish of soft bronze, seemed vulnerable against the deep indigo of the sheets. Indigo . . .

The silk in itself was not alarming. Marcus di Medici preferred the cool feel of silk; all the beds in the palazzo were garbed in silk. It was the color that was so chilling.

Indigo silk. She was in Marcus di Medici's bedroom—and in Marcus di Medici's bed.

HEATHER E. GRAHAM lives in Florida where she indulges her love of swimming and boating. Her work experience has been varied and unusual and includes time spent as a model, an actress and a barmaid. She was once actually tied to a railroad track to create publicity for the dinner theater where she was acting. She is married with four children.

The di Medici Bride is Heather E. Graham's first novel for Worldwide.

The di Medici Bride

BY

HEATHER E. GRAHAM

WORLDWIDE BOOKS
London • Sydney • Toronto

All the characters in this book have no existence outside the imagination of the Author, and have no relation whatsoever to anyone bearing the same name or names. They are not even distantly inspired by any individual known or unknown to the Author, and all the incidents are pure invention.

First published in Great Britain in 1987 by Worldwide Books, Eton House, 18–24 Paradise Road, Richmond, Surrey TW9 1SR

ISBN 0 373 50584 1

09/0587

Printed and bound in Great Britain by Cox & Wyman Ltd, Reading

For Cheryl Keller, Judy Rodriguez –
and the Coral Gables/South Miami Khoury League

Prologue

Oh, no... where the hell was she?

The question pounded in Christina's mind along with the throbbing pain that viciously attacked her temples.

And it was really a ridiculous question. She knew she was at the Palazzo di Medici, in Venice. She was a guest there, of course. A guest of the old contessa... and of Marcus di Medici....

Marcus...

She opened her eyes slowly, cautiously.

The first thing she saw was her own hand, lying beside her face on the silk-covered pillow. For some reason her long fingers appeared very delicate there. Even her nails, with their polish of soft bronze, seemed vulnerable against the deep indigo of the sheets.

Indigo...

Her fingers clutched convulsively against the smooth sensual material of the pillowcase. The silk in itself was not alarming. Marcus di Medici preferred the feeling of cool silk to cotton; all the beds in the palazzo were garbed in silk.

It was the color of the silk that was so chilling.

Christina opened her eyes wider. Without daring to twist her head, she further surveyed the room. Soft Oriental rugs lay pleasingly against a polished cream Venetian tile floor. The walls were papered in a subdued gold that lightened the effect of the deep indigo draperies and mahogany furniture. Across a breezy distance, highlighted by the morning dazzle of the sun streaming through French doors, was a large Queen Anne dresser, its only ornament a French Provincial clock.

Chris closed her eyes and swallowed miserably. Memories of the past night returned in fragments to compound the ferocity of her headache. Marcus . . . exercising his considerable charm. But she should have known. . . . No, that wasn't being honest with herself. She *had* known. She had been as suspicious as he. She had sadly overrated her own competence and confidence with the male of the species.

Not with just any male. With Marcus di Medici.

She had been certain she could be just as charming . . . and just as evasive. But she had played out her hand—and lost.

Lost what? She didn't want to remember, but she had to.

Panic gripped her for a moment. She had no doubt that she was lying in his bed. But when she refocused her eyes on her hand, she felt a tingling of relief. A white lace cuff rimmed her wrist. She was dressed.

Her relief faded. How had she come to be dressed this way? She had left the palazzo in a black cocktail gown.

She remembered him, waiting at the foot of the stairs, elegant and overwhelmingly male in a black tux.

He wore it so well. His shoulders were so broad, his waist and hips so arrestingly trim. His tanned olive complexion had looked almost copper against the crisp white of his shirt; his hair was a jet deeper than the fabric of his suit.

And from beneath the dark arched brows, his eyes had been a startling arresting blue. A deep blue. So deep that they, too, could appear black.

Or indigo . . . like the sheets.

But last night they had been alight with charm and suave pleasure at the sight of her. Still, she hadn't doubted for a moment the measure of cunning beneath the civil facade of the beast. She had been careful, so careful. But not careful enough.

She clearly remembered the walk around St. Mark's Square. She remembered laughing and cleverly avoiding his questions. She could see them now as they tossed bread crumbs to the pigeons that thronged before the ancient cathedral.

And she could clearly see them in the gondola as they skimmed along the canals, listening to the subtle music of the gondolier.

She remembered the restaurant. the aroma of the masterfully prepared appetizers. The mussels, the clams Casino, the scungilli, tiny squid prepared so tenderly in garlic and oil that they were the sweetest delicacy to the tongue.

Chris closed her eyes tightly. She could recall exactly how his arm had rested leisurely on the back of the booth behind her, his hand so relaxed. Yet she had already known its strength. His palm was broad, but he had long tapering fingers that could tighten like talons or touch with tenderness. His hands were tanned to the same golden color as his sharply handsome features, and they had gleamed against the white sleeve that peeked from beneath the black jacket.

She even remembered the look of his blunt black-banded watch against his wrist. The last time she could remember noticing had been 10:05 P.M.

Perhaps it had been the wine. He had ordered a vintage as smooth as the silk of his sheets, and she had been nervous, yet trying not to betray her wariness. Perhaps she had imbibed too freely. She had only thought herself watchful because he had known all along that she was watching him. She had meant to charm and seduce him, but instead he had charmed and seduced her. She had been a fool, easily manipulated. Twice a fool. She had thought herself so competent, confident, bright and sophisticated, a worthy player of the game. But she had known that she was out with a well-dressed panther, one with a frightening veneer of charisma and cordiality.

Sophisticated . . . Oh, what a fool she had been! He had taken her out and given her wine, and she had been as easy to handle as a girl of sixteen. She had thought herself strong and determined enough to trick a murderer, to expose the secrets of the past! She had played with Marcus di Medici. . . .

Her last memories were still a blur she could scarcely straighten out even now within the confused confines of her pain-racked mind.

Another ride along the canals. A hushed stop at the dock of a crumbling old cathedral. Strange, but she could vividly remember the frescoes on the high, gracefully arched ceilings. . . .

He had whispered to her. Murmured gently and tenderly. He had clutched her fingers firmly but without painful pressure as he had led her along. Her hand had appeared so starkly pale and fragile against his strong dark ones.

Snatches of Italian and some other language—perhaps Latin?—haunted her memory, but they had been spoken so rapidly that she couldn't recall a word.

And then, try as she might, she could remember nothing more. Nothing more . . .

Nothing! Except the sound of her own laughter, a mocking echo in her ears.

Chills suddenly raked through her, sending ice and fire hurtling with erratic speed and fever along the length of her spine. He was in the room. She knew it. When she opened her eyes once more and turned, she would find him leisurely leaning against the frame of the French doors. But there would be nothing truly leisurely about him. Even in moments of repose, he was still full of leashed tension. Always he was the panther, stalking, ready to strike. He had been playing with her, toying with her from the very beginning. But now it was time for the kill, time for the sophisticated beast to show his face.

Chris tightened her eyes in a moment's frenzy of fear, anger and reproach.

The man might very well be a murderer, but she had been so sure of herself! She'd thought herself a Mata Hari, and now she was paying the price, lying in a murderer's bed.

No! an inner voice shrieked. *Not Marcus!*

What a fool she was. Even now, when she couldn't believe the price she had paid, she wanted to defend him. She wanted to believe in him.

There was a slight movement in the room. A whisper of sound in the air. He was watching her, Christina knew. Watching her, and waiting. He could afford to wait with amused and taunting patience. She had nowhere to run, nowhere to go.

She didn't want to open her eyes; she didn't want to turn to him. She didn't want to face the consequences of what had passed between them in the misty oblivion of last night.

She heard the quiet ticking of the clock on the dresser. It was persistent. Monotonous. And yet it seemed to grow in volume, mocking her, and suddenly she could bear it no longer. He was there, and the force of his presence caused her to open her eyes and turn . . . and meet his smoldering indigo stare.

He was leaning against the doors, as she had suspected, dressed in a caramel velour robe. The V neck of the haphazardly belted garment bared the breadth of his chest with its profusion of crisp dark hair. A gold St. Christopher's medallion seemed to emphasize the masculinity of copper flesh and muscle.

His legs, too, were bare beneath the knee-length hem of the robe. Long sinewy calves, covered seductively with short black hair, gave way to bare feet. Chris even noted the particulars about his feet. They were long no-nonsense feet, planted squarely on the floor.

"Buongiorno. Buongiorno, amore mio."

The soft taunt of the words brought her eyes back to his. There was no pretense of charm within those dark-blue depths in the demanding light of day, only smoldering fire. Something that warned that the harnessed tension and electricity that seemed to vitalize the air about him could explode too easily.

He began to stalk slowly toward the bed. His full sensual lips were curled into a slight mocking grin of cold amusement. Chris curled her fingers tightly around the bunched-up sheets, her eyes on him with mounting wariness and a fear she couldn't subdue despite her staunchest efforts. She waited to fling harsh questions at him. No, not questions. Demands. But she couldn't seem to form the words she wanted to say.

Because, despite everything, despite the horrible web of deception that had brought her here, she was fatally attracted to him. Like a moth to flame. There was a strength about him that could not be resisted. He mesmerized; he seduced; he wielded an indomitable power with the flick of an eye, a wave of the hand.

He had her cornered. She had to fight, had to resist.

He stood still before her, then calmly sat beside her on the edge of the bed. The faint scent of his aftershave assaulted her senses and warned her afresh of the raw masculine strength that was inherently a part of him. She narrowed her eyes and stiffened, preparing to do battle.

But before she could lash into him, he chuckled, the sound dry and biting. One dark brow rose with cool mockery and cutting amusement.

"What? Can she be angry? Dismayed? How so, my love? You wanted a di Medici man. You said so often enough. Well, you've gotten one. I could resist the temptation no longer. But perhaps you feel that you brought the wrong di Medici to the altar?"

Fury stabbed through her. She raised a hand swiftly toward his ruggedly hewn features, but he moved more swiftly, catching her wrists with a cold gleam of triumph in his eyes.

She felt him as she might a fire. His touch seared her, warmed her, frightened her as she had never known fear before. He was so close, so intimate, so demanding....

She cried out inwardly again. No! Marcus could not be guilty of blackmail—or murder. Not Marcus. For all that she sometimes hated and feared in him, she could not accept that Marcus could be evil, or that he could harm her. She just couldn't believe it. Not in her heart nor her soul. Not when, beneath everything, she was falling in love, and that love just wouldn't allow her to see evil....

Because it wasn't there. Not in Marcus. No matter how dangerous he could appear, no matter what the evidence led her to see, she knew inside that it couldn't be Marcus.

But . . . she had married him. The fragments of the dream that she didn't want to accept were true. She had been conned.

"Why?" she breathed, incredulous and furious and achingly aware of him against her. And as his handsome features came nearer, she hollowly echoed the question within her own heart.

Why? She had always believed that he wanted her. She had also believed that he despised her. So why did he have such a seductive power over her?

Like now. When the triumph faded from his eyes, she caught a glint of sorrow, of tenderness. Like fencers, they had often circled around one another. Like the moth and flame, they had too often come dangerously close together.

What exactly had he done? What had *she* done? Last night . . . could it have been real?

"Cara . . ." he murmured, and the tenderness remained, an apology he would not put into words. He meant to play his hand to the end. "Why? Because it was your wish, of course."

He had duped her. Cunningly. With carefully planned intent. Why? Had it been love, he would never have had the need. The money?

"Cara . . ." he repeated, touching her cheek tenderly with his knuckles. Chris jerked from his touch, lowering her head as tears stung her eyes. He stood up impatiently. "We have both known that something had to happen between us. Did you take me for a saint? I have only given you what you wished. Or perhaps," he said mockingly, "it was truly Tony whom you wished to captivate. He is the more malleable, is

he not? But, alas! As you Americans are so fond of saying, you have made your own bed. Now you shall lie in it."

He had added insult to injury. Anger washed through her like a raging tide, and she hurled her silk-covered pillow in his direction.

He started to laugh. "Another cliché, but you're truly beautiful when you're angry."

"Why?" Chris raged.

An elite brow rose. "Why? You were there, too, my love. Oh, I admit, we were neither of us completely lucid, but . . . that is the course of love, my sweet."

It was a lie. He had planned the entire thing. The dinner, the wine, the gondola . . . the wedding.

But why?

He started to open the door. Chris leaped from the bed, racing toward him. "Wait! What are you doing? We have to do something about this. Surely we can arrange an annulment—"

"An annulment?" He kept smiling, but she sensed his anger, his controlled tension. He caught her shoulders, his grip a shade too tight.

"*Cara*, I am on my way downstairs to make the announcement to the family." His eyes narrowed. Warningly. "If you have any sense, Christina, you will keep your mouth shut. You will give the appearance of a sheepish—embarrassed, perhaps—but very happy bride. For God's sake! Haven't you the sense to stay alive!"

His grip tensed as their eyes clashed in anger. She was certain that he wanted to shake her. He released her instead with a little shove. He opened the door and exited, closing it sharply behind him.

Christina swore vehemently.

The door opened again. He was smiling. "Don't fret, *mia moglie*. I'll come back to you...quickly." His voice was husky, tinged with laughter. She would gladly have struck him.

Mia moglie. My wife.

Christina started to shake.

Why? she screamed to herself in a raging silence. She closed her eyes. Again, despite her anger and confusion, she couldn't bear to condemn him. Perhaps . . . perhaps he *had* married her to protect her. It wasn't love, but perhaps it was, at least, protection. Caring. Perhaps he knew just as she did that things were very, very wrong, that someone near them was guilty of holding deadly secrets. Someone was guilty of blackmail.

And someone was guilty of murder.

Chris bit down on a knuckle, trying hard not to become hysterical. She sank in confusion back onto the bed.

How had she come to this? Trapped in a web that was not of her own weaving, cast into this game where she didn't begin to know the rules.

Falling in love with a man she often thought she hated at the same time.

Hated . . . and feared.

She should have stayed away from Venice. From Contini and the di Medicis. She'd intended to do just that. Chris had never thought she harbored a determination to flush out the roots of her past. . . .

Until the mime troupe had come to Venice. Until Alfred Contini had sought her out, and brought her to the palazzo.

And begged her to help him, right before dying in her arms.

Chapter One

Twilight was coming, and with it a sudden breeze swept through St. Mark's Square. Chris Tarleton looked around, and smiled slowly.

The lights had come on. The last vestiges of a red-and-gold dusk were combining with the soft artificial light to create a shimmering splendor all around the ancient Basilica, the bridges, the Venetian-Gothic elegance of the Doge's Palace and, of course, the water. The Grand Canal rippled and sparkled behind her with the brilliance of a thousand gems. It was a spellbinding moment for her; this was Venice, in all its artistic glory, in all its magical mythical beauty.

Then she shivered, touched by a strange feeling of déjà vu. She had loved the place before she had come here. Before she had seen the multitude of pigeons that flocked to the Square, and the toddlers who screamed with delight and laughter as they chased the birds. Before she had ever raised her head to see the two great granite columns at the water's edge with their respective figures of St. Theodore and the winged lion of St. Mark. Before she had felt the magic that was Venice by night...the laughter and the excitement. This was not just Italy, it was Venice. It was the Renaissance, the Far Eastern influence that had come here in the days of Marco Polo. It was beautiful and totally unique—and by nightfall, absolute magic.

But it was not strange—Chris knew that it shouldn't have been. She had been born here, but until yesterday, when her mime troupe had arrived to prepare for this evening's performance in the Square, she would have said with all honesty that she had absolutely no memory of the place. But then, she thought wryly, she had left when she was four and grown up in Detroit, Michigan—far, far from this world of gondolas and canals and ancient architecture that spanned the centuries and led back to a distant different time.

A shiver ran up her spine again, another whisper of breeze swept by, and near her, a group of the ever-present pigeons burst into flight. Venice. Her parents had seemed to hate the place. And in her conscious mind, she'd harbored no great wish to return to the city. But when she had learned that it was on their schedule, she had been fascinated; she had experienced the first of the shivers, as if she had known she would come back, as if she had been compelled, as if the performance were merely an excuse for her coming here. Venice was her city; she had known it as soon as she had seen it.

"Christina, you are ready, yes?"

Chris started, then turned to smile at Jacques d'Pry, the head of the school in Paris and the leader of a prestigious corps of mimes. Jacques had been a favored pupil of the great Marceau, and he was a rigid taskmaster, an absolute disciplinarian. Chris had never minded the discipline or the hours and hours of physical exercise—sometimes abuse! she added to herself, with humor—that led to the perfection of her craft. She had always felt lucky, even blessed, to have been accepted as a student at the school. She had been stunned to have been chosen as a member of the professional corps that traveled across Europe each summer.

"*Oui*, Jacques," she murmured, tensing and flexing her fingers again and again. The fingers were, Jacques often stressed, perhaps the mime's greatest tool. There had been many sessions of total concentration, total silence, when they had done nothing but draw the thumb to the forefinger isometrically, so that when the performer reached for an individual string, the audience saw the string and felt its pull.

"Then come, please, we begin the show."

Jacques led the way through the milling crowd at the water's edge to a section of the Square, paved with marble and trachyte, that had been roped off for the performance. Tomas and Georgianne Trieste—two Parisian mimes who had fallen in love with the romance of silence—followed behind Chris, and behind them came the last of their group, Roberto Umbrio, a very dedicated and impassioned young man from the Basque Provinces. None of them spoke. Once they had started their approach to their "stage," the law of silence was in order.

A little girl cried out something in Italian and grabbed at Christina's white-gloved hand. Chris restrained a smile, widened her reddened mouth into an "O," and brought her other hand up to it in surprise. The child laughed delightedly, and Chris felt a familiar warmth fill her. The laughter of a child made the often dreary monotonous hours and hours of work worthwhile.

Moments later she was on, into her secret world. The lights, the beauty of the Square, were still there, as were the whispers of the audience, mainly in Italian but spattered with the excitement of many tongues. But they were all part of an outer world. Tonight she played Jacques's wife, alarmed at the prospect of his anger when he discovered a naughty escapade of the children—Georgianne, Roberto and Tomas. There was a door to be locked against him, and then she had to discover that she had locked herself in, rather than him out. There were invisible pulleys to work with, invisible chairs and stairs. And then there was the inevitable confrontation with her "husband," and her efforts to escape his wrath. But, of course, the husband intended no harm to his wife. All her fiascoes were her own, and he was left to shake his head at her foolishness and the disaster she brought upon herself.

There were two men in the audience who had not come to see the show; they had come to see Christina Tarleton.

One was an old man, older than his years. He was short and slim, balding, and the fringe of hair that remained had faded from black to snowdrift silver. His cheeks were gaunt; lines were deeply etched around eyes that defied time—brown eyes, deep and warm, yet sharply alert. And anxious now. Eyes that were focused intently on the girl on the pseudo stage.

It was easy to see that she was slim, as agile and graceful as the cats that haunted the streets of Rome. She was clad all in black: black tights, black flowing skirt, black knit top, black slippers. Only her hands were in white—white gloves. And her face was powdered with white to enhance the eyes, the expression and the mouth. Perhaps that was why he could see the color of her eyes so clearly. They were tawny, part green, part gold. Like the sun, they were alive with expression and warmth, and thickly fringed with honeyed lashes that matched the color of her hair. Her hair was pulled back, and it was neither blond nor brown; rather, it was a tawny shade of sun and honey somewhere in between. The old man was fascinated by her lithe movements, by the elegant strokes of her hands and fingers against the air, by the practiced twists and turns of her supple body.

Fascinated and . . .

Hurt. He clutched his hand to his chest suddenly; the pain, guilt and remorse went deep. For a moment he felt dizzy. She did not have her father's coloring, only his height and slim build. She did not look like James at all, and yet there was a look of him about her.

And standing there in the crowd, with the show proceeding before him, he wanted to reach out. To touch her. Did he feel that he could vindicate his sins against her father? he asked himself sharply. Something inside him cried, and he stared up at the Basilica suddenly, crossing himself and murmuring beneath his breath, "Blessed Jesu, forgive me."

He closed his eyes. In a minute the dizziness left him. He felt the same restlessness, the same *need* he had experienced when he had first seen the paper and read her name in the list of performers. He would make it up to this girl, and sweet, sweet Jesu, it was possible that the girl could help him. He was too old to go on as he had. His conscience could no longer bear the weight of his lie.

She was a Tarleton. A part of the trio. The name Tarleton belonged beside those of Contini and di Medici.

His lips, faded against the weathered wrinkles of his face, relaxed into a smile. A sudden peace had settled over his soul. Now he could watch the show; he knew what he would do at its conclusion.

But in time his smile slipped away. He wondered what she had been told about Venice—and what she might remember. Remember? Bah! She had been but a child.

Still, it was her heritage he intended to give her.

The second man who stood in the crowd assessed the girl with a cool sweep of sharp startling blue eyes. He was not at all old, and though his exact age might be indeterminable, he was obviously in the prime of his life. He was tall, and though his shoulders were broad, he gave the appearance of being a lean man. His suit was designed with impeccable taste; it hugged his trim form. And, despite a certain relentlessness, if not ruthlessness, about the firm square line of his jaw, he was a handsome man. More than handsome. He exuded an assurance that was a power unto itself. When he spoke, it was with the inner knowledge that his quiet words would be taken as a command; when he moved, it was never with any question of where he was going. He was capable of an absolute stillness, of listening, watching and waiting. His intelligence was shrewd; his thoughts were seldom known, for an invisible shield could fall over his eyes with a blink, and the true import of his words could be hidden in a deadly fashion.

Tarleton.

Like the old man, he had seen the name in the papers, and if curiosity had not drawn him here, the suspicion that the old man was coming would have brought him anyway.

He watched the girl and he watched the old man, wondering at the pained expression in the old man's eyes. Something seemed to light a quick fuse to his temper. Contini was an old man now. Old and weary. The Tarleton girl had no right to be here, dredging up painful memories that had been best buried by time.

Marcus di Medici lifted his eyes from the old man to the stage, and he felt as if anger sizzled and seared in each and every one of his nerve endings. His father had died so senselessly all those years ago—at the hands of a Tarleton. And now *she* was back. The sound of her name in his mind ripped open old wounds; the sight of her made him remember until he felt all the pain again, just as if he were once more a boy of twelve. . . .

He crossed his arms over his chest, adjusting his stance, and his lashes fell briefly over the agate of his eyes. He closed his heart and his mind took over objectively. She was good. Lithe, smooth, graceful, like a young animal, composed of fluid sinews and vitality. She seemed to move with the ease of the wind or flowing water.

And then he discovered uncomfortably that he was looking at her too objectively—as a woman. A heat ran through him that had nothing to do with temper, anger, regret or the past. For a moment every thought was washed from his mind except one. She was, in the black mime's outfit that clung so tightly to her supple form, the most desirable woman he had ever seen. She was beautiful. And that beauty was demonstrated in every movement. He discovered that he was wishing he could hold her, feel the vibrance of the liquid curves and hollows of her body beneath his hands, strip away the fabric and the makeup and make fevered love to the woman beneath.

Startled, Marcus gave himself a little shake and smiled dryly at the intimate path his imagination had taken. A comedy was taking place on stage, nothing risqué.

His smile faltered. She was the daughter of a murderer. And not just any murderer. She was the daughter of the man who had killed his father.

For a moment his every muscle went rigid, and then he forced himself to relax. She had come to Venice with the mimes. She would leave with the mimes. She would be gone, and the past would fade into memory once again.

Marcus gazed at Contini, then returned his attention to the show. Without his knowledge, a smile curved his lips again, small and a little crooked. He was suddenly remembering her as a child. Even at four she had been a pretty thing. Willful, spoiled and pert, determined and stubborn. She had driven him crazy. But when he had been half-ready to kill her, she had looked at him wide-eyed, her tawny gaze filled with tears, and his anger had melted away.

He could even remember thinking that James Tarleton was going to be in trouble by the time his daughter reached her teens. At four she had known how to wield her power. A little imp—a practiced seductress with the flutter of her lashes. Pretty and as bright as a star. She'd had an almost uncanny command of both English and Italian—and the powerful ability to use all her feminine wiles.

Marcus sighed, slipped his hands into his pockets and turned away although the show wasn't over. The sins of the fathers, he reflected, did not fall upon the offspring. Contini, Marcus was certain, intended to approach her.

And if he asked her to the palazzo, Marcus decided firmly, he would be courteous. He would make her welcome but hope that she did not stay long enough to rake up the ashes of his past.

"And so ends another season!" Jacques muttered happily in English. He had just shaken hands with the last child waiting in line to meet them; he had only to meet with the producers of the show and the summer's work would be officially over.

Chris smiled a little secretively, watching her teacher and employer with affection and amusement. In class Jacques spoke French exclusively. On tour he spoke English. He was, however, a master of at least five languages.

"What shall we do with the evening in celebration?" Georgianne asked excitedly, laughing. "The night is young, and so are we! And this is Venice!"

Her husband grinned dryly at Chris. "Doesn't she sound just like 'An American in Paris'?"

Chris laughed. "Well, she's right, you know. We're off. We should be doing something."

Jacques lifted a hand to them, then wandered off to finish his business with the show's producers. Only Roberto seemed brooding and intense, as usual, as they waited near the lightly rippling water.

"We've got a month off," he reminded them all. "Tomas, Georgianne, what do you plan to do with the time?"

Georgianne smiled. "Party! We're going to go back to Rome—we did throw three coins in the fountain, you know. Roma, Napoli and then Nice and Monte Carlo." She grimaced very prettily. "We want to gamble away some of our hard-earned money. And you?"

"I will go back to school early and work to improve my craft," Roberto said reproachfully. The others exchanged quick smiles, but said nothing. Georgianne linked an arm with Chris.

"And you, Chris? What will you do? You are welcome to keep company with Tomas and me."

Chris laughed. "No thanks. I can't imagine joining a pair of honeymooners." She sobered. "I was thinking about going home. Jacques wants me to teach next year, you know. And I'm not sure what I want to do. I have been 'An American in Paris' for three years now. And I have to start deciding what I really want to do with the rest of my life."

"Oh, to the devil with the rest of our lives!" Tomas proclaimed. "I say we find a lovely spot for dinner, indulge in rare and delicious wine, dance and—"

"Tomas!" Georgianne murmured, interrupting. "Look, that old man over there is watching us most peculiarly."

"Yes, he is," Tomas murmured. He looked at Chris. "Why don't you go over there and find out what he wants?"

"Me!" Chris exclaimed, startled.

"Of course!"

"I don't speak Italian!"

Tomas frowned. "I thought you said you were born here?"

Chris sighed. "Tomas, I left Italy when I was four. And that," she added wryly, "was over two decades ago. I never had much occasion to use the language on the streets of Detroit, and I've only managed to make my French halfway decent this year."

"It doesn't matter," Roberto interrupted tensely. "The man is coming to us."

The man was coming to them, straight to them, Chris realized. And then she experienced another one of her déjà vu sensations. Before he took another step, she knew that he was coming to her. And although she didn't actually recognize him, she knew that he was Alfred Contini.

Tingling sensations raced through her, and she was left to wonder again if she had really come to Venice because of the mime troupe, or if her coming had really been preordained. For a brief second she was afraid. And then the fear was gone.

She wanted this; she wanted this confrontation. Just as she had wanted to come back to Venice. She was curious—no, damn it, *compelled*—to find out the truth. What had driven her parents from Venice, a city they once had loved?

Contini was old, Chris thought, as he walked toward her. Very old—much too old for her to have remembered him. If she did have a memory of him locked away in her mind, just as she had of the Piazza San Marco, it was a memory that was twenty-one years old. And unlike granite and marble, a man would change drastically in that amount of time.

Small and slim, he still had a look of strength about him like stone. Until he had almost reached her. And then something tender and a little bit . . . frightened? . . . seemed to crumple his old face as he reached out a frail hand to her.

"Christi?"

A quick chord of distant memory caused her to shiver briefly. Christi. Contini's name for her.

She smiled and accepted his hand warmly, strangely touched by a flood of emotion for this worn and aged man who was reaching out to her.

"Alfred!" she replied softly.

"Ah, Christi! So you do remember me?"

"No!" Chris laughed and shook her head. "But I knew who you must be if this is Venice—and it is."

Christina quickly introduced him to the rest of the group. Alfred replied graciously, but his attention was completely for her.

"Christi, you will do an old man the honor of having dinner with him?"

Georgianne cleared her throat, apparently somewhat suspicious of the elegantly dressed, elderly Venetian. "Christina, do you remember our plans?"

Chris hesitated for a second, suddenly and deeply aware that her answer was going to mean everything to her life. She could almost see herself standing at a crossroads. . . .

Ridiculous, she told herself impatiently. She couldn't pretend that she wasn't haunted by the past, and she had never gotten over the vague dream that she could completely solve the mystery of why her parents had left Venice with such sadness in their hearts.

She had known that she herself would seek out Contini.

Chris turned to Georgianne with a bright smile. "Georgianne, I hope you all will excuse me. I haven't seen Signor Contini since I was a small child. Do you mind?"

Tomas shrugged. The two years he had known Chris had proved to him that she was an adult. Charming when she chose to be, competently assertive when she did not.

Chris felt a little like laughing. She could see the emotions darting quickly through their eyes. Suspicion, worry, and then that mutual shrug. What on earth could happen to her in the company of such an old man?

She felt a tug of affection and appreciation for their protective attitude. It was nice to have such caring friends. Their ensemble work made them more than professional associates, perhaps more than friends. A little like family.

"You know how to get back to the pensione, right?" Tomas asked her.

"Yes, yes, thank you Tomas," Chris said.

"Miss Tarleton will be perfectly safe, I assure you," Alfred Contini interjected. "I will see to it. Christi?"

"I'd love to have dinner," she said brightly, and she waved to the others as she moved away with him. "Would you mind, though, if we returned to the pensione for a moment first?" She grimaced. "I'd like to remove this makeup."

"Certainly, certainly!" Contini said agreeably.

Chris would have taken one of the vaporetti, the mass transit boats that moved through the canals, but Contini was already raising a hand to summon a gondola—much more expensive. She would have protested had she been on a date, but she swallowed her words. From Alfred's finely tailored suit, it appeared that nothing much had changed from what little she had learned from her grudging mother. Contini was a very affluent man, able to hire all the gondolas he might wish.

He watched her after they had taken their seats in the small boat. Then he grimaced apologetically. "Forgive me. When I saw your name, I could not help but come."

Chris smiled ruefully. "I believe I would have come to you if you hadn't come to me."

He hesitated a moment. She couldn't see his features clearly, because they had suddenly passed from light to shadow.

"What do you know of the past, Christi?"

"Only what my mother told me," Chris answered honestly.

"And that is—no, no, never mind. We will wait until we sit over dinner, *si*?" He cast a quick glance toward their gondolier.

Chris smiled at him. *"Si."*

Soon they turned off the Grand Canal and followed one of the smaller waterways that led to her pensione. Contini pointed out a number of the grander buildings, and told her the names and histories of a number of the crests on the red-striped poles that guarded many gondolas in their berths.

When they reached her pensione Chris quickly washed her face, then glanced at Contini's very expensive suit. She excused herself and hurriedly changed into a white silk blouse and black velvet pants.

Then they were out on the water again, soon following the Grand Canal to an elegant waterside *ristorante* near St. Mark's Church and the Doge's Palace. It was a very lovely spot, with each table secluded by shrubbery. Theirs was right by the water, with a wrought-iron fence separating them from the brilliance of the canal, sparkling in a multitude of colors beneath subdued lighting.

Contini asked if he might do the ordering for them. Chris lifted her hands, laughed and agreed. The old man was absolutely charming—a perfect escort.

He told her that they would begin with antipasto, enjoy a bowl of scracciatelli, have cappelletti for their pasta, and then veal for their main course.

Chris laughed and told him that in the States, the pasta would be the main course. He grimaced, then suggested a deep red Valpolicella. The antipasto and soup were accompanied by light conversation, and then, when their waiter had left them in their secluded corner, Alfred smiled again and looked at her as he toyed with his soupspoon.

"The show was very good. I enjoyed it. You are a talented young woman. What made you choose to become a mime?"

Chris finished an olive, took a sip of her wine and shrugged. "First, thank you for the compliment. As to being a mime . . . well, I started out at about eight wanting to be a gymnast. But I was behind the kids who had started out at four, five and six, and some of the vaults scared me a little. A few years later my mother was determined that I should have dance lessons—"

"Ah," Contini interrupted with affectionate laughter, "yes, Joanne would have wanted her daughter in dance! She always wanted her little girl to be such a lady, such an angel!"

Chris couldn't help but respond to his warm reference to her mother with a feeling of warmth herself. And though her mother had warned her to stay away from Venice—"it just wasn't a good place for a Tarleton"—she had always seemed sad to have left, sad to be forced into hating people who had once meant so much to her.

"Mother can be a bit much, can't she?" Chris asked ruefully. "And I take it I wasn't exactly an angel?"

"Ah, certainly an angel!" Contini said, his dark eyes sparkling. "But an angel with the devil in her soul! You were . . . spirited."

Chris raised one eyebrow. "Not at all sweet and mannerly?"

"Only when you thought you would get your way. And how is your mother? Well, I hope?"

"Very well. She remarried when I was in college. A very nice man. He's a ranger at a national park out west, in Montana. He and Mom are very happy."

"That is good. That is very good," Alfred Contini murmured, looking down at his soup. "Please, tell me more about your work."

Chris shrugged, paused for a minute, then continued. "I started taking dance. Then we went to Chicago one weekend when I was a senior in high school, and Marcel Marceau happened to be making an appearance. At the time," Chris said with a laugh, "I didn't even want to go. But once I had seen him, I was hooked. I knew I wanted to be a mime. Mother—" Chris paused to exchange a wry glance with Alfred "—had in her heart and mind decided that I needed a complete liberal education, but I was able to combine the two by finding a college in California with a wonderful, wonderful department for the performing arts. Anyway," she said, grinning, "I managed to make a great deal of money with some friends doing street theater, and I came straight over to Paris to audition for the school there. I was very lucky—I was accepted. And so here I am now."

"And what will you do now? The tour is over, isn't it?"

"Yes. I've been offered a teaching position for the fall. I have about a month to think it over."

Contini nodded, but said nothing. Their waiter had returned to clear away their plates and replace them with the pasta dishes. Contini refilled Christina's wineglass.

"So," he said then, "what do you know of The di Medici Galleries?"

"Very little," Chris admitted. "Only that you and my father and Mario di Medici went into business together. And that the galleries are now world famous. And—" she hesitated briefly "—that Mario di Medici died, and my father chose to leave the company and return to the United States."

Contini shrugged. "Yes, simply put, but all true." His dark eyes took on a distant look, as if he were suddenly lost in a mist of memory. "I met your father at the end of the war. And Mario... well, I'd known Mario most of my life. Your father and I were working on certain..." He paused, waving a hand as he searched for the English word.

He'd been talking about the war. "Reconstructive projects?" she asked.

"*Si, si.* He was a wonderful man. He had the power and the enthusiasm to bring men together. And he could sell canal water to a Venetian!"

"He provided the sales and business know-how," Chris murmured.

"Yes. And I—I had the money. I had never liked Mussolini, or his association with Hitler. I'd taken my money out and put it into Swiss francs in a Swiss account long before the downfall of our country. And Mario...well, the di Medicis are one of the oldest and most respected families in Venice. Mario's was a bastard branch of an old family, perhaps, but centuries have a way of forgiving such a thing, you understand."

Chris nodded, hiding a smile. She did know that the di Medicis had been counts of Venice since the Renaissance—certainly long enough to be forgiven an indiscretion!

"Mario gave us his...class. Ah, Mario! He was both a gentleman and a gentle man. He knew art; he had an eye for the truly beautiful and antique. It was a wonderful partnership."

Chris set her fork down and swallowed her wine, feeling a slight tingling sensation that warned her that she was about to ask a question to which she wasn't sure she wanted an answer.

"What happened?"

"The statuette," Contini murmured.

"What?" Chris pressed him softly.

"There was a statuette in the galleries, and it disappeared. Suddenly we were at one another's throats, old friends such as we. Then we determined to talk it out aboard the *Trieste*, di Medici's yacht. We were all there that day. Mario and his wife, your father and mother. Sophia and I. Genovese, Joe, Antonio, Marcus . . ."

He was wandering, Chris realized. She leaned forward slightly. "Alfred? Please, what happened then?"

He looked at her suddenly, as if startled by her presence. But then he smiled sadly.

"Mario was lost. He...disappeared. They found his body days later. They pulled it out of the sea."

"And my father left."

"Yes, soon after your father left."

He drank his glass of wine quickly, seemed to shudder a bit, and then smiled again.

"Christi, you say that you have some time now. Please, would you think about coming to the palazzo to spend some time? To. . . to vacation with us? The galleries, they are your heritage, too, you know."

Chris didn't answer him right away; the waiter had returned to whisk away the pasta plates and serve the veal. She felt absurdly as if she were at a crossroads again—that her life might be deeply changed if she agreed.

But something might be lost if she did not. She was so curious to discover what had happened. She felt the pull of Venice, the irresistible draw that had affected her when she had stood in St. Mark's Square.

And she felt her heart beating furiously. There was a mystery here. It had to do with her life, her past, and she longed to solve it.

"Christi?"

She had taken a bite of her veal; startled by the pleading in the old man's voice, she looked up into his eyes, into a dark pool of misery.

"*Per piacere*, Christi! *Per piacere*. I am an old, old man, Christi. I need you."

"Need me?" she murmured.

"To be my friend."

"I—I am your friend, Alfred."

"Then you must come. You must come to the Palazzo di Medici!"

Chris frowned, setting down her fork. "Forgive me, Alfred, I don't mean to be rude. But I assume that the palazzo actually belongs to Mario's widow and his sons—"

"And they will greet you for me, I promise, Christi." She looked uncertain, and he waved a hand in the air. "The palazzo is very big . . . and it has been my home for decades. And Mario's sons, they are decent men. The palazzo belongs to Marcus . . . he is the eldest and the most responsible. Antonio, he is a little bit too much for the fun of things. You remember nothing about them? As a child you followed them both about and taunted them mercilessly!"

Chris shook her head. "I'm sorry. I was only four. I really don't remember much of anything."

She wondered why she was hesitating and putting this poor man through such anxiety when she knew she wanted to go to the palazzo. Perhaps being there would be like being in St. Mark's Square and her memories would come back to her.

She was determined to find out just what had happened to make any mention of Italy a painful thing in her family for so many years.

"I could come to the palazzo," she said slowly, and Alfred clapped his hands like a boy, then reached out to grasp her hand with a surprising strength.

"*Grazie*, *grazie*, Christi! I am grateful, I need you . . . to know your heritage."

His eyes seemed fevered; Chris felt a shiver of fear grip her for a moment. Why was he so fervent?

She closed her fingers around his, trying to reassure him. "It will be fun, Alfred."

She smiled, tugged lightly at her hand until he released it, and picked up her fork once again. She returned her attention to her food, then paused as the strangest sensation crept along her spine—an uncanny feeling of being watched.

She looked up and was stunned to encounter the bluest eyes she had ever seen. Crystal eyes, ice eyes. And they were locked on her intently.

She didn't realize that she gasped, but the man looking at her was so arresting that he could make a woman's heart falter, then race madly, her breath catch, then sweep through her lungs too quickly.

He was tall. And except for those eyes he was dark. Jet-black hair and brows, handsome features made up of rugged angles and planes turned almost copper from the sun. His suit was dark and extremely well tailored, enhancing a form that appeared lean, yet was well muscled. His shoulders were broad despite the trimness of his waist and hips. He was responding to a question from the maître d', and he almost appeared indolent. But Chris knew, from that very first glance of him, that he would never be truly indolent. If he were to walk slowly, it would never be because he didn't know exactly where he wanted to go. His gaze, she was certain, was a shrewd one, taking in all that could be seen by the naked eye—and some of what could not. He was dressed impeccably and seemed comfortable in his formal attire. She had the strangest feeling that he would be equally comfortable walking through a jungle in worn denims. There was something intangible about him....

A sense of danger, Chris mused, irritated that she shivered at the thought. And yet it was true. His looks—the jet hair, the startling blue eyes, the rugged tan on hard-cut masculine features—were not his greatest attraction. It was something about the way he stood, the way he moved. He could probably be a very ruthless man, Chris thought, and a relentless one. He would go where he wished to go, do what he wished to do with an implacable will and drive. And it was disturbingly exciting even as it was frightening, to feel his eyes on her. Chris thought that he would probably be as charming and as civil as his handsome attire; she was equally certain that, should he be crossed, he could strip away that charm as easily as the suit. And beneath it he would be a man of raw power, as impassioned and determined as a tiger freed from a cage.

"Christi, what is it?" Alfred asked.

"Pardon? Oh! I believe we're being watched. Rather, I know that we are."

Contini smiled. Christi was very beautiful, graceful and sophisticated. If she had not noticed that all eyes constantly turned to her, he certainly had. But he turned around with a frown, then murmured, "Ah, but it is Marcus!" He turned back to Chris. "The women, you know, they worry about me. And Marcus, well, he knows that a man of my age cannot cause much trouble, but he is the responsible one, so they send him!"

Marcus di Medici . . .

Chris felt her heart race once again as he began to move toward them. He was not a stranger who would wander off into the crowd and leave her merely to ponder the strength of the impression he had left upon her. He was Marcus di Medici, and if she was going to the palazzo, she was going to his home. The closer he came to their table, the more aware she became that he exuded something seductive, something dangerous.

Something on a very primal level, despite his sleek allure, which warned her to be on her guard. . . .

Chris shivered. The man was almost upon them; she felt hot one minute, chilly the next.

Stop! she commanded herself furiously. The chills subsided. She intended to be in control of the situation. She had long ago decided that if she wasn't beautiful, she had health and youth, and by the grace of those two, she was passably attractive. And she was certainly no teenager; she had toured half of Europe, was well educated and well traveled and—she thought with a quirk of humor—she even knew which fork to use.

She could be charming herself when she so chose, and if she planned on getting any answers about the past, Marcus was the man she would have to question, possibly haunt.

He had reached the table. He nodded curtly in her direction, but addressed Contini. "Alfred, I'm sorry for interrupting you. The household has been worried. It's quite late."

"Yes, yes, I suppose it is. You haven't interrupted me, Marcus, I'm very glad you're here. Miss Tarleton has just agreed to stay at the palazzo."

"Has she?"

Chris felt his eyes on her again. She forced a smile to her lips, wondering what to say. She had another strange premonition—though of what, she didn't know—as Marcus pulled a chair up to the table and took a seat, then signaled for a glass so he might pour himself some wine.

"Christi! Do you remember Marcus?"

"Not at all," she murmured sweetly, watching the man.

"Christi, Marcus di Medici."

She extended a hand. "It's a pleasure to meet you, Mr. di Medici," she said quietly, almost screaming when his hand touched hers. The pressure was firm, the touch as vibrant as a blazing fire.

He released her hand, sipped his wine and smiled. The smile seemed very, very dangerous. "Since I *do* remember you, Miss Tarleton, let me say that it is a pleasure to see you again."

"Thank you," she said simply.

"So?" He arched one dark brow. "You are coming to the palazzo? When?"

"I—"

"Tonight, Christi!" Contini said. "You must come tonight! Marcus, please, you must tell her that she is welcome, that she must come tonight."

Marcus turned to her and smiled, once again with little humor. "You are welcome," he told her cordially, and she knew that he was lying. "And I see no reason why you should not come tonight. But Alfred..." His eyes turned to Contini, and Chris was certain there was warmth in them then. "You must go home. I can see to Miss Tarleton. Genovese has the boat at the piazza outside the main entrance; please, allow him to take you home."

Contini listened, then sighed. He grimaced ruefully to Chris. "Marcus is right, *cara* Christi. My apologies. You will not mind if I go home to my bed? An old man needs his sleep. You will not mind if Marcus escorts you?"

I mind like hell, Chris thought dryly, but she kept smiling. "Of course not."

Marcus rose along with Alfred Contini, helping the older man. Alfred smiled at Chris one last time. "We will see one another in the morning."

"Yes," she murmured.

Marcus watched him until he was greeted at the entrance by a short wiry Italian man of an indeterminate age. Genovese, Chris assumed. But then Marcus was sitting again, his eyes touching her, openly assessing her with no thought of apology, and she felt tension—and anger. His gaze was very nearly insolent, and yet he gave no indication of reacting to what he saw.

"Would you like coffee, Miss Tarleton? Espresso, tea or cappuccino?"

"Coffee, please," she replied.

He signaled to the waiter and switched easily to Italian to order. A second later they were served.

"Why are you coming to the palazzo, Miss Tarleton?" he asked at last, lighting a cigarette to go with his coffee and leaning back slightly in his chair, his eyes raking blue fire over her once again.

"Curiosity, Mr. di Medici. Is that so unusual?"

"No. And neither is it really unusual to see a very young woman on the arm of a very old man. It's hard to tell what is what these days."

Chris felt her fury growing, but she allowed herself to do no more than flick her lashes briefly.

"Meaning, Mr. di Medici?"

He shrugged, rather eloquently, Chris thought. "Merely that Contini is an old man—and a rich one. Are you out hunting a fortune, Miss Tarleton?"

The question was very smooth, and painstakingly polite. His voice, like his eyes, could touch her with husky velvet—and with fire.

Chris forced herself to smile. "It's quite hard to tell these days, isn't it?"

He laughed and she felt the sudden warmth of it, for it was honest laughter.

"So you intend to leave me in wonder," he said, musing.

"I haven't left you in anything, Mr. di Medici. Whatever you choose to think will be your affair, won't it?"

He smiled and lifted a hand for the check. He signed it with a pen from his inner pocket, and Chris again caught herself thinking about him. He was made for a three-piece suit; he was lean, sleek and dark, like a panther. Negligent, and yet vibrant.

Dangerous.

Not really. *She* intended to be dangerous—if he crossed her.

"Are you ready, Miss Tarleton?"

She nodded uneasily, again noticing in his polite tone and sweeping gaze a sense of his hostility. Leashed, as his tension was leashed. Very, very controlled.

"Then come. The palazzo awaits."

He helped her from her chair. His hand was against her spine as he escorted her from the restaurant, and she felt as if she had been seared through the silk of her blouse. But then, it felt as if his eyes had already stripped her to the soul, as if he could bare both her heart and flesh at will.

"We'll hail a gondola," he murmured, "since Genovese and Alfred have taken our launch."

Soon they were seated in the small boat, moving along the Grand Canal. As had happened earlier, it seemed to Chris that they moved too quickly from light to shadow, back into light, then into shadow once again. Sitting beside the man, Chris again felt the tension in him, the vibrancy, and against her will she felt fear and excitement. He didn't speak, but she watched his face and when he turned to her, she was startled once again by the hostility in his eyes.

"Mr. di Medici," she said, refusing to flinch from his stare. "I cannot imagine what I might have done to you at the age of four. And yet I'm certain that you really don't wish to 'welcome' me into your home at all. Why?"

He shrugged, then leaned away from her, crossing his arms over his chest. She couldn't see his face or his eyes for a minute, only a formidable, very male shape. His voice came from the darkness.

"It's rather hard to welcome the daughter of a murderer," he said casually.

"What?" Chris gasped.

"Surely you knew." His voice grated harshly. "Your father was accused of murdering mine."

Chapter Two

What?'' Chris gasped again, and this time she leaped to her feet to confront him, causing the gondola to sway precariously and the gondolier to gasp something himself.

''Sit down!'' Marcus commanded, reaching out for her and sweeping an arm about her waist to bring her crashing gracelessly back down beside him. ''Do you wish to swim at night? I promise you, the water can be quite cool!''

''Let go of me!'' Chris seethed, tearing herself away from his touch but being careful not to rise again. The gondolier said something in rapid Italian and Marcus answered him with a laugh, but when he turned to look at Chris, the laughter faded and his eyes looked like cobalt fire in the night.

''Can you please behave rationally?'' he asked, his words low and crisp with irritation. ''He's asking me if we would care to be put ashore to finish this lovers' quarrel.''

"Lovers' quarrel! Tell the man that you just accused my father of murder and ask him how he would feel!"

He didn't respond to her anger. He stared off to the left bank of the Grand Canal and said with a sigh, "I am not the first to accuse him, Miss Tarleton."

"Then—" Chris swallowed and lowered her tone to match his, despite an inner turmoil that seemed to make her motions those of a puppet, jerked on a string, and her speech rapid. "If my father were guilty of murder, he could not have returned to the States!"

"I said that he was accused, not convicted."

"Then what—why—"

He spun toward her sharply. She felt the sweep of his cobalt eyes and shivered involuntarily. "Miss Tarleton, it is not a subject that I care to discuss. If you want more information, you'll have to speak with Alfred."

"Wait a minute!" Chris declared hotly. "You can't say something like that and refuse to explain yourself."

"I can, and I intend to," he said briefly. "Where is the pensione?" he asked her.

"Off the Via Pietà," Chris murmured distractedly. "You're wrong!" she insisted. "I knew my father, and I don't know what you think, or why, but he couldn't possibly have committed a murder! I'm telling you—"

He wasn't listening to her; he was giving the gondolier directions.

"Marcus di Medici!" Chris insisted. "You are not listening to me! I'm telling you—"

"You can't tell me anything," he told her with a tired sigh. "You were a child of four when all this happened, hardly equal to the task of sorting the facts. The matter is best left alone. James was dismissed for lack of evidence; there was no trial. He was not forced to leave Italy. He chose to do so. Let's leave it at that. The past is best buried."

"No! Not when—"

"I believe we are here, Miss Tarleton," he interrupted quietly, and Chris realized that the gondola was indeed standing still at the piazza by the pensione. Marcus stood to help her from the boat. He spoke to their gondolier; she assumed he was asking the man to wait for them. The boatman chuckled, and Chris was further infuriated to realize that he assumed that they were indeed in the middle of a lovers' quarrel, which Marcus—the male, the rational member of their duo—would quickly solve, putting her—the female, the irrational one—in her place.

"You needn't tell him to wait," Chris said, fighting for control over her temper and to achieve a cool tone. "I don't care to go back with you, Mr. di Medici. Perhaps you do not care to welcome the daughter of a man you saw fit to condemn when a court of law did not do so. And *I* do not care to enter the household of the man who condemned him!"

He stared at her for several seconds in a way that made Chris wish she could back away from him. He had one foot on the seat of the gondola, one foot on dry land, and though the canal rippled below him, he was perfectly comfortable, perfectly balanced. He was so agile, shrouded in darkness, only his eyes alight with that blaze that subtly invaded her being, causing her to shiver, to remember that her first impression of him had told her that he could be a dangerous man.

He moved suddenly, taking a single springing step with no sound that brought him next to her, staring down at her again, and leaving her feeling decidedly at a disadvantage. But she tightened her jaw and tilted her chin in challenge, determined not to back away from him.

"Do you wish me to give a message to Alfred?" he inquired softly.

She was somewhat stunned, having assumed that he would fight her decision. But why should he? she wondered. He had said he didn't want her at the palazzo.

"Yes. Tell Mr. Contini that I'm very sorry. Tell him that I found you to be intolerable, rude, insolent and arrogant and that I have no wish to 'vacation' beneath your roof."

She thought she saw a smile briefly curve his lips, and his lashes fell momentarily over his eyes. She hadn't insulted him, she had amused him.

"Do I frighten you, Miss Tarleton?"

"Certainly not! You offend me."

"There is no reason for you to refuse to come because of me. The Palazzo di Medici is large, very large. I spend a great deal of time working." He lowered his eyes for a second, and his tone changed; she sensed a sudden warmth and caring in it. "And Alfred Contini is an old man, Miss Tarleton. He wishes to have you there."

"Perhaps he does not believe my father to have been a murderer!" Chris snapped.

"Perhaps not," Marcus agreed coolly. "But that is not the point, Miss Tarleton. Alfred is old and ill; if he wishes to have you at the palazzo, then I do, too."

"No matter what your own feelings, I take it," Chris said dryly.

"I apologize. I never should have spoken."

"But you did!" Chris cried passionately. "Your apology does not change your feelings—"

"Then," he interrupted smoothly, "perhaps you have to come, Miss Tarleton. Since you are your father's passionate defender, perhaps you can change my feelings."

"I really don't give a damn about your feelings," Chris muttered.

He arched a brow, and she realized he was still amused by the entire encounter. "If I were you, Miss Tarleton, I would be very interested in discovering the truth."

His voice seemed to rake over her soul, rough and intimate velvet. She longed to push him backward, right into the canal. But she realized with sinking dismay that he was right; she had to go to the palazzo. It was no longer a matter of curiosity; she *was* her father's "passionate defender."

He was still watching her; she didn't know if it was with tolerance and scant interest or a great intensity. All she knew was that she felt his strange power once again; there was something primal and raw beneath the immaculate tailoring of his suit. She shivered, all too aware that his sexuality was a part of the danger he represented. He didn't need to touch a woman to make her tremble; all she needed to do was see him, inhale his subtle scent, feel the brush of his words or his eyes....

She smiled, like a tiger released from a cage herself. He was ready to condemn her father, but she was not. She was suddenly determined to discover the truth and then rub his nose in it. And she'd use him—and any member of his family—in any way she had to in order to discover that truth.

"If you'll wait here, Mr. di Medici, I'll get my things," she murmured coolly.

"If you wish some assistance—"

"I do not." Chris smiled grimly, then left him.

In her room, Chris hurriedly assembled her things, then paused to write a note to the others, explaining that she was going to the Palazzo di Medici to stay with old family friends. She added cheerfully that she hoped they all enjoyed their vacations, and that she would see them in the fall.

Chris was about to hurry back downstairs when she paused and walked down the hallway to the single window that overlooked the small canal. She could see Marcus by the poles of the piazza, talking with the gondolier. He laughed at something the other man said, shrugged, then paced across the piazza, obviously impatient and curious as to what could be taking her so long. Moonlight cast a cold glow over the piazza. She realized then that he really didn't walk at all; he stalked. Fluidly, smoothly, like a shadow through the night, or a sleek beast through the jungle. He lifted his head suddenly, staring up toward the window as if he knew she was there. Chris ducked back quickly, but she kept her eyes on him, studying him, trying to determine what it was that made him so compelling. Perhaps it was the lean form that touched chords of both primal excitement and fear; perhaps it was his face, the angles and lean planes so masculine, strong and striking.

She didn't know. She gave herself a little shake and reminded herself that she was going to beguile Marcus di Medici into doing her will—and make him swallow his own words like muddy canal water.

She forced her eyes from him and hurried downstairs. He saw her as soon as she stepped outside, and he moved toward her, silently taking her suitcase. "It's very late," he muttered. "I hope Alfred asked that a room be prepared for you."

"I'm sure I can prepare my own room," Chris replied dryly. They were at the gondola, and she tried to step ahead; she felt his arm at her elbow, steadying her anyway. She sat as far from him as possible. The gondolier was grinning again. Chris sat in silence until she lost her cool.

"Oh, good heavens! Will you tell the man that this is no lovers' quarrel—and not at all amusing!"

Marcus laughed. "Why spoil his evening?"

Chris fell silent and once again watched the magnificence of the buildings they passed in the moonlight. Baroque palaces, Gothic palaces, one after another. And then they were passing St. Mark's Square again, and Chris could have sworn that the winged lion, high on its granite column, was laughing down at her. They passed beneath the Bridge of Sighs, then turned and traveled beneath a number of small bridges, the pedestrian highways of Venice.

Suddenly she swallowed and caught her breath. She would have sworn she never would have recognized it, but she knew the Palazzo di Medici as soon as the gondola swung along the canal. It was huge, rising several stories out of the water and, unlike the majority of its neighbors, it did not sit wall-to-wall with the next building. Venice was a city created of islands; the Palazzo di Medici was an island in itself. An expanse of marble steps led to it from the water; it was set back, separated from the canal by those white gleaming steps and a garden enclosed by a wrought-iron fence. There were four graceful columns on the landing of the stairs, and the overhang formed an inverted V, with the family crest of the di Medici—St. Mark's winged lion in the center, Neptune rising to the left and a thorned rose to the right—fixed on a huge bronze shield in the center of the V. Chris allowed her gaze to sweep southward; she knew that she would see a bridge leading from the second story of the piazza across a slender waterway to the back of another building, similarly fenced, and of the same baroque design. The second building was where the galleries were housed.

"You do remember it," Marcus observed.

"No, I don't," Chris replied curtly.

She felt Marcus shrug. She wasn't on the right side of the gondola to escape unassisted to the landing, so she silently accepted Marcus's touch once again as he helped her out. He paid the gondolier—tipping him well, Chris assumed from the man's fervent thanks.

"Prego, prego!" Marcus murmured, her suitcase in one hand, the other coming resolutely to her waist once again to usher her up the steps.

Despite Marcus and her own stalwart determination, Chris felt a twinge of unease as they started up the stairs. Alfred Contini wanted her here but did anyone else? If the general consensus was that James Tarleton had murdered Mario di Medici, it was unlikely that his widow would be glad to see Chris. Or that Tony, Marcus's younger brother, would be thrilled to pieces, either.

She heard her own footsteps on the marble stairs. They seemed to echo loudly. How many steps were there? Fifteen, sixteen, seventeen . . .

She was still three steps from the landing when the intricately carved wooden entrance door swung open. From inside a massive chandelier cast a glow over the entryway.

There was a woman standing there, tall, dark and slim, and very proud, judging from her posture. For a moment Chris thought that she was young, and she wondered if either Marcus or Tony had married and Alfred had neglected to tell her so. But Marcus kept ushering her along, and she saw the woman's features. She was very beautiful, with a slim heart-shaped face and huge deep-set dark eyes. But she was not young; she was, Chris thought, either in her late forties or early fifties.

"Sophia," Marcus murmured, and Chris frowned fleetingly. The name had touched a chord in her memory.

"Ah, Marcus, Miss Tarleton, you have arrived," the woman said, and Chris could discern nothing from her voice. There was no warm note of welcome, but neither was there anything hostile in the words.

"Come in, come in. Genovese will take the bag."

They stepped into the grand entryway of the palazzo. The short slim man of indeterminate age whom Chris had seen helping Alfred Contini earlier was quickly at their side, taking the suitcase from Marcus.

"*Grazie*, Genovese," Marcus murmured.

"Prego," was the muffled response. Genovese left them, striding across the marble-tiled entryway to a curving staircase that led to the second landing. Chris gazed up at the chandelier. It hung from a majestic cathedral ceiling adorned with frescoes.

"So, you are Chris Tarleton. You've grown a great deal since I saw you last."

Chris started, then stared at the woman. She smiled sweetly. "I left twenty-one years ago. I certainly hope I've changed."

"You are a performer, Alfred tells me."

Chris lowered her lashes quickly. It was obvious that Sophia—whoever *she* was—thought that performers were of a lower class than average citizens.

"I am a mime," she replied.

"A very talented one, Sophia," Marcus said from behind her, startling Chris again. She spun around to look into his enigmatic cobalt eyes.

"You were at the show?" she asked him.

"Yes," he said, and for some reason she shivered again, knowing that he had watched her when she hadn't been aware of him.

"Ah, there you are at last!"

The cry came from a male voice at the top of the stairs. Chris gazed upward to see a handsome young man with a dazzling white smile staring down at her. "It's about time, Marc! I've been dying of curiosity to see our mystery guest—our prodigal daughter!"

Marcus laughed. Chris glanced his way and felt suddenly warm. There was open amusement in his eyes, and his smile was as full and inviting as his brother's. His teeth were white against the copper of his features, and when he met her gaze with a teasing light in his eyes, she knew that he was definitely capable of being charming.

"Come down, Tony. Miss Tarleton, my brother, Antonio. Tony, Miss Christina Tarleton."

Tony quickly came to them, offering Chris his hand. His touch was warm, his smile genuine, and she almost felt like crying. At least someone besides Alfred was glad to see her.

"Hello, Tony," she murmured.

"Hello yourself, gorgeous!" Tony laughed. He was in jeans and a blue denim shirt; his eyes were blue, but a lighter shade than his brother's. He was very handsome, and he seemed . . . fun. Not at all like Marcus, with his underlying elemental streak of danger.

He kept her hand and swung around to Sophia. "She did turn out just beautiful, but then, you're the one who always said she would!"

"Yes," Sophia remarked dryly.

Tony slipped an arm around the older woman. "It takes a beautiful woman to judge another, *si*, Sophia?"

"*Grazie*, Antonio," Sophia said, slipping from his embrace. "Since you two are here, I will beg leave to retire. I haven't the energy of your youth. Marcus, there is coffee in the rear courtyard, if you wish, and I've had the crystal room prepared for Miss Tarleton. If you'll excuse me, I'll say goodnight."

"Of course, Sophia. It is very late. Good night," Marcus said.

She waved to him as she started for the stairway, seeming to sail regally.

"Thank you, thank you very much," Chris called after her.

She received a dismissive wave in return.

"Where's Mother?" Marcus asked Tony. "Sleeping?"

"Yes, she said she'd have to see Chris in the morning," Tony replied. Then he grinned broadly at Chris again. "Are you up to coffee?"

She could feel Marcus standing behind her. She gave Tony a brilliant smile. "I'd love some coffee."

He caught her arm in his and led her through the grand marbled entryway. "Do you remember the palazzo, Chris?"

"No, not really," she replied.

"Then I'll tell you a bit about it so you don't get lost! The music salon and den are to the left; the dining room and kitchen are to the right. You can reach the courtyard by going either way. All of our rooms are on the second floor, Alfred and Sophia are on the third. There's an elevator at the rear of the stairs. The bridge to the galleries is on the second floor, but you mustn't use it now; it's in urgent need of repair! There are subterranean tunnels, too, but again, you really mustn't use them. Marc is busy saving them—and everything else in Venice!—from the sea."

Chris turned around a bit. Marcus was following them, but he was at a distance. She frowned and lowered her voice, bringing her lips close to Tony's ear. "Please, Tony, help me quickly. Who is Sophia? I don't remember her."

Marcus was closer than she had thought. Either that, or he had closed the distance between them with uncanny speed.

"Sophia Calabrese has been the housekeeper here since my father invited Alfred into the house," he answered for Tony. "Don't you remember her? She lived here when you were born."

"She seemed familiar," Chris murmured. "Of course. The housekeeper..."

Tony broke into soft laughter. "Marc! Chris is an American, a worldly woman. Sophia is Alfred's *mistress*. She has been so for thirty years. Not that I think much can go on between them anymore."

"Tony!" Marcus said sharply.

Chris laughed, linking her arm more tightly through Tony's. She was aware of the beautiful hallway they were passing through. It was wide enough to be a room in itself, and lined with chairs and love seats, pedestals, statues and paintings. And then they came to a huge room with four sets of French doors, all standing open to a beautiful tiled patio. Chris could see a circular table there, set with a snowy cloth, a silver coffeepot, cups, saucers and plates.

"Sophia must have thought we needed supper!" Tony laughed, very gallant as he led Chris onto the patio, seated her and handed her a napkin with a flourish, and poured her some coffee. Marcus silently took a chair opposite her.

Chris looked up at Tony and returned to their earlier topic of discussion. "Sophia has been Alfred's mistress for thirty years? Now that's definitely Italian! Why didn't he marry her?''

''I don't really know—'' Tony began.

''Nor is it any of our business, is it?'' Marcus interrupted. He sipped his black coffee, watching Chris pointedly over the rim of his cup.

She shrugged, then smiled at Tony again. ''People are fascinating, aren't they, Tony?''

Tony seated himself and caught her hand and her eyes across the table. ''*You're* fascinating, Christina.''

She laughed, quickly retrieving her hand. She wanted to taunt Marcus di Medici, but with his eyes on her, she only dared to go so far.

''Thank you, Tony,'' she said a little breathlessly, then allowed her eyes to roam over the courtyard. ''This is the most land I think I've seen in Venice. All the other buildings are built so close together.''

''Oh, most of them have courtyards,'' Tony said. ''I guess that we do have more property than most, though. But there isn't much space, you see. It's a bit like New York City—''

''You've been to New York?'' Chris interrupted.

''Oh, yes, of course. We—Marcus and I—travel extensively. It's necessary to keep the galleries going.'' He started lifting the silver domes from the serving platters on the table. ''Pastry, cookies and cakes. What would you like, Miss Tarleton?''

''I liked 'Chris' better,'' Chris told him, ''and I really don't care for anything at all. I had a huge dinner.''

Tony didn't press her. He selected a large anise cookie himself and eyed it as he continued to talk to her.

''We're opening a gallery in the States soon,'' he told her.

"Really?" Chris inquired politely, a little annoyed that they traveled so frequently and had never bothered to check into the state of her welfare or her mother's.

"Yes. We've already opened a place in Paris, and one in London. Next year will be the States."

"Where?" Chris asked.

"We haven't decided yet. Either New York or Boston," Tony replied.

"And it probably won't be next year," Marcus contradicted his brother. He glanced at Chris as he lit a cigarette. "We've just opened a new exhibition here. Something quite different."

"You'll love it!" Tony assured her.

"Actually, it's more of a show than an exhibit. We're using robotronics, something that's pretty widely used in some of your American amusement parks."

Tony snapped his fingers. "Like the Hall of Presidents!"

Marcus grinned tolerantly at Tony. "Something like that," he agreed. "Only we depict Venetian life through the centuries, and the costumes and jewels on the animated figures are real."

"It sounds fascinating," Chris murmured.

"Oh, you'll see for yourself," Tony assured her, munching his cookie. "In fact, I'll take you through tomorrow—"

"No, you won't," Marcus interrupted smoothly. "You're going to Florence tomorrow, remember?"

"Ah, Marcus! You could go! You really should go; you know the tapestries much better than I."

"You know them well enough, Tony. And I can't go. The workmen are coming to look at rot in the catacombs. And I have an appointment at the bank at eleven. *And* the engineer is coming from the computer company to work on the latest figures."

Tony grimaced, but gave in gracefully. He winked at Chris. "Alas! We get a beautiful guest—and I'm out on my ear. But I'll make it up to you, Chris, I promise."

She smiled. "I'm sure you will. How long will you be gone?"

He shrugged. "Two days, three at most. Whatever the gorgons upstairs and this whip-cracker do to you, see that you wait for me!"

"Gorgons?" Chris queried, frowning.

"He's referring to Sophia and our mother," Marcus said with a sigh. "And I'm sure they'll be very gracious."

"But of course," Tony said to his brother. "Chris is here because of Alfred, isn't she?" There was something peculiar—amused, but nevertheless resentful—in his tone.

"Yes," Marcus said simply. He crushed out his cigarette and sat back in his chair as if he were removed from the group, an observer only.

"Ah, well then, Alfred will be wanting your company."

"And she his," Marcus commented dryly.

"Whatever for!" Tony laughed. "She'll spend hours sitting in the courtyard...oh, perhaps it will not be that bad. We have a very unique pool on the roof. Do you swim?"

Chris nodded. She felt suddenly very wary of Marcus; she knew he was watching her carefully.

"I believe she wishes to be with Alfred," he said lightly. "After all, it is at Alfred's invitation that she has come." He looked straight at Chris and smiled, but spoke to Tony. "She might be after his money, you know."

Tony laughed. "Are you?" he asked Chris.

She returned Marcus's blatant stare. "Oh, possibly, Tony. I haven't decided yet."

Tony was taking the entire thing as a joke. He laughed again. "Well, you needn't bother with Alfred. Seduce Marcus here—or better yet, seduce me! We've both got a share in it all."

Chris set down her coffee cup, still eyeing Marcus carefully. There was nothing to be read in his cobalt gaze, yet she still shivered at his undaunted perusal of her. She smiled slowly and turned to Tony. "What a lovely idea. If I fail in coercing the whole thing from Alfred Contini, I'll just have to con a share of it from one of you."

Tony's eyes were a dazzling shade, like a summer sky, as he laughed again. "Marriage, my dear Miss Tarleton. Take us for all we've got."

"I'm certain she'll try," Marcus murmured.

Chris cast him a quick hostile glance, then grinned sweetly at Tony. "Do you think I should? Go after one of you, that is."

"Why certainly! And, Marcus, think of the gain to us! Anytime one of the robots went out, we'd have a mime, talented flesh and beautiful blood, to slip into the show! We wouldn't have a worry in the world."

Marcus smiled politely. "I think we'd still have plenty of worries, Tony. Most assuredly more." He rose suddenly, as if he had tired of a game. Perhaps he had, Chris thought; he had tired of the game of watching her.

"Miss Tarleton, I'll show you the galleries myself tomorrow." He raised a dark brow in his brother's direction. "I have a few papers to go through before the morning, and I'm sure Tony will be happy to show you to your room."

"I'd be happier to show her to mine," Tony commented.

Chris laughed, but Marcus was not amused. "Antonio!" he said rather sharply. "Miss Tarleton is Alfred's guest."

Tony glanced at Chris and shrugged sheepishly. "I'm sorry for the comment. I can't help the thought."

"You're forgiven," Chris said flippantly. Marcus was behind her; she could feel his eyes, like blue fire. Good. Let him think she'd be willing to hop into his brother's bed. At least Tony hadn't greeted her by condemning her father.

"*Buona notte*, Signorina Tarleton," Marcus murmured. His voice was low, a brush of raw silk. When she turned to reply, he was gone.

"Sinister chap, isn't he?" Tony inquired affectionately, referring to his brother.

Chris spun back around, looking at Tony with surprise. He laughed. "Marc sometimes takes life a bit too seriously," he told her. He lifted his shoulders and allowed them to fall, then grinned. "Marc had to grow up very suddenly—at twelve. My father was gone, and your father was gone, and even then Alfred was ailing. It all fell to Marc. He did a remarkable job of keeping things together through the years. So forgive him if he's a bit brusque at times. He's also . . . well, he's used to speaking and being obeyed, you know. And . . ."

"And what?" Chris pressed Tony.

He gave her his infectious grin. "Half the time he doesn't need to speak to be obeyed." He shook his head as if grasping for an elusive answer, then laughed. "Women! It's a pity I wasn't the son to inherit that dark charisma of his. I could have taken it much, much farther! Marc loses interest so easily, you see. If he inclines his head to get them, he inclines his head once more when he wishes them gone! Ah, to have been the eldest!"

"I'm sure you do quite well on your own," Chris told him dryly.

Tony chuckled. "I do try."

"Tony," Chris murmured, suddenly very serious. It was all well and good to joke with Tony and goad Marcus, but that wasn't why she had come to the palazzo, nor was it to take anyone's money. She swallowed suddenly. "Tony, please..."

"Christina! What is it?"

He lost his lighthearted manner very quickly; his question was caring and concerned, and Chris decided that although Marcus might be a thorn in her side, she liked Tony di Medici very much.

"Tony, Marcus said something to me tonight that was very upsetting. He said that my father murdered yours."

Tony instantly withdrew from her; a pained expression flashed through his eyes as he leaned back in his chair.

"Chris, *per favore*, leave the past alone."

"Tony! I can't. I can't believe that my father was a murderer! I knew him, Tony. He was gentle and kind, and any mention of Venice was like stabbing him with a knife."

"Chris, Chris!" Tony moved forward again, taking her hand in his. "Whatever happened, I'm certain James did nothing on purpose."

"But what happened?" Chris almost screamed.

"I—I can't tell you. Don't ask me this, Chris, please. I can't say anything. I was barely eight at the time. Please, Chris, I can tell you nothing. I will tell you nothing."

There was an implacable look in his eyes, very similar to his brother's. Chris sighed and cast herself back into her chair. "I've got to find out somehow, Tony."

He hesitated uncomfortably. "Christina, please, if you have any mercy, don't speak of this to my mother."

She closed her eyes and shook her head wearily. She didn't want to make promises that she couldn't keep.

"Christi, *per favore!*"

The soft entreaty brought her eyes open again. Tony smiled a little ruefully. "I—I really can't tell you anything, Chris." The teasing light returned to his eyes, and he suggested, "Plague Marcus if you must; he was older at the time. More aware of what was going on."

"Marcus..." Chris murmured bitterly. "It's like talking to a granite wall."

Tony laughed, his easygoing nature apparently restored. Or perhaps he felt that he had put himself in the clear; if Marcus chose to answer her, that would be his privilege.

"I've heard my brother accused of being many things, but never as cold as a granite wall!"

Chris merely lifted a brow, then stared at her coffee cup again, suddenly bone weary. It had been a long day, and an even longer night.

"Ah, Christi! *Bella, bella*, Christi! You could melt the strongest wall! Charm Marcus."

"Umm," Chris murmured dryly. Then she offered Tony a weak smile. "Would you mind showing me to my room now? I'm very tired."

"Of course, of course! Come." He stood and courteously pulled back her chair. He led her in silence back through the hallway and up the stairs. Chris noticed curiously that the stairs here were wooden when most of those she had seen in Venice were constructed of marble, granite or some other type of stone.

"What's the matter?" Tony asked.

"The stairs . . . they're unusual."

"Unusual, and a pain," Tony agreed. "We're always fixing them. I don't know what got into our ancestors. I don't even know where they got the wood!" He sighed. "These old palaces, they eat you alive. What with the constant battle with the sea and the salt in the air . . ."

"I guess it is very hard to preserve things," Chris said.

"Very. But it's fascinating." He smiled. "We're active in a group to preserve all of Venice. The sea threatens to engulf us, and it is only in modern times that we have realized this. Marcus or I will show you some of our efforts one day."

"Thank you," Chris said. "I'd enjoy learning."

Tony grasped her face lightly between his hands and kissed her cheek. "*Buona notte*, Christi," he murmured. Then he pushed open the door they stood in front of and switched on the light.

"*Buona notte*, Tony."

He smiled and left her. Chris turned around and immediately understood why it was called the crystal room. The chandelier was almost as large as the monster in the entryway. Enormous, and beautiful. The swirling pink-and-white tiles on the floor gave the bedroom a feeling of being even larger than it was. There was a huge old bed with a massive carved headboard in the dead center of the room; to either side were French doors leading to an outer terrace or balcony. The white muslin drapes flowed in the night breeze. There was a breakfast table, as well as a gateleg table and two large dressers to match a huge wardrobe. A door to the far left, Chris quickly discovered, led to a modern bathroom.

Her suitcase lay on the foot of the bed, and she moved to it quickly, undoing her blouse as she went. The abject weariness that had struck her when she was sitting with Tony remained with her. All she wanted to do was bathe and fall asleep...and stop wondering how she could prove that her gentle kindly father had never murdered anyone.

To sleep...and forget the disturbing effects of her confrontation with Marcus di Medici.

She opened her suitcase and smiled absently at its contents. One nice thing about living in Paris had been the acquisition of a marvelous lingerie wardrobe. Her nightgown was a gauzy fluted pink silk. It went perfectly, she decided, with the elegance of the room.

But she could really come up with little appreciation for anything at the moment. Her mind was spinning on a terrible course: how could they be saying these things about her father? Even Tony, who had been so ready to greet her, seemed to believe that James Tarleton had killed Mario di Medici. And no one would even talk to her about it.

She set her lips grimly as she ran a quick bath. There would be ways to find out. She'd study her Italian dictionary until she had a strong enough command of the language to check the newspaper morgue, the city records and whatever else she could get her hands on. Damn them all! She would find out the truth.

Chris sank into the warm water and tried to relax, but soon gave up. She washed quickly and slipped into her nightgown, feeling refreshed in body, if not in mind. She pulled back the embroidered spread and literally slid into bed. The sheets were pink silk, just like her gown.

"What a match," she murmured aloud, then she doused the antique bedside lamp and determined firmly that she was going to sleep.

"Charm Marcus," Tony had told her. But how should she set about charming a man with a deadly fascination of his own? He was capable of being completely courteous—and completely intractable, implacable and as hard and cool as stone. He could look at her and light a fire in the very center of her being.

She tossed and turned and discovered that she was sliding again on the sheets. Damn! she thought. They didn't go with her gown at all!

Concentration was the name of the game, she reminded herself. And as she had learned in several classes, she started contracting her muscles tightly starting with her toes, then forcing them to relax. Finally either the exercise worked or exhaustion took over, and she drifted into a deep sleep, one from which she was awakened with a startling jarring thud.

Chris's eyes flew open. It was dark except for the moonlight. Still night. Then why. . . ?

She sighed. She had awakened because she had fallen to the floor. Sleeping on silk in silk was like being on a slip 'n' slide. The top sheet and spread were tangled around her, and she was a disheveled mess on the tile. Probably bruised in a dozen places, she decided ruefully.

"What are you doing, Miss Tarleton?"

The deep husky voice was so startling in the night that Chris gasped. She stared at the doors leading to the terrace and saw a tall form there. A man. Marcus di Medici.

He moved into the room silently and turned on the bedside lamp. Light flared all around her and Chris realized that a nightgown was hardly the attire she wanted to greet someone in, especially him. His eyes were raking over her in amusement and no sign at all of humble apology. He was still in his suit. His arms were crossed casually over his chest, and his lips were curved in a wry smile.

"I fell!" Chris snapped, but when she tried to rise, she discovered that she was too tangled to do so. He laughed and reached for her hands, pulling her from the welter of bedding. Chris found herself swallowing as she was set on her feet—too close to Marcus, too aware of his lean sinewed physique and his heated sensual power. He smiled as he held her there for a moment, and suddenly she was also all too aware of her own lack of clothing. The nightgown cut a deep V between her breasts, and the material hid little if anything from his imagination.

He kept smiling. He still had her hands, trapping her just inches away from him. "I'm sorry. We have nothing but silk here. It seems so cool when the air is hot."

She wasn't really touching him, yet she could have sworn that she felt the entire hard length of his body against her own. Suddenly she broke the searing contact of his eyes and tore her hands away.

"Where did you come from, anyway?" she demanded irritably, dragging the sheet and spread from the floor and hugging them in front of her. His lashes flickered and his grin deepened as if he were completely aware that her action had been caused by an uneasy fear.

"My room is next to yours. The terrace connects them. I heard the crash and came to see if you were all right."

"I—I'm fine. I'll just have to learn to sleep in the center of the bed."

He laughed huskily. "Or without the nightgown."

"Yes, quite. Well, if I con one of you fascinating di Medicis into marriage, I won't have a worry in the world, will I?"

She had the pleasure of seeing the amusement fade from his features. But then she was sorry that she had been so flippant because his hands were on her again, drawing her to him, and this time the length of her body was crushed to his, and she did feel all the strength of his well-muscled shoulders, arms and thighs.

"Christi, *cara*, take heed. All the di Medicis do not care to be conned."

His breath warmed her cheeks, and violent tremors, hot and insistent, ravaged the pit of her abdomen. She was about to do something, anything, to escape his touch when he released her, brushing her cheek with his knuckles in a surprisingly tender gesture.

"Again, Miss Tarleton, I wish you *buona notte*."

And then he was gone, silently disappearing into the night.

Chapter Three

They were talking about her when Chris came down to the courtyard the next morning.

She hadn't the least idea what they were saying because they were speaking very rapidly in Italian, and it was only her name that she caught, assuring her that she was indeed being discussed.

She had been walking along the same great hallway she had followed the night before, and she paused when she reached the large inner patio. She wanted to get her bearings before joining the group.

Marcus and Tony were both there. Tony was talking excitedly; Marcus was reading a newspaper and sipping espresso, apparently paying little heed to the discussion. Alfred was at one end of the table; Marcus at the other. Tony was to his brother's left, while Sophia was near Alfred. The other woman at the table had to be Gina di Medici, Mario's widow. The hardest of the lot to face calmly, Chris decided.

No, Marcus would always be the hardest of the lot to face calmly.

There were two girls who appeared to be little more than teenagers serving the group. The offerings seemed to be coffee, rolls, fruit and cheese. Breakfast, Chris realized, was not a major meal to Italians. But then, she had accustomed herself to nothing but coffee and croissants in Paris.

She cleared her throat and moved into the morning sun. All talk immediately stopped, and she was glad she was also accustomed to being stared at, since it seemed that everyone was staring at her now.

"Buongiorno," she murmured, stepping forward confidently.

"*Buongiorno*, Chris, *buongiorno!*"

Bless Tony! He was instantly on his feet, rushing around to greet her. Marcus closed his newspaper more slowly and stood; Alfred would have done so as well, but Chris quickly begged him to remain seated.

"Christi," Alfred said to her as Tony seated her on his other side, "Sophia tells me you met last night; now you must meet Gina di Medici and you'll have no strangers in this house, eh?"

Chris nodded. No strangers! These people were strange even for strangers. But she smiled down at Gina di Medici, praying fervently that Gina would accept her smile at face value.

Gina di Medici was a striking woman and, like Sophia, she had aged very well. It was difficult to believe she could have grown sons, except that it was quite obvious that Marcus and Tony were her sons. Gina's eyes, too, were a beautiful blue—a shade more like Tony's than Marcus's—and stunning in their clarity. But whereas Marcus and Tony had hair as dark as midnight, Gina di Medici was fair. Her hair remained a true blond, with no hint of gray. Her face was a lovely oval, hardly touched by the lines of age.

She smiled at Chris in return, and yet it was as if she wasn't smiling at all. Rather, it seemed that she had curved her lips in an automatic gesture. There was no malice in her eyes when she looked at Chris, but something that hurt far more deeply: sorrow, and the deepest remorse.

"Christina, child," she murmured softly. "It is good to see you again."

Chris swallowed, fully aware despite the gentle words that Gina di Medici wasn't happy to see her at all. To Gina, Christina's presence was like having gravel scraped over an open wound.

Chris decided right then that she could make a promise to Tony never to harass his mother with questions. She would never intentionally hurt Gina.

"*Grazie*, Gina," Chris murmured, lowering her eyes. When she raised them, she found Marcus staring at her. Strangely, it was he who looked away first.

"Does the palazzo bring back memories, Christi?" Alfred boomed out.

"I'm, uh, not sure yet," Chris murmured. She shook her head. "I don't think so."

Sophia was rising. "What would you like, Christina? Tea, coffee, espresso, cappuccino?"

"Coffee, please," Chris said. Sophia lifted a hand and murmured something in Italian. One of the girls brought Chris a delicate china cup and filled it with pitch-black coffee. Tony pushed back his chair, glancing at his watch. "I've got to go. Christi, don't forget, wait for me!" he teased her. He kissed her hand, then moved around the table to kiss his mother's cheek.

"Marcus, if you decide we need anything else, call me," Tony told his brother.

Marcus replied with another of his rare genuine smiles. "I'll be lucky to find you in, Tony."

Tony laughed, waved to the group and left. Alfred asked Marcus something about the workmen who were coming, and Gina di Medici leaned across the table a little to talk to Chris.

"How is your mother, Christina?"

"Fine, thank you," Chris replied. She told Gina about her mother's remarriage, then paused awkwardly. She didn't really know what to say to Gina.

Sophia said something a bit sharply in Italian. Chris looked at her blankly, and thought that Sophia was smiling a little smugly. "Christina, answer me!"

She shook her head. "I'm sorry, I can't. I don't speak Italian."

"But it was your first language!" Sophia exclaimed.

"Sophia!" Alfred remonstrated with a frown. "Leave the girl be."

"I never knew it was my first language," Chris said a bit stiffly. "And I haven't had occasion to use it since I left, I suppose."

Marcus stood, tossing his newspaper down again. "Mother, Sophia, Alfred, have a good day. Christina, I'll be back for you right after lunch."

"Back for me?" Chris murmured with more confusion than she would have liked to have shown him. But there had been something a little less disturbing about Marcus seated than Marcus standing. Looking up at him, all Chris could remember was the way he had touched her last night, and she wasn't at all sure whether she disliked the man, or was totally fascinated by him.

Strangely, though, she already felt as if she had known him for a long, long time. As if their relationship had been formed on a distant intangible level where all that mattered was an elemental heat.

His lips curved just slightly, and she wondered if he was aware of her disturbing reaction to him.

"The galleries, Christina. I told you I would show you the galleries. Will two this afternoon be all right?"

"Fine, thank you," she said, glad to have regained a cool voice and her senses. Marcus, she reminded herself, was going to have to be the direct line of her attack.

He gave them all a brief wave and disappeared in Tony's wake. Chris felt as if both Sophia and Gina were watching her. Alfred started talking again as soon as Marcus had disappeared from view.

"Would you care to join me on the roof this morning, Christi? You can bathe in the pool while enjoying the sun."

"Certainly," Chris told him.

"You haven't eaten anything, Christina," Gina commented. "You must eat something."

Chris automatically reached for a roll. Gina smiled at her again, and Chris felt that Gina was trying very hard to get past her memories in order to make her feel welcome.

Alfred asked Chris about Paris as she ate, and Chris was glad to talk about her time in that city. It seemed like a safe subject.

She had a second cup of coffee while Gina and Sophia agreed that Rome offered more than any city on earth, to which Chris made no comment. But when they all rose at last and Chris returned to her bedroom to change into her bathing suit, she let out a long sigh of relief.

She had survived her first morning at the Palazzo di Medici.

Survived. It was a strange word to use, but that was exactly how it felt, she mused.

The pool on the roof was unlike anything Chris had ever seen, and she loved it immediately. It was tiled all in black, red and gold, and the family crest was set in the center beneath the water, shimmering in the sun. The pool was surrounded by a little wall, making it entirely private. There was a Jacuzzi in one corner that created a cascading waterfall running into the main body of the pool. It was wonderful, and Chris was pleased to stay there, swimming lap after lap and convincing herself that she had rid herself of what she was beginning to think of as the "di Medici tremors."

At length, though, she pulled herself from the water to lay out a towel on a bench at Alfred's side.

"How was your swim?" he asked her, his dark eyes sparkling with happiness. Chris was amazed that her presence could mean so much to him.

"Wonderful," she said, smiling. "This—" she waved a hand around to encompass the palazzo "—is wonderful. Thank you so much for inviting me here."

He gazed at her, and his smile slowly faded. "You did not come just to amuse an old man," he told her.

Chris shook some of the water out of her hair and smiled. "I'm very glad that I've met you, Alfred—as an adult, that is. And I'm very happy if I'm making you happy. But you're right; I came because I want to know what happened."

He shrugged, looking uncomfortably upward. He stared at the sun when he spoke. "Can it matter now, Christi? Can any of it really matter now?"

"It matters to me," she said quietly. "Alfred, you didn't tell me that my father had been accused of killing Mario di Medici."

Alfred lifted a slim hand, then allowed it to fall helplessly back to his lap. "It was so long ago. And . . . and I do not blame your father, Christi. I—I do not believe that he killed Mario."

"Alfred, won't you tell me about it?" Chris pleaded. "I need to know what happened. I can't make any sense of it if I don't know what went on!"

"Sometimes I think it is best that family skeletons remain locked away," he murmured. "And then . . ."

"Alfred," Chris pressed him urgently.

He shrugged. "It was that damned statuette!"

"Why was one little statue so important?" Chris demanded.

"Because its value would be immense—if it was what we thought it was. A Michelangelo, Christi! It was, we believed, a working model for a tomb relief."

"And it just . . . disappeared?"

"Yes, but the statuette was not what really mattered in the end. It merely brought on the clash of tempers on the ketch that day and—"

"Mario di Medici died," Chris finished. "But, Alfred, it sounds like there were a number of people on board that boat. My father and mother, Gina and Mario, Sophia and you. Genovese . . . and didn't you say there were others, too?"

"*Si*, *si*, Christi. Fredo Talio and Giuseppi—Joe—Conseli. They are . . . they are still with us."

"Still with us?"

"Yes, they work for Marcus. Or the galleries." Alfred closed his eyes and leaned back. "Marcus heads it all now. I have no more interest. Too many deaths . . . Christi, what of your father? What happened to him?"

Chris looked down at the brick deck that rimmed the pool. "He died of a heart attack right after my thirteenth birthday. It was...instantaneous, they told us."

"That would be God's way to depart this life," Alfred murmured. "God knew him to be innocent."

"Then he was innocent! Alfred, help me prove it!"

He sat up suddenly, staring at her intensely, then looking all around them like a startled rabbit. "Christi," he murmured, and she was concerned because it suddenly seemed that he was breathing much too fast. "Christi, we will not talk about it here, *per favore*? Even the air, it has ears. The walls here, they listen. Didn't you hear that?"

"Hear what?" she asked him.

"The sound . . . someone coming. Christi, swear to me that you will not talk about it here!"

His face had grown very flushed, and Chris could still sense his too-rapid breathing.

"I swear, I swear!" she promised solemnly. "Please, Alfred, *per favore*, don't upset yourself! I won't say another word."

Slowly he seemed to relax. At long last he smiled again and swept out an arm to encompass Venice.

"Venezia! Ah, Christi, once she was the jewel of the sea. All merchants knew Venezia! Marco Polo brought back his gifts and crown jewels from Kublai Khan. It was from here that he left for his journeys, and it was here that he returned. Ah, what a great city! The doges kept power, but the merchants were princes! She was a city where people lived and breathed and laughed and knew the beauty of song and the great artistry of her Italian sons! But we weren't always 'Italian.' Did you know that Venice belonged once to the Austrians?"

"No," Chris murmured, watching him and smiling but feeling as if his sense of unease had become hers. She had the horrible feeling of being secretly watched.

"We were a young state once. A Venetian republic, Romanized in the third century, of course! The French put an end to our independence in 1797, and we were provisionally assigned to Austria. We joined the new kingdom of Italy in 1866."

Though Chris was listening to him, she felt as if she were in a fog. The unreasoning uncanny fear remained with her. And it was absurd. They were on the roof. There was only one place where someone might be—in the marble archway that protected both the new elevator shaft and the ancient winding stairway to the roof.

Chris looked quickly to the arch and swallowed.

Gina di Medici was there, standing with the breeze catching her hair and her skirt. She might have been a young girl, anxiously looking for her lover. She shielded her eyes from the sun with her hand.

"Alfred! Christina! You must dress for lunch!" she told them.

"Coming!" Chris tried to call, but the sound that came out of her mouth was more like a croak.

How long had Gina been standing there, watching her and Alfred?

Chris rose and Alfred did the same. She started toward the arch ahead of the old man, forcing a smile. She almost started violently when she realized that Sophia was there, too, hidden in the shadows behind Gina.

Gorgons. Tony had called the two women gorgons. Perhaps that was just what they were, like the multitudes of imps that guarded Notre Dame in Paris, these two guarded the Palazzo di Medici and all its secrets.

Chris gave herself a firm mental shake. They were two middle-aged ladies, very attractive at that, and she was the intruder here, not the two of them.

"How was the pool?" Gina asked her.

"Lovely!" Chris replied, and she wrapped her huge towel about her like a cape and hurried past the two women.

She felt a hand grasp her elbow just before she could enter the elevator. Startled, Chris spun around. It was Alfred, anxiously looking back over his shoulder.

"Christi. Meet me at the galleries at closing time on Friday."

Friday was three days away. She wondered what his message was, and why he was willing to wait so long before passing it on.

"Friday, Christi."

"Yes, yes, Alfred. Whatever you wish."

"I need you, Christi. I need you."

"Alfred, I..." She wanted to demand to know what made him so nervous. She wanted to clutch his hand, pat it and assure him that everything was all right.

"I can—" He looked around again, lowering his voice. Chris saw that Gina and Sophia had walked out on the brick deck to stare out to the sea. "Christi, I can tell you about your father then. The galleries, right after closing time. I'll see that the main door is open."

"I don't even know where they are yet!"

"You'll know. Marcus will show you today."

She did squeeze his hand then. "I'll be there, Alfred. Don't worry, I'll be there."

"Bless you, Christi."

She frowned, then squeezed his hand again. "And I promise you, Alfred," she said softly but very firmly, "I will help you."

He smiled. She felt like an angel—for the moment, at least.

Alfred wasn't at the courtyard table when Chris came down to lunch. Sophia told Chris that he had decided to eat a light lunch upstairs; he intended to spend the afternoon resting. It sounded natural enough; a number of Italians, like Spaniards, liked to rest during the heat of the afternoon and work or stay active in the evening.

But it did leave Chris alone with 'the gorgons' for lunch.

Whereas breakfast at the palazzo was small, lunch seemed to be a meal that could fill Chris up for the next two weeks. There were endless antipasti, as well as soup, cannelloni and rigatoni, and a choice of fish or veal for the main course. Chris was sure she'd never get to the main course, but she surprised herself by being almost famished. It had been the swimming, she decided, and determined not to turn into a blimp during her stay.

She was also glad of the food because it gave her something to talk about when she was trying to stay away from uncomfortable subjects.

Halfway through lunch, though, Chris found that she didn't have to keep the conversation going. Sophia was determined to do so.

"Christina," she said, pointing to one of the young dark-haired girls who were serving the meal, "this is Liggia; that is her sister, Teresa." Chris smiled warmly at the girls, who gave her shy tentative smiles in return. But she realized quickly that she wasn't being given a casual introduction when Sophia spoke next, sighing dramatically.

"Liggia and Teresa are our only live-in help these days. The world . . . it is not what it was. We have a service to do the floors and furnishings once a week, but otherwise . . ." She paused and stared pointedly at Chris. "I do hope you understand, Christina. You will help."

Chris smiled very sweetly. "I love to clean."

"Sophia!" Gina di Medici gasped. "You mustn't ask Alfred's guest—"

"Guest! She's James Tarleton's daughter, isn't she? She is a part of all this. She shouldn't mind giving—"

"Sophia!" Gina di Medici could put quite a ring of authority into her voice when she chose, very much like her elder son. "I am the Contessa di Medici, and the last I heard, this is still the Palazzo di Medici! You'll not ask a guest—"

"Please! Please!" Chris interrupted, somewhat stunned by the sudden hostility between the two women. "Gina, I'm quite accustomed to looking after my own things and my own surroundings, which is what I believe Sophia is asking. And I'd rather not be a noncontributing guest. Really, I don't mind at all!"

Both of them were silent for a moment, staring at her as if they had just remembered that she was there. Sophia sighed first. "I am sorry. I shouldn't have spoken. If Marcus would just hire more help—"

"Marcus can't afford more help," Gina interrupted impatiently.

"Can't afford! Alfred would gladly—"

"Marcus will not accept Alfred's money for use in his private concerns," Gina said flatly.

"His reasons make no sense to me!" Sophia said, and then she continued speaking in rapid Italian that left Chris completely out in the cold. She turned her attention to the espresso she had chosen for after lunch and picked at a piece of cheese. Should she admire Marcus for refusing to take Alfred's money for his 'private concerns'? No, she thought dryly, why should she? Who else was there to eventually inherit everything—the Swiss accounts and the galleries—except for Marcus and Antonio di Medici?

Chris wondered a little sourly if the whole thing might be a show, put on entirely for her benefit. Perhaps the di Medicis wanted her to think that they were in the midst of financial difficulties. Exactly why, she wasn't sure. Maybe Marcus wanted her to think he was broke . . . just so she wouldn't go hunting for a di Medici husband! It was hard to believe that any of this lot were really facing poverty!

"What a lovely discussion for luncheon . . . with a guest in attendance!"

The words, drawled in icy English, stopped both Sophia and Gina cold. They—and Chris—stared up in horror at Marcus, who was making a swift entrance across the courtyard.

He ignored them, and their obvious discomfort, as he sat down and smiled at Teresa. "Teresa, espresso, *per favore*."

The girl bobbed to him and ran to do as she'd been told. He thanked her warmly, then caught Christina looking at him. She couldn't read the expression in his eyes; they were simply as sharp as midnight gems as he smiled slowly. "Well, it seems you have had a wonderful introduction to the palazzo. I assure you, we are not customarily so rude."

He was apologizing to her, and yet she felt that he was angry—also at her. Because he had heard the remarks regarding his finances?

Chris swirled the espresso in her cup, withdrawing her eyes from his. "I am just that, Marcus: a guest. I shouldn't interfere with the family."

"Marcus, I—" Gina began to say, but he waved a hand in the air. "*Per favore*, let's drop it! Christina, how was your morning."

"Lovely," she replied. "The pool is just beautiful."

Marcus stared down at his own espresso. "It *is* beautiful," he murmured. Then he looked at her. "Your father designed it."

"He did!"

"Yes, he was able to tell the workmen how to create it from an existing fountain and small fishpond."

Chris heard the sound of a chair being scraped back. She glanced up quickly to see that Gina di Medici was rising. "Marcus, Christina, you'll excuse me, please. I—I've acquired quite a headache."

Marcus was instantly at his mother's side, speaking to her softly in Italian. She smiled at him; he kissed her cheek and she left the courtyard.

"I really do not mean to give offense, Christina," Sophia said, "but it was terribly cruel of Alfred to ask you to this house."

"Sophia!" Marcus snapped.

Perhaps because Chris had had it with the accusations—unfounded, as far as she could see—being thrown so easily at her father, she was ready to fight her own battles.

She leaned across the table and gave Sophia a straightforward glare. "Perhaps it will prove to be a very good thing for the contessa that I am here. Maybe she has been blaming the wrong man for all these years. At any rate, Sophia, I am here, and I cannot leave until I understand it all—or until Alfred, or the contessa, ask me to!"

Sophia stared at her in return, apparently stunned. Then she emitted a furious oath, which Chris didn't understand, since it was in Italian. She did, however, get the general meaning.

Marcus said something very sharply. Sophia threw her napkin on the table and stalked back to the house, her high heels clicking loudly on the tiles.

Chris lifted her hands a little helplessly. "I, uh, I'm sorry. I really am causing quite a disturbance."

He laughed and sat down beside her again, idly drawing a finger over the back of her hand. "Perhaps, as you say, disturbance is good."

"But your mother..."

"My mother has lived too long with her memories. And I do not think that she blames you. Mother would not find fault with a child."

Chris was absurdly tempted to wrench her hand from the table because his touch was both lulling and far too evocative. She felt herself tensing, so she forced herself to relax and smile sweetly. She was out to win Marcus to her side, one way or another, and charm had been his brother's suggestion.

"It would be nice to prove that my father wasn't to blame, either," she said softly.

He grunted impatiently and pushed back his chair to rise. "Are you ready to leave?"

"Yes. I just have to get my purse. Shall I meet you at the bridge?"

"No, meet me back here. We'll walk."

"Walk?"

"Yes, we'll go the long way, since the bridge has been closed off for repairs. The galleries are actually on a little peninsula."

Chris nodded and hurried back through the house. She ran up to her room and grabbed her handbag, then paused briefly at her mirror. She'd chosen a short candy-striped halter dress with a wide band around the waist, hoping that the outfit would emphasize the nice color she had picked up that morning. It was summery, casual and, she added hopefully, smiling at her image, alluring. Her hair was freshly washed, full of sun and the light rose scent of a French shampoo. Unwilling to ponder her seductive powers or possible lack thereof, she quickly hurried out of the room and raced back downstairs.

Marcus was still standing in the courtyard, waiting for her. When she reached him, she was a little breathless. He smiled and took her elbow to lead her down a long set of steps to a slim pedestrian pathway marked, Via di Medici.

"You have your own road?" Chris asked.

"We've even got a canal," he replied lightly.

"Umm. Your mother said that she was a contessa. Does that make you a conte?"

"Yes, but it doesn't mean anything these days. Except—" he grinned down at her "—that we do get invited to have tea with the Queen when we're in London."

Chris laughed. He could be charming when he chose. Frighteningly so.

She walked in silence at his side for several seconds, noting that they passed a small flower stall, a cheese shop, a bakery and a boutique. Then they turned a corner, crossed over a small bridge and were in a square with the inevitable church to their left and the di Medici galleries before them and to the right.

Chris gasped softly. The building was, she thought, even more magnificent than the Doge's Palace. Eight massive columns decked the porch; row upon row of elegant terraces ringed each floor, evidence of a heavy baroque influence. The length of the roof was lined with colorful flags.

"My God, it's grand!" Chris murmured.

"Do you think so?" Marcus inquired politely. "We grow rather accustomed to such things here."

Chris laughed. "In Paris I grew accustomed to Notre Dame. But it's still grand. And so is this."

He smiled. Tolerantly, she thought. "Come on, I'll show you what I can. The left wing holds the pieces that are for sale. The right wing is a museum. The new exhibit is there. I'm sure that will interest you."

They started with the left wing. Chris wished she had a better education in art than she did. As Marcus pointed out several of the more valuable paintings, lithographs and sketches, the only names she recognized were Picasso and Dalí. Hoping to sound intelligent, she asked Marcus why such works were for sale and not in the museum.

He shrugged. "Because we have to keep the place afloat," he told her. Then he smiled again. "Our crowning glory here is a very unique Rembrandt. And we have a number of small sculptures made by the students of Michelangelo."

They walked through another gallery filled with tableware: flatware in both silver and gold, china and crystal. Another room featured love seats, a third bedroom furnishings.

"And this is all for sale?" Chris murmured.

"Of course. We acquire to sell. Only when a piece is extremely unique can we afford the luxury of adding it to the museum. But come, you'll see our private treasures now."

After crossing an inner courtyard to the right wing, they were stopped by a rotund jovial man. Marcus greeted him quickly in Italian. When the man turned to Chris, grinning like an old friend, Marcus quickly introduced her in English. "Christina, you probably don't remember Joe—Giuseppi Conseli. He has been with us since the galleries were opened. Joe, Christina Tarleton, all grown up."

Joe broke into a quick spate of excited Italian, then apologized profusely. "Chris, little Chris! But of course, you were so little! You cannot remember old Joe, eh?" He took her hand between both of his, then sighed, glancing at Marcus. "Ah, all will be well now, perhaps. The three names are joined again: Contini, di Medici and Tarleton. Christina, it is a pleasure!"

"Thank you," she told him, wincing a bit at the pressure of his handshake. "It's a pleasure to see you."

And it was definitely a pleasure to see someone who was pleased to see her.

He smiled at her warmly again. He was almost completely bald and his head gleamed like a dime.

"Marcus, I do not like to disturb you, but can you come?"

"Yes, of course." He turned to Chris. "Why don't you go through the history display with the robotronics, Chris? It takes about twenty minutes, and I will be back by then."

She frowned. "Is there trouble?"

"I need to see the workmen below," he told her briefly. Then, to her surprise, he kissed the top of her head and hurried away with Joe.

She stood there watching his agile broad-shouldered form walk away. Stood there shivering inwardly, fascinated by his touch.

She forced herself to turn and find the historical exhibit. It was not an auditorium, as she had imagined it would be, but rather a theater-in-the-round. The center stage was alive with light, while all around there was shadow. Chris watched the figures, fascinated. There were Roman soldiers, medieval knights, the doges or duces of the Dark Ages and Renaissance, elegantly dressed ladies, milkmaids and even several of the more notorious courtesans.

The exhibit was marvelous. The figures were incredibly lifelike as they moved on their pedestals and spoke in soft Italian.

When Chris left the exhibit she immediately ran into Marcus again. The rotund Joe was still at his side, as was another taller and swarthier man.

"How did you like it?" Marcus asked her quickly.

"Breathtaking," she told him.

He turned to the swarthy man with the very lean face and very dark eyes. A man, Chris decided, right out of an Edgar Allan Poe poem.

"Chris, I wanted you to meet Fredo Talio. He and Joe are my most valuable assistants. Fredo, like Joe, has been with us since the galleries opened."

Chris said hello and discovered that the swarthy man was capable of a decent smile. Even so, he made her uneasy.

She wondered why, then realized that Alfred Contini had told her that both these men had been aboard the sailboat the day that Mario di Medici had gone overboard and died. She was anxious to know them . . . and also frightened.

They stood for several seconds talking to the two men; then Marcus took her arm again. *"Con permesso,"* he murmured to the two. "You will excuse us. I wish to show Chris the gem salon before the galleries close for the day."

Fredo and Joe quickly moved out of the way, murmuring that they had things to do before closing. Marcus led her quickly down a long hallway that opened onto an immense room with only five or six waist-high cases. A massive glass skylight let in what remained of the afternoon sun and caused the jewels in their cases to sparkle with rainbow brilliance.

"Dear God!" Chris gasped, and Marcus laughed.

"No, Chris, we do not own all of these. Most are on loan from the Italian government. These are all crown jewels from various principalities and duchies."

She couldn't help but ooh and aah as they walked past the various display cases. She didn't consider herself much of a jewelry fanatic, but these were magnificent. Crowns with every conceivable stone: diamonds galore, rubies, sapphires, emeralds. Opals and pearls, aquamarines and other semiprecious stones. Bracelets, medallions, necklaces—even a set of toe rings that had belonged to a Renaissance Veronese duchess.

Not until they reached the last of the exhibits, the one directly in the center of the room beneath the skylight, did she realize that Marcus was watching her. And then, as she stared at the tiara and medallion in the case, something registered in her mind. The emblem on the medallion, the coat of arms, was familiar. The winged lion was in the center, a thorned rose to the right, and Neptune rising to the left.

"di Medici!" she proclaimed, and Marcus grinned.

"Yes," he said simply. "We do own those."

He led her out of the salon and toward the stairs to the courtyard and main entrance. "Would you like to have dinner out?" he asked her casually.

She glanced up at him. "Would I like to have dinner out . . . or would you prefer not to return to your own palazzo?"

He laughed. "All right, I'd just as soon not go back right now. Do you mind?"

Chris lowered her eyes quickly. "Not at all," she told him quietly.

"There's a small . . . intimate . . . place right around the next corner," he told her.

She forced her eyes up and kept smiling. From where they stood, she could see the bridge that led from building to building, from The di Medici Galleries to the Palazzo di Medici. Marcus was holding her arm, and she could feel another onslaught of tremors, hot and cold, thrilling and weakening. She spoke quickly. "Did things work out well?"

"Things?"

"With the workmen?"

"Oh, yes. They believe it's quite safe. Only minor repairs."

"What?"

"The tunnel . . . and the catacombs, of course."

"What's down there?"

His lips curved slightly; his eyes held a definitely wicked cast, all the more beguiling as the sun slipped lower and the sky was bathed in orange and scarlet. "Family secrets and skeletons," he told her. "What else would a di Medici keep buried below the earth? If you have the courage and heart, Chris, I'll take you one day."

She laughed, shaking off his macabre tone. "Oh, I've got the heart. And in daylight, I'm loaded with courage." She frowned then. "What was Joe saying when we first met him, when he was talking so enthusiastically in Italian?"

He watched her for a moment, his eyes partially hidden by the darkness of his lashes. "He was saying that you had grown like a flower. Like a rose. Very beautiful."

"Oh!" Chris murmured.

"A thorny rose, I told him."

"Did you?"

"Of course." He paused for just a minute, then smiled dryly. He started walking again, pulling her close, and murmuring to her in a warm stirring whisper. "You are beautiful, Christina. But then, you know that, don't you? You're relying on that fact to wheedle every bit of information out of me that you want."

"What!" she demanded, wrenching away from him. His tone had been so seductive that she hadn't realized for several seconds that she was being mocked.

He appeared undaunted by her anger, only challenged. He pulled a pack of cigarettes from his inner jacket pocket and lit one, watching her over the flare of his match.

"I told you, Christina, I do not care to be conned. But . . ." He shrugged, then smiled slowly, and in the darkness she couldn't tell if the smile was sardonic, or merely amused. "But perhaps I will not mind being charmed. We will have dinner alone, away from the palazzo, and perhaps I will tell you why your father was accused."

"Perhaps!" she snapped. "You owe it to me! Damn it! Someone owes me an explanation."

"Don't tell me what I do or do not owe, Christina," he warned her quietly, but she sensed the granite behind his words, the warning . . . or threat.

She didn't feel like backing down, even if she was shivering again, outwardly and inwardly. And she didn't know if it was with anger or the sense that she had fallen prey to something beyond common sense or logic.

Fallen prey to Marcus. His excitement and danger.

He didn't allow her time to answer. He slipped an arm around her, pulling her close to his body, its strength and riveting heat. "You're cold," he told her. "Let's get to the *ristorante*. Because I choose to, I'll explain what happened. Though you really should know."

"How could I?" Chris cried out.

He hesitated again, and she could feel him looking down at her, his cobalt eyes raking over her. She cast her head back to meet those eyes, now cold as the moon.

"Because you were there," he said softly.

Chapter Four

What?"

"Could we go inside, please? You're shivering again. And I'd appreciate it if you'd quit shouting."

"I'm not shout—"

He laughed, bringing his hand from her shoulder to clamp it lightly over her mouth. "You were shouting. *Per favore!* Can we go inside?"

Chris nodded, and managed to maintain a tense silence while he led the way into a restaurant called Le Grotto. The place gave the appearance of a cave—or a cellar, at the very least—but it was decorated with warm wood and plants, and each of the booths was very private, in its own little enclave. They were seated immediately, and when the waiter spoke ingratiatingly to Marcus, he glanced at Chris.

"Wine?"

She shrugged. "When in Rome . . ."

"This is Venice," he reminded her.

"Close enough."

He spoke to the waiter in quick flowing Italian, then faced Chris again, his hands folded on the table. "You really have no memory of Venice?" he asked her.

"No, not really," Chris murmured, wondering suddenly if that meant that Marcus intended to lie to her. "Just...images now and then. A sense of déjà vu. When I got to St. Mark's Square I knew what it was going to look like, although I didn't really remember it, if that makes any sense."

The wine arrived, and the waiter poured a small amount in Marcus's glass. He tasted it and nodded. A glass was poured for Chris, and small crisp loaves of Italian bread were set before them. Marcus caught the waiter before he could leave, asking Chris quickly if she liked shrimp.

"Yes," she told him.

"It's their specialty. Shall I order?"

Why did she feel that it wasn't really a request? Because it wasn't, she decided. It was an assumption that she would comply. He was just showing a facade of courtesy.

She lifted a hand. "It makes no difference."

He placed their order, and the waiter moved away. Somewhere a violinist was playing, but it seemed that they were very much alone. They were across the table from one another, but her kneecaps kept brushing his and even that contact seemed to start her heart racing.

"Would you care to go on?" she asked him, watching him over the rim of her wineglass. He raised one brow, but kept silent. "Would you please go on?" she murmured with a saccharine edge, smiling as she added, in a softly warning tone, "Before I start shouting again and leap across the table to strangle you."

He chuckled, a warning in itself. "Why do I doubt, Christi, that you could do such a thing?"

She ignored the comment. "All right. Alfred Contini and Sophia were there on the yacht that day. My parents and your parents. Genovese was there . . . and Joe Conseli and Fredo Talio. Right?"

"Yes. And so were Tony and I . . . and you."

Chris took an overlarge drink of her wine. The dry liquid burned her throat and abdomen. She swallowed a second time and set her glass down, wanting to watch him but unable to. She traced a finger around the rim of her wineglass.

"So why my father, Marcus? All those people were there . . . yet it's pinned on my father. How? Why?"

"Because your father was the last person to see him alive."

"The last person to admit to seeing him alive!" Chris exclaimed indignantly.

"Because," Marcus said, and his voice seemed to grate impatiently, "they'd been fighting."

"Fighting?"

"Yes. They'd come to blows. Your father had a black eye and a cut lip. He told your mother that my father looked worse." He was silent for a minute, then added bitterly, "And, oh, he did! By the time they found him, he was hardly recognizable."

The waiter came over then, leaving a typical antipasto tray piled high with olives, small tomatoes, celery, anchovies and slim pepperoni. Chris looked at the platter, feeling a little ill.

The waiter moved away.

"You're not eating," Marcus commented.

She stared up at him furiously. "No, I'm not. And you've got no right at all to condemn my father on such slim evidence!"

"Slim evidence?" he asked quietly as he selected a piece of pepperoni.

"Damned slim...and even an Italian judge thought so, too!" Chris exclaimed. "All right, they'd been fighting. But like two men, Marcus. My father came in with a black eye, not with a denial. He didn't do anything cold-blooded or conniving. He got into a fight. Where is your sense of reason? Obviously someone else killed your father!"

"Who?" Marcus demanded flatly, and she felt the full blue flame of his gaze. "Myself? Or Tony? You? Perhaps you're up to strangling men these days, but you were only four at the time. Your mother? She never left the cabin."

"You're neglecting Alfred, Genovese, Joe and Fredo, and Sophia," Chris said stiffly. "And your own mother."

His hand shot out across the table, encircling her wrist in a painful vise. "You would accuse a woman who has lived in a tomb herself since his death? My mother?"

"Why not?" Chris demanded heatedly, ignoring the burning hold around her wrist and meeting his gaze with fury of her own. "You accuse my father."

He emitted an impatient curse and practically threw her wrist from him. "You refuse to face the facts, Christina," he said wearily. "Your father left. The rest of us . . . we have all been together for the past twenty-one years. I'm sorry. Everyone believes that your father killed mine. If he hadn't, somewhere in all these years, something would have come up. Some type of evidence or proof of guilt. It has not."

Chris took a deep breath. "You're wrong about one thing, Marcus. Not everyone thinks my father was guilty. Alfred Contini doesn't think my father killed yours."

She had the supreme satisfaction of seeing stunned surprise filter across his customarily guarded and implacable features.

"What?" he demanded with a quick harsh breath.

"You heard me."

"Alfred told you this?"

"Yes, quite flatly." Chris smiled, picking up her wineglass to swirl the liquid around. "It's rather amazing, isn't it? All these years, Alfred Contini has been cared for into his old age by the powerful di Medicis. His loving mistress stays by his side...but he came to me, a near stranger, to ask for help."

"He asked for your help?"

"He said that he needed me." Chris just stopped herself from telling him that Alfred intended to meet her alone at the galleries to talk to her and impart secrets that he didn't want the "walls" or the "air" to hear. She wanted to rub Marcus di Medici's nose in his own arrogance, but she reminded herself that Marcus could be the very "walls" or "air" that Alfred had meant.

Marcus lowered his head. A lock of his jet hair fell across his forehead, and when he raised his eyes to Chris once again, they were filled with amusement. The candlelight was caught in his eyes, making them look like blue diamonds, and something about his expression caused Chris to catch her breath and reminded her with a little shock that she should never have forgotten her first impression of the man. He was elementally dangerous on many levels, not least of them sexual.

Her hand lay on the table. He reached out to touch it again, but this time without painful strength. She found that she was staring at his fingers as they stroked her flesh. The nails were neatly bluntly cut. His hands appeared slimmer than they were because his fingers were long. Long, and filled with a shocking strength . . . and stunning tenderness. Now his touch grazed lightly, almost absently, over her knuckles, and he warned her with humor, "I wouldn't take anything that Alfred has to say too seriously. His health is poor, and I think that he is often bored with life these days."

"Bored, perhaps, but not senile," Chris objected quietly. Her eyes were still drawn to his fingers where they stroked her hand. She could snatch it away, she knew, but some part of her refused to do so. She couldn't help it; she had never pretended to herself that she had been anything but fascinated by him from the first. If he had walked away she would have been fine. But instead he had become, within hours, the focal point of her life.

"Then, Christina," he murmured lightly, "perhaps you should be very careful. If any of what you are saying is true, Alfred could well be casting you straight into the fire!"

Her eyes flew to his. "What?" she demanded.

He shrugged. "Oh, Christina! I wasn't being serious! Alfred is old and lonely. Perhaps he craves a little intrigue or excitement in his life, and perhaps he also feels this is a time for peace. He has you here; he does not want you hurt. It's very possible that his plan is simply to give you a sense of well-being so that in your mind, and your heart, you can clear your father."

"I don't . . ."

She paused when the waiter arrived, and watched as their pasta and shrimp were served. The pasta tonight was a spaghettini with a light sauce. The shrimp had been broiled in oil and garlic, then topped with crispy cheese and bread crumbs. Everything smelled delicious, and Chris hoped she could find an appetite.

Among other things, she was acquiring a headache. The white wine that Marcus had ordered was extremely potent.

The waiter refilled their glasses, and apparently asked Marcus if there would be anything else. Marcus glanced to Chris. She hadn't understood many of the words, but she had grasped the question. She smiled at the waiter.

"No, *grazie*."

He left them. Chris picked up her fork to poke at the shrimp. She started when she felt Marcus's hand on hers again, and when she looked into his eyes this time, she felt as if something as haunting as Venice itself swept through her being. There was, she thought, guarded concern in his eyes, something gentle where there was so often anger and mockery.

"Christina, let it all lie," he told her quietly. "Let the past go. You are here, you are welcome. Enjoy Venice, enjoy the galleries. My father is dead, so is yours. Let them rest."

"I . . ."

She wanted despertely to break his spell over her. She tossed back her hair and offered him a very cool smile. "Have you forgotten? I'm really after Alfred's money."

He slowly withdrew his hand from hers, and she saw the ice rise in his eyes again. "Ah, yes. Alfred's money. Or a di Medici husband, didn't you say? Actually, we're not worth much . . . financially."

"Oh, but you must be! All those gems! Those paintings!"

He smiled, white teeth flashing in the candlelight, copper features harsh and drawn. "The galleries and the palazzo, they are hungry, Christina. They consume money like sharks prey upon the weak."

Chris chewed a shrimp and deliberately ignored his comment. "This really is delicious, Marcus. And you needn't worry too much. I'll go after Tony, I believe. He has a much sweeter disposition."

"Really? Perhaps I should try to exude a greater charm."

"You could try," Chris murmured noncommittally, and she began to wonder what she was doing besides playing with fire.

He seemed to be thinking the same thing. Smiling laconically, he reached across the table, grazing her cheek with his thumb.

"The irony of it, Christina, is that I do find you fascinating," he murmured, and a flash of pure heat assailed her. "So if you choose to flirt with fire, *cara* Christi, see that you do not do so carrying casks of petrol, eh?"

Chris caught his hand and placed it on the table, smiling sweetly. "I always flirt carefully, Marcus."

He laughed, freeing her from his spell.

"Eat your shrimp, Christina. *Manga. Manga.*" Smiling with a slight curl of his lips, he tapped her glass.

"Bicchiere," he said, and she smiled, finding herself repeating him. *"Pane."* He picked up the bread, then pointed to her shrimp. *"Frutti de mare."*

"Fruit of the sea?" she asked.

"Literally, yes. Seafood."

Chris did manage to eat as the meal turned into a lesson in the Italian language. And—the déjà vu again—many of the words rolled off her tongue very easily.

Despite the fact that the evening had begun with tense anger and rigid determination, she discovered that she had a nice time. She laughed, smiled and was, she was certain, charming . . . to an extent, at least.

But then, he had already told her all that he could. Or had he? She didn't feel like dealing with it anymore that night. Her headache had become lightheadedness, and the idea of playing with fire had become very seductive.

By the time they left Le Grotto Ristorante a full moon had risen over the city. Chris smiled slightly as she stared up at it. Venice, Venezia . . . it was a city of romance, touched by the years and by the future. She loved the water, the bridges, the gondolas and everything about the city.

And Marcus . . .

Dark, handsome and intriguing. The perfect host when he chose to be. Courteous, charming, polite.

But always . . . mysterious. It was his eyes, she decided then. So deeply, deeply blue against his dark complexion. His features were so ruggedly defined, his movements so smooth. What was it about the man? She liked the casual touch of his hands, the feel of the fabric of his suit. His casual laughter, his negligence and . . .

And his intensity. It was always there, lurking beneath his smile or his laughter. In the way he looked at her, touched her with his eyes.

The narrow roads were almost empty as they sauntered slowly back to the palazzo. She didn't mind his arm about her at all, and that thought made her smile again.

She was going to have to watch out for the local Venetian wines. They were a potent brew.

It seemed that he could read her mind. As they neared the palazzo steps he asked her, "Did you like the restaurant?"

"Yes."

"The shrimp?"

"Yes."

"The wine?"

She wrinkled her nose. "It was a little dry."

"Ah, well, there is a similar sweeter vintage," he murmured.

"I'll have to try it sometime."

"Yes," he murmured. He opened the gate and locked it behind him. Then, in the shadow of the steps, shrouded by vines and shadowed by the moon, he pulled her into his arms.

Startled, Chris stared upward into his eyes. She felt his palms grazing her bare shoulders, then fitting themselves to the base of her spine, pulling her hard against him. His lashes fell briefly over his cobalt eyes, darker than the night, hypnotic, and then he returned her gaze with a probing depth.

"If it's Antonio you're after," he whispered, "I'll have to sample what I might be missing . . . now."

Chris knew that she should resist him, yet she had no desire to. She watched his eyes as they came closer and closer to hers, then disappeared altogether as she closed her own and felt the hot provocative touch of his mouth, firm against hers. Ah, yes, she had charmed him. Done such a wonderful job that she was in his arms, losing sight of everything but the perfect feeling of being there. This kiss was no mild thing, stirred and fanned to grow deeper; it began as a tempest. She felt that she melted at the steel of his arms about her, fusing to his length. And yet she was real and alive, and aware that as he held her, she pressed her length to his, arching to appease the hunger of his mouth and her own. His tongue moved wickedly, fluid and demanding; his hand moved to her cheek, then caressed her throat. Blue fire sizzled within her, sweet and urgent, lapping along her spine, burning into her limbs. She played with the dark hair at his nape, touched his cheek, savored the scent and taste of him, barely aware that in all her life, she had never been kissed like this. So deeply, so passionately. Never had a man made her feel so alive, so hungry herself.... She felt the warmth of him beneath his jacket, the taut musculature, rippling, powerful beneath her fingers. The feeling grew that this was something wild and beautiful, as old as original sin, but absurdly right.

It was the full moon over Venice, she decided vaguely. Erotic, romantic, decadent...casting a light of intrigue and fascination. But no, it wasn't the moon or Venice, she admitted somewhere in her heart. It was the man. Marcus di Medici. Tall, sleek and sinewed, unleashing his power, the intangible strength of the sensuality she had known she would find and shiver beneath since she had first seen him....

His mouth drew gently away from hers, and his hands tangled in her hair as he held her close, kissing her cheeks and her throat, holding her, feeling the erratic racing of her pulse. Then, at last, he stepped back and she almost fell; he righted her, then released her.

And smiled.

"Christina..." he murmured, and the sound of her name had never sounded so raw and exotic before. But then a cloud passed over the moon, and when she could see his face again, it was cast in shadow and his eyes were elusive indigo. He smiled, and even before he spoke, she knew that the cloud had taken something away, that he had changed.

"It's a pity," he said lightly, "that you're after money...and I really have so little."

She was dying to slap him, but she knew he would be amused, and prepared to stop the gesture before she could complete it.

She managed to smile very icily instead. "Don't worry about it. I still find Tony by far the more...charming...of the brothers di Medici. *Buona sera*, Marcus. *Grazie*, for dinner—and for the... entertainment."

Chris was pleased with her control, proud of her dry reply and relieved that she had held her temper in check.

But she was raging inside.

She walked up the steps and across the courtyard with slow and amazing hauteur... but she ran up the steps to her room, and hurled her purse onto the bed with a streak of pure violence.

Marcus di Medici... she would truly love to strangle him. Just what the hell was his game?

Her anger fled suddenly, leaving her so weak that she sank down onto the bed.

His game...

Yes, Marcus was playing a game. But there was something deeper here, too. Something that went beyond their words, beyond circumstances. Words could easily be lies, and yet...

It was no lie that he wanted her. That, too, she had known from the first time their eyes had met.

And yet he was like a dark panther. Accustomed to stalking, accustomed to the kill. Aware of his own strength. Wasn't she just like any other prey that he had set his eyes upon?

Chris took a deep breath and began to pace her room, riddled with confusion, doubt and fear. Half the time she was certain that he despised her. But then he would smile, or he would laugh... or he would touch her. And she would feel again that his touch couldn't be a lie, that the electricity that had sparkled between them and flourished at every new meeting was flaring toward an explosion that was inevitable, that she could never deny. That she would never want to deny. He made her ache with anticipation, made her long to delve past the mysteries or ignore them, just to be with him.

Chris sank back onto the bed again. Mysteries. The palazzo was filled with them, shadowed by the past. Guilt was the family skeleton.

But already, absurdly, her heart was rebelling against her mind. There might be evil somewhere, but Marcus could not be that evil.

He was innocent. Totally.

Innocent of what? she asked herself.

Then a sense of foreboding settled over her so chillingly that she had to rise again, running her hands over her bare shoulders and hugging herself for warmth.

Something was going to happen. She had come here to find out about the past. Well, she had found out. And now she was going to prove that her father had never been a murderer.

Chris smiled grimly to herself. So what if she was fascinated by Marcus—he had admitted to being fascinated in return. She would be damned if she would be a pawn; he would be forced to play that position.

Determined, Chris showered and changed for bed, then crawled between the silk sheets, very carefully remaining dead center. She assured herself that she would find out the truth. Alfred Contini would be able to give her all the information she needed.

If Alfred said that her father was innocent, then it seemed very obvious to Chris that he was.

But proving it wouldn't be that easy. As she tossed about—carefully—trying to get comfortable so that she could fall asleep, she realized that she had acquired a very real sense of fear. Of foreboding.

And she couldn't shake it until sleep at last claimed her.

Chris awoke in the middle of the night, wondering why she had done so. Then she was touched by the chilling feeling that someone was in her room, watching her.

She opened her eyes carefully. Moonlight was pouring in from the terrace in a soft glow. She could easily see everything but the farthest corners of the room. She didn't realize that she had been holding her breath until she exhaled shakily with relief. There was no one there.

She hesitated for a few moments, then crawled from the bed, carrying her pillow with her. She wasn't sure why, since a pillow wasn't much of a weapon. But even when she checked out the corners and the bathroom, there was nothing to imply that anyone had ever been in the room or anywhere near her.

Puzzled, Chris sat on the corner of the bed, trying to fathom the strange feeling that had assailed her. She had been so certain....

But why would anyone in the di Medici household want to come in and stare at her as she slept, anyway?

She shrugged, then stood and walked slowly, as if drawn, to the terrace. She had never been out on it before; she knew it connected her room with Marcus di Medici's.

The gauze drapes drifted around her as she stepped into the night air. The moon was still shining beautifully. There were no clouds, and it was a silver orb hung against black velvet. Or indigo velvet, really. A blue darkness just like...

Chris took a few steps along the terrace, her bare feet silent. The French doors to Marcus's room were open. Curiosity compelled her to step closer to them. She hesitated when she reached them, then peered around one door. Was Marcus, too, out on a silent stalk in the night?

The moonglow filtered into the room. She saw his bed, placed against the opposite wall. The sheets, a striking masculine indigo, were drawn back invitingly, but there was nobody in the bed. She gazed at the drapery beside her hand. Indigo.

But the Persian area rugs that lay scattered about the floor were light, and there was a white French Provincial clock on his heavy dresser. It was a striking room, much like its occupant.

But where, Chris wondered, was Marcus di Medici? Had he been in her room, silently moving about? Looking for something? What?

She inhaled deeply, then exhaled. She shouldn't be here. She had been disturbed by a possible covert invasion of her privacy, but wasn't she doing the same thing? It was ridiculous to be here, barefoot and scarcely clothed, peeking into a man's room.

Chris turned to tiptoe back to her own room, but from the other side of the door a hand shot out, capturing her arm, spinning her back around. Terrified, she screamed—but her scream was choked off by a hand quickly clamped over her mouth. Shivering with dismay, she heard Marcus speak just as she looked up and saw his eyes, devil dark, yet blazing where they caught the moon's glow.

"Will you shut up—unless, of course, you wish to explain to the entire household why you were sneaking about my room in the middle of the night."

Rigid, she shook her head. He released her and planted his hands on his hips. Chris noted that he, too, was barefoot. And clad only in a belted knee-length robe. A gold chain around his neck gleamed. She followed its line down the V of his robe to a medallion nestled in a thick mat of dark hair on his chest.

"If you had knocked, I would gladly have let you in," he drawled insinuatingly.

Chris instantly decided to go on the offensive. "What were you doing in my room?" she demanded.

"*Cara*, this is my room."

"But you were in mine!" Chris declared.

"Doing what?" he demanded impatiently.

"I—I don't know. Standing, sneaking around . . ."

"I believe I just caught *you* sneaking around."

"That's exactly the point. You were hiding behind the door—"

He sighed with exasperation. "I was behind my door because I heard someone prowling around the terrace."

"I wasn't prowling. . ." Chris began to protest, then she asserted, "Someone was in *my* room!"

He laughed. "Christina, I promise, if I'm ever in your room, you'll definitely be aware that someone is there . . . and that it is me."

"Oh, go to hell!" Chris muttered, turning to walk back along the terrace to her own doors. She entered her room, then turned around to give the moon one last suspicious glance. Instead she started, gasping as she crashed into Marcus.

"Shhh!" he warned harshly, bringing a finger to his lips, holding her bare arm with his other hand.

"What are you doing?" she whispered a little desperately. Not only was she half-naked, but so was he. And he was so close that she could feel the coarse hair on his chest teasing the flesh of her breasts through the silk of her gown. A trembling heat, the sensation that engulfed her when he came too close, threatened to overwhelm her.

"We'll check out your room," he told her.

"I already did," she murmured.

Nevertheless he released her, then moved around the room, a stealthy silent shadow. For a moment he disappeared into her bathroom, then reappeared, hands on his hips once again, one brow laconically raised. "Your door is locked, isn't it?"

"Yes."

"Are you quite certain that you don't have strange imaginings?" he asked her. "Or fantasies?"

"Will you get out of here, please?" Chris demanded irritably.

He chuckled softly. "Certainly, *cara* Christina . . ." He didn't touch her again. But at the doors, he paused and gave her an amused grin. "I do like your 'prowling' mode of dress, Christina. In fact, I'm growing very fond of that gown."

She was glad that she was in the darker shadow of the room, because a flush rose to burn her features. There was nothing to her gown. She had known it last night; she knew it now. Sheer, spaghetti-strapped and long, but with high slits along each leg.

She had no reply; he wasn't expecting one.

Chris crawled back into bed, determined that she was going to get to a boutique in the morning and purchase some puritanical neck-to-toe cotton nightgowns.

And then, of course, she wondered why she should be so determined. How many more clandestine meetings was she expecting to have with Marcus di Medici?

"I should lock those damn terrace doors," she muttered to herself. But it didn't occur to her to get up again and do so.

It was almost eleven o'clock by the time she went downstairs the next morning. Once she had fallen asleep again, she must have slept like a rock.

There was no one around when she reached the courtyard, but the snowy tablecloth, with a single flower and place setting for her, waited invitingly.

Chris wandered to the serving cart to pour herself coffee.

"*Buongiorno*, Signorina Tarleton."

Startled, Chris spun around. Genovese was coming across the courtyard toward her.

Chris studied the man. He was no more than five-foot-eight and slim, but wiry. His eyes were dark, and his dark hair was untouched by silver, but seeing his weathered olive face up close, Chris knew he was either in his late forties or early fifties. But of course. He couldn't really be a young man. He had been with Alfred Contini for at least twenty-one years.

"*Buongiorno*, Genovese," Chris murmured a little awkwardly, taking a sip of her coffee. "I, uh, I'm sorry to be late. I appreciate the coffee you've kept for me."

"There are croissants in the basket," Genovese said, his English heavily accented.

"Molto grazie," Chris told him softly.

He smiled, then chuckled. "No, signora. *Molto bene*, as in food, eh? *Mille grazie.* A thousand thank-yous."

Chris laughed, too. "Thank you for the lesson, Genovese. Maybe one day I'll get it all right."

He pulled out her chair. "Once, when you were a little, little girl, you had it all right."

Chris sat, wondering why she felt so uneasy to have the man behind her. Alfred trusted him implicitly. But it seemed that since she had come to Venice and the Palazzo di Medici, she didn't like having her back turned to anyone.

"Strange, isn't it?" she murmured. "Some things are easy to remember . . . and some things are not."

He was still behind her. "You remember nothing of your years in Venice?"

Did she? Yes, bits and pieces, a fragment here and there . . . or perhaps it was only the pretense of memory, something totally subconscious that surfaced without her command.

"No, absolutely nothing." She lied cheerfully. "Where is everyone?"

"Alfred and Marcus are out on business; Tony has not returned from Firenze. Sophia has gone shopping; Gina is in the chapel."

"The chapel?"

"*Si*, she . . . meditates."

"In other words, she wishes her privacy?" Chris asked him.

"Ah . . . yes," Genovese murmured, at last moving around the table. "If there is anything that you need . . ."

"There is nothing at all that I need, Genovese. *Mille grazie*."

"Then I will leave you," he murmured.

Please do! Chris thought silently, and was angry at herself for allowing the man to make her uneasy. He'd never been anything but perfectly courteous and polite. She was allowing herself to become frightened, and that bothered her.

Chris was glad to be alone. She ate a croissant and sipped two cups of coffee, then decided to spend the afternoon following the path she had learned last night. She would find that boutique and purchase new nightgowns. She would also find a bookstore and buy herself a good English-Italian dictionary. Then, if Alfred couldn't help her, she would find out what newspaper morgues and record offices she could get to so she could study the media coverage of Mario's death and see what had been written about the involvement of her father, and everyone in the household.

So decided, she ran upstairs for her purse, then found Genovese in the hallway and told him that she'd be gone for most of the afternoon.

He was like a very concerned parent, offering to accompany her so that she didn't get lost. Chris assured him that she was a seasoned traveler, and that even if her command of the Italian language was close to nil, she knew enough to get around the streets.

He still appeared unhappy when she left.

But Chris loved her afternoon out. She found exactly what she wanted in the boutique: nightgowns so all-encompassing that only her face and hands were left bare. On impulse she also bought a stunning black cocktail gown that had been greatly reduced in price.

It was fun to wander around. She adored all the alleyways and little bridges and the beautiful old churches she came to on almost every corner. She stopped at a little sidewalk café and bought herself cappuccino and some bread and cheese for lunch, and tried to think out all of the things she had learned since coming to the palazzo.

But uneasiness settled over her again, the feeling that something was about to happen. Ridiculous, she told herself. It was just Venice. She was allowing herself to get wrapped up in the past, and it was nothing less than ridiculous.

But she was convinced that someone had been in her room last night. Marcus? He had been up; he had caught her as easily and stealthily as if he had been waiting for her....

No, he wouldn't lie. Why not? she charged herself. Because he was Marcus. Because she . . .

Was falling beneath his spell. Thinking about him in the bright sunlight made her shiver, then grow hot.

Impatiently, Chris paid her bill and started to wander back toward the palazzo. Alfred would tell her something on Friday, she was convinced. She would prove her father's innocence, then bow regally out of the picture and return to Paris, where she could decide what she wanted to do with the rest of her life.

Thinking about her life reminded Chris that she had spent a day with no exercise at all. When she returned to the palazzo she hurried straight to her room, changed into a leotard and worked out on the floor to limber her muscles.

When she decided she had practiced long enough for a seasoned mime on vacation, she was thirsty. Not trusting her system to Italian tap water—even in Paris, she drank only bottled water—Chris decided to find the kitchen and get a drink. She drew a skirt on over her leotard and tights and hurried down the stairs in her dance slippers, remembering to follow the arched hallway to the right.

She found the formal dining room—a huge place containing a grand old table with enough chairs for twenty people—and knew the kitchen must be right through the archway behind it.

But at the archway, Chris paused.

People were arguing in the kitchen. Violently. Two voices were rising in very rapid, very vehement Italian.

One of the voices belonged to Alfred Contini. The other, Chris realized slowly, belonged to Genovese.

She paused for several seconds, then decided that she didn't want to be caught eavesdropping, even if she couldn't understand a word. She hurried back through the dining room to the entryway, then decided to wander out to the courtyard. There might be something to drink set out on one of the serving carts, and she hoped that Alfred would make an appearance, and possibly explain something about what had been going on.

But Chris never reached the courtyard. She noticed a wrought-iron gate in the center of the hallway that she hadn't registered before. She paused, then walked toward it.

It led to a sweeping set of marble steps that went downward into darkness.

There was something about the steps that touched a chord in her memory. Wide white marble going downward into darkness. They were probably like a hundred others in Italy, Chris reminded herself, leading beneath the main level of the palazzo to the catacombs...and the chapel, she assumed. Gina had been down there earlier, wanting privacy. But that had been hours ago. Marcus had warned her that the subterranean tunnels weren't safe, but surely the chapel was or else Gina would not have been there.

Chris shrugged a little uncomfortably. None of it really mattered. She knew she was going to go down the steps. There was simply something there that... beckoned to her.

She opened the gate and started down, her footsteps very silent in her slippers. Her breath came quickly, and yet she wasn't frightened at all, just very curious and anticipatory.

Darkness quickly fell around her, but then she saw light ahead of her coming from one side. She reached the last step. It was cavernous here; great unadorned arches swept away in perfect symmetry to her left. They faded into darkness, and Chris knew that they marked the tunnel that led beneath the water to the galleries. To the right, from where the light came, was the chapel.

She walked quickly to it.

It was a simple chapel; there was an altar with a large gold cross, and several pews. The ceiling was frescoed, and various religious paintings lined the walls. Chris walked forward to stare at the altar, shivering a little. She knew that she had been here before.

"You recognize our chapel?"

The question was softly voiced. Chris spun around. Gina di Medici was kneeling in the last pew. Chris hadn't seen her because she had been hidden from view by the doorway.

"Yes," Chris answered Gina. Then she added, "I'm sorry to disturb you. I—I didn't think you'd be here so long."

Gina smiled—sadly, Chris thought—and stood to walk up to Chris.

"When you were a child you loved to come here to play. We tried to tell you that it was a place for sanctity, but you did not care to listen. Someone told you that the original di Medicis claimed to have built their altar with a tiny bone fragment belonging to St. Mark at its center. You wanted us to tear up the altar so that you could see the bone."

Chris grimaced. "I'm afraid I must have been a rather irreverent child."

Gina waved a hand in the air. "All children are irreverent, yes?"

"I hope," Chris murmured. Gina's words were quiet, and they seemed friendly. But her eyes, so crystal blue, held the sadness that never failed to touch Chris. Suddenly she wanted to leave as desperately as she had wanted to come.

She backed away from Gina. "I'll leave you now, Gina. Truly, I didn't mean to intrude."

"Christina . . . wait. A moment, please."

"Yes?" Chris murmured, forcing herself to stay still. It seemed as if the chapel were shrinking, closing in around her.

"I—I want you to know that I am glad to have you here. I missed you very much when you were taken away. I had no little girl of my own to dress up and your mother and I . . . we were very close. I—I apologize for my manner. I do not seem to be able to let go. . . ."

Chris paused, holding her determination to clear her father in check. "Gina, for yourself and no one else, you must let go. You're a beautiful woman; there can be more happiness."

"Yes, so they say. It was just that Mario . . ." She hesitated and her eyes were astute as they stared bluntly into Chris's. Her voice was very soft when she spoke. "Marcus is very much like his father. You will know what I mean."

"Both of your sons are wonderful, Gina. You should be very proud."

She smiled dryly. "Tony . . . he is a fine son. I bless God each time I see him. But you cannot deny that you feel the strange power that belongs to Marcus. It is a power that compels women, yes? He is a man who harbors his secrets, and not even I know him well. He is intense, and perhaps there lies the fascination. Such a man was Mario. I loved him with all my heart, with all of me, and I have not found that which I lost with him yet. But, Christina, you are welcome here."

"Thank you," Chris murmured, but more than ever she wanted to flee. The candlelight in the chapel was flickering; for a moment Gina's eyes seemed very wild and Chris wondered if she hadn't lost a bit of her sanity. Any woman who spent hours and hours closeted in an ancient chapel . . .

She began backing away and Gina was still smiling.

"I'm terribly thirsty," Chris murmured. "The stairs just seemed to beckon. . . ."

"There will be lemonade in the courtyard," Gina told her.

"Thank you," Chris said, nodding. She tried a brilliant smile, then turned and walked away from the chapel. She didn't even look to the left, to the dark subterranean tunnels, as she hurried to the steps.

But once she was halfway up the marble steps she started to feel ridiculous again. She had literally almost run away from Contessa di Medici, gentle lovely Gina.

Chris shrugged as she turned to reclose the gate.

Had she really been frightened? Or had she, perhaps, been merely ill at ease because Gina had seen—and commented on—her reactions to Marcus di Medici.

Oh, God! Just what was her reaction to the man? Yes, he was compelling; yes, he was intense. Yes, he could touch her and make her feel as if her blood sizzled and her soul drifted on clouds....

And he was secretive, too. Dark and intriguing. She didn't trust him; he made her wary. She was also willing to swear that he was innocent when she didn't even know of what he might be accused!

She emitted an aggravated little sound to herself and hurried down the hallway to the inner terrace, then out to the courtyard. She smiled then, because Alfred was sitting at the table, alone. His old head was leaned back, the waning afternoon sun shining on his bald spot. His eyes were closed as if he were resting.

Christina walked over to him. She was about to speak when he murmured something in Italian. She frowned, thinking he had dozed and was talking to himself. Then he murmured aloud in English. "Blackmail, blackmail... never pay a blackmailer."

He seemed very disturbed; his face was growing a mottled color. Chris knelt at his side, loosening his tie.

"Alfred! Alfred! Wake up, you're distressing yourself!"

His eyes flew open. For a moment he appeared absolutely panicked. Then he saw who was there, and his color faded back to normal. "Christina," he said, sounding relieved. He caught her hand and patted it.

"Alfred, what's wrong? You said you needed me. Let me help you."

"Never pay a blackmailer, Christi. Never live with a lie."

"Tell me about it, Alfred."

He lowered his voice. "I will, I will, at the galleries Friday. When we are alone. Absolutely alone!" He was looking over her head. Chris spun around quickly.

The house had seemed so empty for so long. But now, it seemed, everyone was coming to the courtyard.

Gina was smiling and heading toward them. Sophia was right behind her with Genovese, apparently giving him instructions in Italian. And behind them was Marcus di Medici.

His eyes, dark and intent, stared searingly—warningly?—straight into her own.

Chapter Five

Fifteen minutes later Chris was still trying to decide just who in the household frightened Alfred Contini.

They were all seated around the table, sipping drinks, lazily watching the sunset. Alfred was querying Marcus about a trip he had made that afternoon to an old church, and Sophia—all friendliness and charm this evening—was asking Chris numerous questions about the United States. Genovese had served the drinks, then disappeared.

It seemed to be nothing more than an easy social gathering.

But each time Chris looked at Alfred Contini, she thought the old man was still disturbed. It made her unhappy to see that; in the little time that she'd had with him, she'd come to like him very much.

Blackmail . . .

He'd been muttering away about blackmail. Who would be blackmailing him and why?

Unless, she thought fleetingly, it had something to do with Mario di Medici's death. Someone might know that James Tarleton hadn't murdered Mario. And that same someone might know who had. And they could be blackmailing Alfred....

She shook her head unconsciously. Why blackmail Alfred...unless Alfred had been the murderer. She couldn't accept that any more than she could accept the accusation that her father had been the murderer. Was he protecting someone, then?

Who?

There was a rustle of sound from the gate to the Via di Medici. Dressed in their solid business suits, Joe Conseli and Fredo Talio were coming to join the group. Fredo's smile was wide across his robust face. Next to him, the sallow Joe seemed saturnine even though, Chris realized, he was smiling, too.

"Fredo, Joe!" Sophia rose to greet them, linking arms with both men and bringing them to the table. Gina also rose to accept kisses on the cheek. Both men greeted Chris cordially, then apologized and began to speak quickly in Italian to Marcus. Apparently the discussion was strictly business. And then everyone was speaking Italian. Chris was glad to realize that she was beginning to recognize some of the words. It was obvious to her that they were discussing the galleries. First, something about one of the figures: it seemed that a costume had been completed for Catherine di Medici. Second, the tourist board had asked that the galleries be kept open on a certain night in August for a student affair. Chris was rather proud of herself for having followed the conversation that far. But apparently it wasn't quite good enough, because Alfred lowered his voice to speak in an aside to her.

"You must study your Italian, Christi! Study it well."

"I will," she murmured, again getting the feeling that Alfred Contini—the de facto patriarch of the family—was desperate.

Who frightened him? she wondered again. Was it Genovese? After all, Alfred had been arguing with Genovese earlier. But he had also clammed up when he had seen Sophia and Gina. And if he did need help, one shocking question remained: why not go to Marcus or Tony?

"How did you like the galleries, Miss Tarleton? Did you have a chance to view them all?"

The question came from Joe Conseli. It was politely asked, but she had the strangest feeling that it wasn't a casual question, that he was listening intently for her answer.

"I saw a lot, and of course, I was wonderfully impressed," Chris told him. "I suppose it would take days to really see it all."

"Ah, yes, of course! To study each piece!" Fredo said.

"I'm sure she'll get the chance to study everything as thoroughly as she chooses," Marcus said, and Chris found his speculative gaze on her.

She smiled. "I do plan to study everything," she told him levelly.

He smiled briefly in return. Then Fredo asked him about something, and he replied in Italian.

Chris suddenly felt like screaming. Everything that was said, every glance in her direction, seemed filled with intangible undercurrents. Was it just her? she wondered. Or had all this been going on for years?

"Would you care to come?"

"What? Pardon?" Chris murmured, startled. The question had come from Marcus. For once she had been completely unaware of his eyes raking over her.

"I said, would you like to come with me?"

"Uh, where?" Chris murmured uneasily, fully aware now that everyone at the table was staring at her.

Gina di Medici laughed suddenly. "Christina, where have you been? Gathering wool? Marcus has been talking about the Church of the Little Flower."

"Oh? I'm sorry. I suppose I was lost in thought. What is the Church of the Little Flower?"

"Just what it sounds like: a church," Alfred said with a grunt. "A sinking church, at that. But Marc is on a committee that tries to save old buildings."

"You really should go with him," Sophia purred, smiling at Chris with rather icy eyes. Chris assumed that Sophia would love to see her anywhere except there.

"Yes," Gina said, suddenly grasping Chris's hand. "Go with him. You will enjoy the trip."

You *are* both gorgons, Chris thought fleetingly. Both Sophia and Gina were looking at her as if they were sending her off to be fed to a dragon and were very pleased with the idea.

Or were they? Perhaps they were just being polite. The "dragon," in this case, was Gina's son.

And Gina knew that something was going on between Chris and Marcus. Did she approve, or disapprove?

She seemed a lot like Marcus, welcoming her and repelling her, all in one breath.

"Christina?"

Marcus was on his feet, waiting. Chris shrugged. Marcus was behind her, pulling out her chair. "We go by the front," he murmured, so she waved goodbye to the others, feeling that they were all relieved to see her go.

Chris started to walk ahead, then decided it was too unnerving not to know where he was. She paused and turned, only to discover that he was right at her elbow.

"Where are we going?" she asked him.

He laughed. "Down to the Grand Canal, and then we take a left."

Chris smiled. He opened the carved front doors and caught her hand to lead her down to the di Medici *pali* that guarded the boats.

"The motor launch," he told her, and she felt lighthearted for a change as he led her to a small motorboat. He hopped in, caught her about the waist and brought her down to him. She sat on a plank at the rear of the boat, by the tiller.

Chris stared out at the buildings they passed. Venice was beautiful by day, she thought, but it was magnificent by night. Even the shabbier palaces appeared beautiful, cast in soft light. The water shimmered, and the air seemed exceptionally cool and fresh, and subtly exciting.

And Marcus...

As ever, he held his own excitement and fascination.

They turned into a small canal, and a moment later he murmured. "There she is, the Church of the Little Flower. What do you think?"

"What do I think...?" Chris murmured, and she stared at the church as they approached it. The architecture appeared to be Venetian Gothic. It was a pretty church, with numerous coats of arms displayed along the rooftop. It was small, though, and the steps seemed particularly close to the water.

"It's... nice," Chris murmured.

He smiled at her. "Take a closer look."

She did, and he waited, killing the motor and letting them drift toward the building. "The walls!

They're crumbling...and the steps are too close to the water."

"Exactly," Marcus murmured. Then the double doors—richly carved with saints, but with warping wood—swung open.

"Conte di Medici! Marcus! *Buona sera*."

There was more, spoken in a deep male voice, but Chris lost the flow of words. It was a young man who spoke, about the same age as Marcus or Tony. He kept up a smooth flow of words until he saw Chris; then he broke off suddenly. Chris could follow his next words. He asked Marcus who the beautiful woman might be. She smiled a little dryly. Italian men did tend to be flirts.

"*Una Americana. Parli inglese*, Salvatore."

"Hello, hello, hello!" Salvatore said, reaching to help Chris from the boat. She liked the firm grip of his hand, his flashing dark eyes and his smile.

"Hello, Salvatore," she said with a smile. She instantly felt Marcus's hand at her waist; he had lost no time moving behind with a single lithe step from the boat.

"Sal, Chris Tarleton. Chris, Sal Astrella. A very old friend."

They smiled at one another. "Come, come, and see what you think," Sal said, ushering them into the church.

Chris followed them, not at all sure what they were looking for as they walked around the small building. The sides of the room were lined with small altars, and there was, of course, the main altar. There were numerous beautiful paintings, and a magnificent pulpit near the main altar, but like the facade of the building, it appeared to be rotting. The stone floor was worn smooth.

"Eh, *mi parla*, Marcus!" Sal murmured at last.

Marcus looked at Sal with a grimace. "The committee has refused to take it on?"

Sal nodded.

"I can see why. The costs will be atrocious."

"I'm willing, if you are."

"What are you talking about?" Chris asked at last.

Both men turned to her and laughed. "We both belong to a committee that works to preserve our buildings," Sal told her.

"But the committee has refused to take on this church. They say it is too far gone."

"So you see, sometimes Marc and I try to save buildings ourselves."

"But usually," Marcus murmured, grimacing once again, "we do so to resell."

Sal laughed. "Often to Americans at that, those who wish to have a second home in Italy."

"But you can't resell this time?" Chris asked.

Sal slipped an arm around her shoulder and walked her toward the main altar. "Christina, see that altar? Cardinal Valotti of the sixteenth century is buried within. He is a saint to these people! You see, this is a parish. Father Donato came to me when the building was condemned. The people do not want to lose their neighborhood *chiesa*."

"I see," Chris told him, and she did. It would be a terrible thing to see people lose a place they held so very dear.

Sal turned around. "Well, Marcus?"

He shrugged. "It will need pilings. All the wood has worm rot. The frescoes must all be refinished. There is nothing that doesn't need work."

Sal grinned. "I know. Well?"

"It's a challenge."

"Then you agree?"

He shrugged. "Why not? You'll put me in the poorhouse yet. When the Palazzo di Medici starts to sink into the sea, I hope you'll be there to bail me out!" He smiled as he approached them, spoke lightly to Sal and caught Chris's hand to pull her back to his side.

"Bene, bene!" Sal laughed. "Shall we celebrate with something?"

"Chris?"

"Why not?" she murmured.

They left together, and Chris was glad of Sal's company. He was serious, but young and entertaining, and she liked to see the easy repartee he and Marcus enjoyed.

It was, she decided, the first time she had ever seen Marcus appear so young himself. He smiled frequently and relaxed.

They went to a slightly rowdy bistro. Pop music was being played loudly, most of it American or English. Chris learned that Sal was an attorney, that he didn't really know a thing about art, and had no association with the galleries. She liked him all the more because of it.

She told Sal that she was a mime, and he demanded a demonstration so beseechingly that she laughed and tried to teach him the principles of pulling a string. He was hopeless using only his fingers.

"Sal!" She laughed. "You must bring down the wrist first, and allow the hand to follow."

She showed him again, and he shook his head, watching her admiringly. "You must be very good."

"She is excellent," Marcus said softly, and Chris was amazed by the tenor of his voice; his words were spoken with no mockery, and nothing danced in the cobalt depths of his eyes except for what appeared to be honest admiration and affection.

They ordered German beer and thick Italian pizzas, the original pies baked in pans and loaded with tomatoes, fresh cheeses, oregano and parsley. Chris danced with Sal, and then she danced with Marcus. As it happened, the music slowed for them; it was an Italian love song.

With one hand he clasped her fingers to his chest; he rested the other at the base of her spine. Her cheek leaned against the fabric of his jacket, and she felt her heart beating painfully.

There were things going on at the palazzo; intrigue shrouded in the shadows of the past was surfacing again. She knew it. Marcus was a part of it all, a dark and dangerous part. Twenty-one years ago there had been a murder of which her father had been accused; this very afternoon Alfred Contini had cried in his doze about blackmail.

But here, held so close to Marcus, feeling the heat and hardness of his body, letting the arresting male scent of him flow over her, Chris could only believe what her heart cried out.

Whatever it was, Marcus was innocent.

She heard his words whispered in her ear as his head dipped to hers. "You move like a gazelle, Christi.... Did you know that? Or a cat, ever graceful. Or a floating swan."

She tilted her head back and smiled, dazzled by the warmth in his eyes. "No, Marcus, *you* are the cat. A panther, stalking in the night."

He laughed, startled by her comparison. "Do I stalk you, Christina?"

"I don't know," she replied honestly.

His slightly secretive smile remained on his lips; he lowered his head slowly, and his lips touched hers lightly. She didn't think to twist away; his mouth was warm and fascinating, and it was the merest brush of a kiss, gone very quickly yet leaving her aching for more of that almost speculative and musing—but tender—touch.

His eyes touched hers with their intriguing glitter. Before either of them could speak he pressed her head back to his chest, and they swirled with the dance.

"How are you doing with Alfred?" he asked her.

She stiffened a bit, angered by his caustic tone—especially since he had just kissed her. "How am I doing?" she asked sharply.

"Have you convinced him to leave all his money to you?"

Was he teasing her? she wondered desperately. She was so easily lulled by him. She had to remain on guard against him. "I'm trying," she said sweetly.

"Umm," he murmured noncommittally. "It will be a pity if he leaves it to you. Then you will not need to try for a di Medici husband."

"A pity?" she demanded, casting her head back again. "But I told you, I would opt for Tony, anyway."

Chris thought that his smile was very grim. The music hadn't stopped, but he led her from the dance floor. Sal had ordered another round of beer, and the evening remained pleasant, but Chris felt as if a special warmth she had touched upon briefly had disappeared before she'd known it was within reach.

They dropped Sal off in front of the church. He said something in Italian to Marcus, and Marcus shrugged, then spoke. Chris thought he said that Sal should say to someone named Anna whatever he wished.

Sal told Chris that he hoped he would see her again soon; Chris echoed the sentiment, and then she was alone with Marcus once again as he steered the boat toward home.

"Who is Anna?" she asked lightly.

He cast her a noncommittal glance. "A friend," he said briefly. Chris fell silent. She felt as if a tension were growing within her, getting stronger the closer they came to the palazzo. Suddenly she wanted to challenge Marcus. She desperately needed to know where he stood about things.

"I think that Alfred Contini is being blackmailed," she said flatly—and calmly, she hoped. "Do you have any idea who might be doing such a thing to him, or why?"

"Blackmail?" He frowned as he gazed at her, as if drawn from his own distant thoughts. "Good Lord, no. Who would blackmail Alfred? And as you say, for what?"

Was his surprise genuine? she wondered. Or had his eyes narrowed a little suspicously?

"I don't know," Chris said, looking out at the water and wondering if she weren't a complete fool. "Something that happened in the past, I would think."

"Think!" Marcus muttered with annoyance. "Christina, your imagination is wild. You play in the field of illusion so frequently that you see things that do not exist."

"I do not! And my father didn't kill your father, which means that someone else did. And maybe Alfred knows who and—"

"Damn it, Chris, stop it! Stop it, do you hear me?" His hand left the tiller to catch her chin and tug it around roughly so that she met his eyes, harsh now as they reflected the water. "Don't run around with your idle accusations."

"Why? If they *are* idle, what do I have to fear?"

He began to swear vigorously in Italian. Chris pulled her chin from his grasp, feeling ridiculously close to tears. She barely noticed as the boat docked;

she only became aware of where they were when he stepped over her, reached for her hands and practically dragged her to the steps.

"Let go of me," she muttered.

"No, not until you listen to me. You cannot change what happened; you can only cause trouble. Keep your mouth shut, Christina."

"I—"

"Just what are you out to do, Chris? Is this to be a form of vengeance? Do you feel that your father was cheated, and so you will torment us all? Are you after Alfred's money? Or perhaps you really have determined that having a di Medici husband would be the best vengeance for the wrongs supposedly done the Tarletons!"

"What?"

"What are you up to, Christina?"

"I'm trying to find out the truth!" she raged. And then she wrenched her hands from his. "*Buona sera*, Marcus. Thank you for the outing."

Chris left him and hurried to the elaborately carved doors of the palazzo. She wrenched them open and hurried up the steps to her room.

She changed into one of her new ultramodest gowns and lay down to go to sleep.

But sleep was elusive. All she could think of was Marcus's dark eyes. The threat in them, and the barely leashed intensity of his anger. And the warmth that had burned so briefly...

And Alfred. Muttering so disturbingly about blackmail.

When she did sleep, it was restlessly. She woke sometime during the night and opened her eyes slowly. She almost started when she realized that someone was definitely at her terrace doors. She was so frightened at first that she couldn't move or scream, and then she didn't want to.

It was Marcus. She recognized his tall dark form, the silence of his movement. He walked across the room and checked the lock on her hallway door, then paused briefly to glance at her. Chris hurriedly slitted her eyes, watching him from the shadow of her lashes.

He seemed to accept the fact that she was sleeping peacefully and turned to disappear onto the terrace.

She lay awake for a long time again, afraid to wonder if his anger had been a bluff...and if he might really be concerned for her safety.

With the morning sun pouring through the terrace doors, Chris stretched and slowly wakened, a frown furrowing her brow.

The loud strains of a rock song by Duran Duran seemed to be shivering through the very walls of the palazzo.

Duran Duran? Chris smiled, hurried out of bed and decided on a light knit dress for the day since it was Friday at last, and she would finally get to meet Alfred at the galleries. Then she hurried downstairs to find out why the house was filled with music.

As soon as she reached the courtyard she knew. Tony had returned from Florence.

He was sitting at the table, rocking to the beat with a knife and spoon. He saw Chris when she entered, grinned like a minor-league devil and jumped up to give her a hug.

"Christi! You waited for me to return. You didn't let any of the demons or gorgons chase you away."

Chris laughed and hugged him in return, then stepped away from him, lifting a brow to indicate the music that filled the courtyard. "A bit loud, isn't it?"

"Only a bit. Eh, Christi, the gorgons are all out. I can blare to my heart's content and offend no one. Unless, of course, it's bothering you?"

Chris shook her head. Tony poured her a cup of coffee and extravagantly pulled out a chair.

He smiled at her as he pulled his own chair close. "You see, the palazzo only looks as if it's old enough to sink into the sea. It's been totally rewired—except, of course, below—and Marcus and I put in sound systems and speakers years ago. I mean, it's as necessary as indoor plumbing these days, you know."

"Umm, sure," Chris murmured. The Duran Duran tape ended and something by David Bowie began. "How was Florence?"

"Lovely. . . except that her name is Angela."

"Oh, and you had me languishing away here with the gorgons!"

He teased the back of her hand with a playful finger. "Ah, but I lost you before I ever had the chance to meet you, didn't I?"

He spoke softly, looking over her shoulder. The music danced around her with a rhythmic sensual beat, yet that wasn't what made her tremble.

The song playing was called "Cat People." Chris thought it was rather apropos.

She spun around. As she had expected, Marcus was standing there, hands in his pockets, watching her and Tony. He was in dark jeans and a navy denim work jacket that was dusted with a little plaster. How long had he been standing there? she wondered. Not long, she decided, as she realized he was walking over to them. But his movements . . . it seemed as if he moved in step to the sexual beat of the music, as if he could turn into a black panther at any minute and continue after his prey.

"Hey, Antonio, are you coming down?" he asked his brother, passing them and going to the serving cart to pour himself some orange juice. He didn't sit at the table but leaned against it, nodding at Chris and giving her a crisp, "Good morning."

Tony grimaced. "Yeah, I'm coming. What have the workmen said so far?"

Marcus shrugged. Chris watched the ripple of his shoulder muscles. "They say it's not as bad as we thought. The tunnel is good, and the construction is sound there, and in the foundations for both the galleries and the palazzo. We have no leaks. There's just one section they say should be reinforced, down beneath the galleries."

"The land of deep dark family secrets!" Tony teased Chris.

"Come help, Tony," Marcus prompted his brother irritably. "I've got to get to the galleries and take a look at the books; we do have a problem somewhere. You've—"

"Trouble with the books?" Chris interrupted him. Did he suspect embezzlement?

He sighed. "Chris, it isn't your concern. Just something that I have to look into." He turned back to Tony, dismissing her query. "Tony, you've got to be there by this afternoon to check in the tapestries that you bought in Florence. Right now the workers are plugging up some holes in the inner wall and the tunnel. They could use some help and supervision . . . to make sure it will be done."

"Okay, okay!" Tony grinned. "No rest for the weary!" he groaned to Chris. "Eh, Marcus. Let's do something tonight, shall we? You could give Anna a call, and Chris and I—"

"I think you'd better give that a little thought, Tony," Marcus interrupted him, grinning. "Katrina

Loggia has called the galleries at least five times in your absence. Once to tell me I was aiding and abetting your wanton life-style by sending you out of town so frequently." He paused a minute. "Maybe you'd better call Katrina. She's the best woman you've found yet."

"Ah, but I can't leave the 'Bella Christi'!"

"You won't. Chris and I will come with you."

"What about Anna? Shall we allow her to lie languishing?"

"Anna never languishes," Marcus said dryly.

"Hey, hey!" Chris interrupted. "I'm an adult. They told me so when I turned twenty-one, and that was several years ago. You both go out with your friends. I'm perfectly capable of taking care of myself. And good heavens," she teased, smiling as she looked at Tony, "if I'm going to con Alfred out of all his money, I'm going to have to spend some time with him."

"True, true," Tony mused, responding to her teasing. "But, in case all fails with Alfred—"

"And you wish to entrap a di Medici husband," Marcus interrupted, rising fluidly, coming behind her and playing gently with her hair, "then you should be working on the di Medicis."

"Seriously," Chris murmured, very aware of his touch, of his presence behind her, "I've . . . got some shopping to do this afternoon. If I went out it would have to be late."

"Everything is late in Italy," Tony told her.

"Yes, as in work," Marcus reminded him.

"I'll be right down. Can I just finish my coffee, master?" Tony asked his brother, grinning.

"If you can drink fast," Marcus replied, chuckling.

"I could help," Chris offered.

"And delve into the family closets? Never!" Tony said. "No, Christi. When it's all fixed up, you can come through."

Chris turned around with a strange feeling. Marcus was gone.

"He's like a damned panther!" she muttered. He could move without a sound.

Tony laughed. "Brother Marcus, you mean? No sound upon the step and all, eh?"

"Umm. Stealthy."

"And the eyes . . . kind of searing?"

"Deadly and dangerous," Chris agreed with dry solemnity.

Tony laughed again, truly enjoying her comments. "Well, if you're handling a black panther, you'd better pull out your whip and chair! And I'd better get down there." He reluctantly pulled out his chair to rise, then said, "Chris, I almost forgot. Alfred left you a note. It's on the serving cart. Ah . . . here it is."

"Thanks," Chris murmured, accepting the note. She glanced at it a bit quizzically. It was in an envelope, and though the envelope hadn't been ripped, it looked as if it had been opened and resealed. She opened it quickly herself, waving absently as Tony murmured again that he had to get below.

"*Cara* Christi," it read. "Make it the gem salon, six-thirty this evening. *Per favore*. I'll see that the doors are open. Alfred."

Something made Chris call out quickly to Tony. He paused just before entering the inner terrace, shading his eyes from the sun with a hand as he looked back to her.

"Tony, who has been around this morning?"

"Around?" He sounded mystified.

"Yes. Around the courtyard. Besides yourself."

"Marcus, of course. Sophia, Genovese. My mother. Oh, Fredo and Joe were even by." He shrugged. "Everyone, I suppose. Why?"

"Oh, nothing. I was just wondering." She smiled sweetly. "If you all want to go out later, nine or ten o'clock would be fine with me."

Tony nodded and waved again. Chris sat pensively at the table for a while, drank her coffee without tasting it, then went back upstairs.

She spent an hour exercising, then paused without really knowing why and looked around her room.

Things seemed . . . different. Nothing major, and nothing seemed to be gone. But a brush seemed to be placed at a different end of the dresser. She had tossed her handbag on the pillows after making the bed; now it was below the pillows.

Chris shrugged, but tingles burned along her neck and down her spine. She stood and looked through the drawers. Her things were all in order, but they, too, seemed . . . different.

Uneasily she showered, redonned her knit dress and determined to leave the palazzo. Until it was time to meet Alfred and find out what was going on, she didn't want to be around the di Medicis or their home.

Chris took herself on a sight-seeing trip, visiting a number of art galleries, museums and cathedrals. She also went into one of the tourist offices and asked about getting access to public records. The friendly girl on duty gave her a map and a list of libraries and offices, and Chris decided that her day had been well spent.

She had been using public transportation—the vaporetti—and they hadn't been running exactly on time. By the time she reached the square in front of the galleries—the Piazza di Medici/Contini, she noted dryly—it was closer to seven o'clock than it was to six-thirty.

And it was growing dark.

Chris hurried up the steps to the main entrance; not until she was almost there did she slow her pace.

There were lights within the galleries, but they were pale and muted. The ancient building suddenly seemed sinister beneath the moonlight.

What am I getting myself into? Chris wondered belatedly. She had never really stopped to think about personal danger, even though it seemed that Marcus was constantly warning her to be careful. Was that because he *did* know something she didn't?

Chris gave herself a serious shake. She had come this far because she wanted Alfred to talk to her, to confide in her and let her help him. There was nothing sinister about a building. Even an ancient building, filled with cavernous passages and shadowed archways and the secrets of the centuries....

"Quiet!" she warned herself aloud, and hurried up the last of the steps. But she found herself looking around when she reached the main doors. The piazza was empty except for a few pigeons. In the distance on the water, a pair of gondoliers were shouting to one another. In the other direction, down the via from the piazza, a couple of lovers were disappearing arm in arm down an alleyway.

Chris pulled at the door; as Alfred had promised it was open. She slipped inside.

It was even eerier to be inside the galleries at night than it was to look at them. She inhaled deeply and the sound seemed to echo. She held her breath, then exhaled very softly.

She could have sworn she heard her heart beating like thunder.

The inner courtyard was in front of her with its empty concierge stands, shadowed marbles and tiles, statues and archways. Chris closed her eyes for a minute, leaning against the door. It would be after seven o'clock now. She was lucky that Alfred hadn't chosen to leave.

She might be uneasy—she refused to even think the word "frightened"—but she might also be within an inch of clearing her father's name.

With that in mind Chris straightened and headed for the left-hand stairway. The banister felt like ice beneath her fingers. And despite all her reasoning, the higher she climbed, the more furiously her heart seemed to beat.

She passed the doors to the historical exhibit. They were open, and as she glanced in she shivered. All the figures stared out at her from the darkness, posed, eyes wide, arms outstretched.

Almost as if they were beckoning to her to join them.

Chris shivered, then was furious again with herself for being ridiculous.

She hurried on. The gem salon would be next.

But as she neared those doors she slowed her pace, then came to a dead standstill. Someone was whispering in the salon, and someone else was replying furiously. They were speaking in Italian, low but vehement.

She should run, get the hell out of there, Chris thought. But logic didn't seem to have much control over her actions. Without conscious thought she moved closer to the doors, until she was staring into the salon.

Alfred was there, standing right in front of the case with the di Medici jewels and directly beneath the skylight. Moonlight pouring in like quicksilver displayed his features clearly. They were strained and angry, and tinged with an unhealthy pallor.

But despite the moonlight, Chris couldn't see the features of the other person at all. She couldn't even tell if it was a man or a woman. It might have been a gargoyle that had crawled down from the ceiling for all that she could tell; the figure was clothed from head to toe in a hooded cloak.

"No, no, *no*!" Alfred exclaimed, slamming a fist down on the glass case. Chris flinched, expecting it to shatter. But it didn't and she noted that a piece of paper floated to the floor, unseen by either Alfred or the hooded figure. What was it? Chris wondered. The subject of the argument?

Alfred threw his hands up and stalked to the left side of the room. The figure followed. The words were coming more and more quickly between them, more and more vehemently. Chris swallowed, certain that her presence would break up the argument. She should just burst in with a cheerful "hello" and a broad smile on her lips.

She started to do just that, but suddenly Alfred stood dead still and shouted in English to the figure, "*Murder! Blackmail!* Where and when does it end!"

Chris was halfway across the room. Something about his words warned her of imminent danger. Instinctively she pitched to the floor and rolled silently until she was hidden behind the case containing the di Medici jewels. How well she was hidden she didn't know, because the moonlight was almost like a flashlight on her, streaking through the skylight.

With her heart pounding at a fevered pitch, she crept to her knees to look beyond the case and a scream froze in her throat. Alfred was screaming, *"No!"*

And the moonlight, powerful, glowing quicksilver, was reflecting off the blade of a raised knife.

"No!" Alfred shouted again, and then he was running past the cloaked figure and out of the salon. The figure followed him with a whirl of flowing fabric. Chris heard their footsteps clattering on the stairs; she heard the great front doors being thrown open and falling shut.

She left her hiding place behind the case with little thought and tore down the stairs herself, not realizing until later how foolish the action had been. But Alfred was out there being chased by a figure in a flowing robe who was wielding a knife.

She didn't notice a thing about the courtyard as she raced through it; she, too, yanked open the doors with a vehemence. Heaving, panting, she raced down the steps to the piazza, and there, right beside a little fountain, she saw Alfred suddenly pause in flight, clutching at his heart.

The cloaked figure was nowhere to be seen.

"Alfred!" Chris screamed, and sobs tore from her along with her breath as she raced to him.

"Alfred! Alfred!" She curled her arms around him, trying to help him stand. The piazza was absurdly empty in the glowing moonlight. He was too heavy. He began to sink to the ground; she sank along with him, trying to protect his head and keep him warm with her own warmth.

"Help!" she screamed to the night.

"Christi, Christi..." His eyes were open, dazed, but deep-brown and luminous, staring into hers. "Help me...."

"I'm here, Alfred, I'm here. I'll help you. I have to attract someone—"

"Oh, God, Christi! The sins of the past. They catch us all." With a sudden burst of energy he grasped her shoulder, his fingers painful and desperate. "Careful, Chris, careful. It was my fault. I paid. I hid the truth. Be careful. Marcus—"

His voice broke off. A terrible chill swept over Chris. Was he telling her to be careful of Marcus or to go to Marcus for help?

"Alfred, don't try to talk. I've got to get help!"

At last, Chris saw people emerging from the alleyway. A man, a woman and a child, chattering as they ambled along in the night.

"Help!" Chris screamed, hoping the fear in her voice would atone for her lack of Italian. She racked her memory furiously for the right words. *"Attenzione! Attenzione! Dove un medico? Per favore, un medico!"*

The woman began to cry something excitedly to her husband. The husband raced toward Chris, while the woman started to scream, *"Polizia! Polizia, un medico!"*

The hand that was grasping Chris's shoulder slowly began to relax. She stared into Alfred's eyes again, tears blinding her own. "Christi, *bella* Christi, I brought you into danger. Find the new will. I tried to make reparation.... But watch out. Watch out for—"

"Alfred, don't worry! Rest easy, help is coming."

He shook his head and tried to moisten his dry cracking lips. "Come closer!" he gasped, and she could barely hear him. She lowered her head to his mouth. "I took care of you, Christi. Find the will. You must be careful...you know the truth. Your father didn't kill Mario...you know he didn't. It was my fault. All my fault. And now the years have caught up with us all. They've—"

"Alfred! Stop!" Chris begged. "I'm getting help." She couldn't understand his ramblings; all his words managed to do was steal his remaining strength.

"Christi . . . watch out for . . ."

There was nothing more. Numb with pain and fear, Chris raised her head. Alfred was still staring at her. But his eyes were completely glazed. She realized that his chest was moving no more. "No, Alfred!" she cried, and she pressed her ear to his chest.

There was nothing. Not even the faintest beat of hope.

The Italian man was standing beside her; she tried to nod that she understood when he told her that the *polizia* were coming.

And then there was a big commotion on the piazza. It seemed that people were springing from everywhere. Chris could only stare at the ground. She saw a pair of feet and black jean-clad legs coming toward her.

A man bent down beside her, taking Alfred's head from her lap and placing it very gently on the ground. She looked around, still dazed, and saw that it was Marcus. "Goodbye, old friend," he murmured softly. For once his indigo gaze held nothing but tenderness, caring and sadness. His dark features were drawn and strained, his hands, on Alfred and on her, were gentle.

"He is gone, Chris," Marcus said. And he reached to close the lids over the dark-brown eyes of Alfred Contini. When that was done he set his arms around Chris and helped her rise. She was staggering. He drew her very gently against him and smoothed back her hair with a deep protective tenderness.

She broke into tears and turned her face into his chest. "Marcus, he was murdered," she garbled out.

She felt his body stiffen, but barely noticed. "No, Chris, it was a heart attack. Chris, a heart attack."

"No," she murmured.

"Hush! Christina, before God! Hush!"

Swift sizzling fear swamped her senses. Dear God, she couldn't tell anyone what she had seen. If the murderer—the cloaked figure with the gleaming knife who had pursued Alfred until his heart gave out—if he or she knew what Chris had seen . . .

She began to shiver. There were shrill whistles and a flurry of activity. The police came, and a doctor, and a stretcher. A million questions were being thrown at Marcus in Italian; he was answering them all calmly. Chris vaguely heard him explain that she was an American, Alfred's guest, his guest. And she vaguely heard the respect for Marcus in the voices of the officers; she heard them addressing him by his title—and they believed every word he said, and didn't pressure him once. Someone asked something about Alfred, and he hesitated several seconds, then softly said, *"Si."*

Alfred Contini was gently swathed in a giant sheet, then taken away. The piazza began to clear.

Chris watched, shivering. She buried her face in her hands, and of all things, absently realized that she had lost an earring. What could an earring matter when Alfred had died . . . ?

Marcus gave Chris a little shake.

"Alfred is gone, Chris. We must go home. You must rest from the shock, and I . . ." He inhaled deeply and exhaled sadly. "I must tell my mother, and Sophia."

Chris nodded again. Somehow she was able to walk beside Marcus.

Marcus . . .

Oh, God! What had Alfred been trying to tell her? Was Marcus truly her friend, or was he the dark and sinister danger that she should be fearing?

Marcus . . .

She closed her eyes and swallowed a new rush of tears. Now, feeling his touch, his warmth, his tenderness and his strength, she could believe no evil.

It was strange. With shock and pain foremost in her heart, still she was comforted, and yet trembling again in another way. It felt right to be with Marcus now. But it had always felt somehow right to be with Marcus. Since that first night when she had seen him she had felt the draw, so powerful. . . .

Was she falling in love with him?

Or falling into a trap—from which there would be no escape?

Chapter Six

Three days later Alfred Contini was taken down the Grand Canal one last time.

His gondola was shrouded in black; behind the coffin, keeping a silent vigil, were Sophia Calabrese and Gina di Medici. They, too, were shrouded in black.

Chris, in the next boat between Marcus and Tony, realized that she was more a part of the scene than she would perhaps have been willing to be had she not spent the hours and the days following Alfred's death in an absolute daze.

Like Gina and Sophia, she was clad in black. And she wore a low-brimmed black hat with a black veil.

Everything had been draped in black: the galleries and the palazzo, even the small *chiesa* or church near the galleries where Alfred had attended Mass almost every Sunday for thirty-odd years.

Contini had been a name of importance in his city of merchant princes. And his city had turned out for him. As the parade of gondolas and launches in funeral black traveled along the canal, people lined the streets to throw flowers into the water and murmur prayers for his soul.

Bells were chiming across the city; they seemed to toll heavily upon Chris's heart.

In the days of Alfred's wake she had carefully withdrawn. Sophia had not cried; she had retired to their quarters, begging to be allowed to grieve in private. Gina had cried; Chris had been impressed by her earnest emotion. Alfred Contini had enjoyed one true friend in life, at least.

Tony had been uncustomarily somber; Marcus had been quiet—and completely efficient. He had closed the galleries for several days so that the last of their original founders could be mourned.

The gondolas came to the little *chiesa*. Chris slipped into a pew, between Marcus and Tony once again.

Only Gina could be heard, weeping during the long service and the Mass. Sophia held to her silence.

When it was over the mourners filed from the church. Chris could see a workman tearing at the stones of the floor to the left of the altar; Alfred would be interred in the church he had patronized, as he had planned during his lifetime.

The gondolas, still shrouded in black, began their slow journey back to the palazzo.

But this night no one would be grieving in private. The numerous friends and acquaintances of Alfred Contini would all be pouring into the palazzo. Food and wine would be served in abundance, and Alfred would be eulogized by one and all.

Chris had never felt so lost in a foreign land in all her life. There were so many people there, and they were all speaking in Italian. Marcus never faltered as a host; Chris was introduced to everyone. She noticed that a number of people stared at her peculiarly when they heard her name. Why not? They all assumed that she was the daughter of a man who had murdered a di Medici—it probably did seem strange that she was in the household.

One name in particular caught Chris's attention: Anna Garibaldi. The woman appeared to be in her late twenties; she was very confident in herself and in her movements, which made sense because she was beautiful in a fashion that only an Italian woman could be, Chris thought. Her deep-brown eyes were huge and hidden by luxurious lashes. Her waist was tiny; her hips and breasts flared like any man's fantasy.

Although none of her actions was overt or the slightest bit in bad taste, it was obvious to Chris that she knew both Marcus and Tony very well, and that she was warmly welcomed by Sophia and Gina.

Perfect wife material? Chris wondered, and she couldn't help but feel a horrible stab of jealousy. She didn't really know Marcus at all; she should mistrust him like a snake. He seemed unwaveringly positive that her father was a murderer and Chris wasn't at all certain that he didn't really totally dislike her.

But, she decided, watching him move smoothly among his guests, exchanging quiet words here and there, she must be in really bad shape. No matter what logic said, no matter how sternly she warned herself that he had more reason to be her enemy than her friend, she could not stop her feelings. In her heart she was sure that Marcus could be trusted.

Chris sipped a glass of dark dry wine, wondering if anyone would notice—or care—if she escaped to her room. But right when she was feeling so lost and lonely that she was ready to fly to the stairs, Sal came to her, kissing her cheeks and smiling in warm greeting.

"Chris, how very sad this is for you. I hope you are bearing up all right."

"Yes, yes, I am. Thank you, Sal."

"What will you do now?" he asked her.

She hadn't really thought about it. She should leave; Alfred had asked her here, but now Alfred was dead. Yet how could she leave when she knew he had been murdered and that he had been paying a blackmailer?

Yet how could she stay? she wondered with a shiver. She hadn't been asked to talk to the police. They had simply assumed that he'd had a heart attack while she was with him.

Chris hadn't told a soul about the figure with the knife. Instinct had warned her that her life might depend on her silence.

She hadn't even tried to talk to Marcus. He had been extremely remote. And in the darkness of the night she had begun to doubt herself. Marcus was a di Medici. He had been awfully close—and come awfully quickly—to the scene of the crime. And he needed money.

No, no, no. Marcus would not hide behind a hood and cape; he would not sink to blackmail. He would never have raised a knife against an old and ailing man like Alfred....

But who, then? The deeper she went, the less sense any of it seemed to make.

"Christina?"

"Oh, Sal, I'm sorry. I was thinking, I guess. I—I'm really not sure what I intend to do yet."

"Well, you've got to stay a week, at least."

"For what?"

"The reading of Alfred's will."

"Why? What could it have to do with me?"

Sal smiled. "Alfred was my father's client for years and years. Right after your father left the company, he set up a small trust fund for you."

"Oh," Chris murmured. Then she quickly asked, "Sal, Alfred murmured something to me about a new will once. Does that mean anything to you?"

Sal frowned. "Yes, come to think of it. Last week he called my father at the office and asked him a lot of questions about wills. Dad told him that his was all in order, and Alfred asked what he had to do to legally constitute a new will. But as far as I know he never made one out." Still frowning, he turned around. Chris paled as she saw that Marcus was right behind him. "Marc, did Alfred say anything to you about making out a new will?"

Indigo eyes immediately fell scathingly on Chris. They flickered over her features briefly. "No, he said nothing to me. But that isn't to say that he didn't. Why? Did you manage to persuade him to bequeath his money to you after all, Christina?"

"He mentioned a new will right before he died, that's all," Chris said, stiffening, but keeping her voice sweet. She smiled at Sal, who appeared ill at ease and startled by the animosity between them. "I assume that the di Medicis inherit the majority of Alfred's holdings?"

"A majority, yes. Sophia, of course, receives her pension. And, as I mentioned, there are various trust funds and the like."

"You'll have to remain on the prowl for a di Medici husband then, Christina," Marcus said blandly, then added, "Excuse me, I believe Tony needs some assistance with the wine."

He nodded, stiff and straight, dark and immaculate and as cold as the moon, and joined Tony behind a serving cart.

Anna wandered over to him. Chris saw his smile flash brilliantly, and she wished she could throw him—bound and gagged—into a canal.

She turned back to Sal and handed him her wineglass. "Sal, I've got a terrible headache. I don't think I'll be missed here. I'm going to try to slip upstairs."

Very nicely, he lifted her fingertips and kissed her hand. "I will miss you, Christina. But go, get some sleep. I'll see you soon."

She smiled her thanks and made a quick disappearance up the stairs. In her room she quickly pulled off her hat and flowing veil and stripped off the depressing black dress.

When her own father had died she had worn light purple. Her father had hated black. And her mother had ordered the church filled with white lilies, smiling through her tears to say that James had always told her that death was but a new life, and she must always think of it that way.

Tiredly, Chris crawled into a white gown, but she couldn't sleep, so she prowled around her room. She stopped in front of her dresser, puzzled as to why she was staring down at it. Then she realized that she was looking at a single earring—a pearl that dangled on a long loop.

There was only one earring because she'd lost the other on the day Alfred had died. She had barely thought about it at the time . . . how could she, when a man had died?

But now it disturbed her, and as she stared at its mate, she slowly understood why.

She had lost it the day Alfred had died. But she could remember playing with it absently on the vaporetto that had taken her to the galleries. She'd had it on then.

And both earrings had bounced against her cheeks when she hurried up the steps. Yet she had realized it was gone just before she walked back to the palazzo with Marcus.

Dizziness swept over her. There could have been only one place where she might have lost it. In the gem salon, when she had pitched to the floor and rolled.

Chris caught her breath, suddenly remembering the sheet of paper that had fallen right by the di Medici jewel case. Right where her earring would be. What had been on the paper? Something to do with the blackmail . . . or the murder?

She shook her head vehemently. She would love to have the paper, but the earring mattered more. If the cloaked figure got into the jewel salon before she did, her earring would be found. And the wielder of the knife, who had sent Alfred running terrified to his death, would know that she had seen everything.

She had to get into the salon and find her earring.

Chris forced herself to lie quietly and tried desperately to figure out how. She couldn't very well ask for a key.

She lay there, closing her eyes tightly, trying to visualize the galleries. All she could see in her mind was the skylight and the moonglow reflecting on the di Medici jewels.

Restlessly she tossed and turned until she realized that the skylight was her only chance. She was a mime, with training in gymnastics. If she was careful she could climb to the roof and descend through the skylight, then find her earring and scurry back up.

The idea terrified her, but it was her only chance.

By the next morning it seemed that the household was beginning to return to normal. The galleries were still closed, but when Chris came downstairs—as late as possible, in the hope that she would be alone—she learned from Genovese that Marcus and Tony had gone to direct some workmen at the Church of the Little Flower.

She thanked Genovese, and felt a little unnerved when he hovered near her. She thought that he was about to say something, but Gina came out to the table. Genovese seated her, then left.

Chris tried to talk to Gina, but Gina wasn't in the best of moods. Or perhaps she had dropped all pretense of courtesy for the day. She looked at Chris and murmured, "It is surprising how people die when you're around, isn't it, Christina?"

Chris excused herself immediately. She left the house and searched the streets until she found a shop where she could buy some strong cord and a grappling hook.

Chris waited until midnight, feeling all the while that she was an idiot. She was going to dress in dark clothing and break into the di Medici galleries like a sneak thief. It was a truly idiotic plan—it was just that she couldn't see any other way. She wanted to trust Marcus; she just didn't dare. She didn't dare let anyone know that she had been in the galleries the night Alfred Contini had died.

She wasn't expecting anyone to be up and around at that hour, but she still planned her exit carefully. The stretchy black outfit she wore could have been street clothing; it was composed of a leotard and knit pants. And her gym slippers could have passed for regular shoes. Her hair was bound at her nape so as not to get in her way, and she carried her rope and grappling hook in what could have passed for a large leather purse.

But she needn't have feared for her appearance as she left the palazzo. She didn't pass a soul when she crept out of the still crepe-decked mansion.

Once she reached the via Chris felt a real case of nerves coming on. Not only was she going to try to scale walls and avoid the alarm system of the galleries, she was walking through streets that were darkly shadowed and might be plagued by an ordinary mugger.

Chris grimaced as she hurried along, closely hugging to the walls. It would be just her luck, she decided, to be knocked out cold before she ever reached her real destination, to get into real trouble.

But if she didn't go back . . .

If the cloaked figure with the lethal knife discovered the earring that was so easily identifiable as hers . . .

She started to shiver again, then took a deep breath and gave herself a mental shake. She was on her way; all she had to do was carry through. Get into the gem salon, get out again.

It would probably make more sense to get out of Venice.

But she couldn't leave. Not now. For her father, for Alfred Contini, the truth had to be known. Even if that truth might include Marcus di Medici.

Chris blocked her mind to all but the task at hand when she reached the square and stared up at the galleries. Even the flagpoles were still draped in black crepe.

She stared at the columns, but knew she didn't want to go in by the front. On the side near the water was a workman's scaffold; she could climb that to the first-floor overhang, scurry up to the skylight, secure the rope on one of the gargoyles facing the canal and lower herself to the floor. Easy?

So easy that she was shaking again once she had climbed up the scaffolding. She looked below her. The canal was dark; no gondolas were slipping by in the night. She couldn't hear a sound from the square. Inhaling, then exhaling, Chris stared at the overhang that would take her to the skylight. It wasn't particularly steep, she assured herself. If she fell, well, she would be one American lost in a Venetian canal. But she wasn't going to fall. She was going to hold tight to the roof tiles until she reached the skylight.

Chris began to climb. She felt grit on the tiles and was glad, because it gave her a better hold. She didn't look down. Inch by inch she edged along, a hand, a foot, a hand, a foot. And then she was there.

She hurried along the roof, forced herself to slow her pace, and then pulled the bag from her shoulder to secure the rope around a particularly macabre gargoyle—one with its tongue out and twisted—before moving to the skylight. The hinge was stubborn, but there was no lock on it. With a little grunting and maneuvering Chris managed to pull it open. She lowered herself through, wincing as she felt the rope tighten around her body. She had judged things just a little short; her feet dangled about six inches from the floor.

She freed herself from the rope and dropped those six inches with a little thud. Just like a cat, she thought, a cat burglar! Oh, don't! she wailed to herself. Find the paper, find your earring, and get back out!

It was dark in here again tonight; the only light in the room was from the moon. Chris looked up. With the skylight open she could see the moon itself, still almost a full circle.

She had landed less than a foot from the case with the di Medici jewels. Starting to feel a little frantic again, she began to crawl around on her hands and knees. The floor felt a little strange, she thought. As if it were made of wood here, instead of marble. But the jewel case sat on a rich throw rug, so it was impossible to see what was beneath. And did it matter? All she needed to do was find the—

Paper. There it was. It had fallen to the rear. Chris reached for the note. She had to stare at it hard in the moonlight, and then she saw what was written. She didn't have to know Italian to understand it. Alfred's name was on it, and an unsigned demand for umpteen million lire.

Chris couldn't begin to compute the sum in American dollars; she only knew that it was vast.

A cloud moved over the moon, blocking some of the light. Chris hurriedly tucked the note into her waistband, then kept crawling around. Here, right here, was where she had been the other night. The earring had to be here.

And then she saw it, too. Almost directly beneath the case. In the almost complete darkness that shrouded the place now that the moon was covered, Chris could see the gleam of gold. She stretched her fingers far beneath the case.

And then suddenly she screamed in amazement and terror as the floor opened directly beneath her. She vaguely heard a snap, as if a hinge had given way.

And then she was falling, rolling, sliding helplessly through what seemed to be an absolutely endless chute, so amazed and totally stunned that she couldn't even scream again as she desperately tried to stop her wild flight.

She gasped for breath as the chute began to level off; then she gasped again as even the chute disappeared and she went into a free-fall.

But not a long one. In total darkness she landed hard on a cold stone floor.

Shocked, shaken, shivering and trying to regain her breath, Chris closed her eyes while the question of where she could be raged violently through her head. She opened her eyes. Oh, God, was it dark! She closed them again. When she opened them a second time she could make out shapes in the darkness. Boxes, it looked like, with something on top of them. Long rectangular boxes.

She shivered and swallowed, testing her limbs carefully for breaks or bruises. She seemed to be okay. There was a scuffling noise near her, and she bit her lip, panicking at the thought of rats or snakes or other creatures. She moved, and gave a little scream as something soft and clinging brushed her face.

Spiderwebs! Chris clawed them from her face with a vengeance, shivering as she wondered what might be crawling through her hair. Then she warned herself that she was about to panic and she closed her eyes, shuddering one last time, and yelling silently at herself that if she was ever going to get out of wherever she was, she was going to have to figure it out first.

She groped her way to her knees, then crawled up to the nearest box. It wasn't a box. It was some kind of stone. She ran her hand over the thing on the top, and then paused, another scream forming in her throat.

The box was a tomb—and the "thing" on top was a sculptured relief of whoever was lying inside.

All the boxes were tombs. Ancient tombs, carved by stonecutters in centuries long past.

She had fallen into the family crypt.

A spider crawled over her hand where it lay on the stone breast of a long-deceased di Medici count. Chris did scream then; she tried to rise, only to bump her head against the low archway of the catacombs.

And then she thought that she would have a heart attack herself; her blood seemed to congeal, her breath to stop, and her muscles to become paralyzed.

She heard a long low chuckle from the darkness. From the graveyard of the di Medicis.

A blinding light flared in her eyes, and a husky male voice murmured, "*Buona sera*, Christina. What an odd way for a guest to spend her evenings."

"Marcus!" Chris screamed, and heedless of anything but the desperate desire to escape the dank aura of death, she hurled herself into his arms.

He stiffened immediately, holding her from him. "Christina, what are you doing here?"

"I lost my earring," she babbled quickly.

"You lost your earring, so you broke into the gem salon?"

Oh, God! He doubted her! He was going to force her to stay down here; he sounded so terribly remote, and in the artificial gleam of the flashlight his eyes seemed like blue flames, filled with an implacable fire.

Marcus...perhaps Marcus couldn't have murdered his own father. But he did need money. He had been in the square just seconds after Alfred had died. She didn't want to believe him guilty, but someone in his household was. Why not he? Just because she was a woman who had fallen foolishly in love?

The way he was looking at her right now...as if he'd gladly crack her over the head with his flashlight and leave her to reside among his ancestors forever after...

"I swear to you, I lost an earring, nothing more. I wasn't trying to steal any gems."

"Then why didn't you just ask me to let you into the salon?" he demanded pleasantly.

"Because, because..." She couldn't tell him it was because she hadn't been sure that he hadn't been the one running around in a cloak and brandishing a razor-edged knife.

She swallowed quickly, thinking desperately. "Because of Alfred's death. I—I didn't want you to open the galleries. You haven't been particularly talkative lately, you know." She tried to add a tremor—not difficult—and a great deal of sweet plaintiveness to her voice. Georgianne had once given her a great French philosophy: when all else fails, flirt like hell.

He didn't seem at all ready to let her off the hook. He leaned casually against one of the tombs, resting the flashlight on top of it and crossing his arms over his chest.

"You might have killed yourself, you know," he told her flatly. But then he smiled, and in the eerie surroundings of the tomb his smile was both disturbing and frightening. She might truly have met a demon among the dead. "But what the hell, if you're missing one earring, scale a wall and a roof and drop twenty feet from a skylight. No big deal. Especially when you might have just asked."

Chris carefully ducked from below the arch and moved closer to him, moistening her lips and trying to avoid staring at the symmetrical rows of ancient sarcophagi. "Marcus, please get me out of here. If I was almost killed anywhere, it was coming down that chute from the trapdoor."

He shrugged. "You wouldn't have been killed." He smiled again. "The fall down that chute isn't a lethal one. Scary, and a little bumpy, but certainly not lethal. I pulled the trap."

"You!"

He hiked a brow curiously, still as relaxed as if they were carrying on their conversation at a sunny kitchen table. It was absurd, Chris thought, that he could still appear so absolutely arresting, so dark and fascinating, when she wasn't at all sure that he didn't mean to leave her there and when he was telling her that her predicament was his fault.

"Tell me, if you thought you had a sneak thief in a position to be snared, what would you do? Trapping the thief would seem an intelligent thing to do, don't you agree?"

Chris didn't respond. She forced herself not to back away from him. "What—what are you doing here yourself?"

He patted the stone relief beneath him. "Visiting Great-Great-Great-Great Uncle Francis?"

"Marcus!"

He smiled again, coldly, and picked up the flashlight, throwing its glow to the right. There was an archway there, but it had been bricked in. The di Medici crest was on the bricks.

"There were a number of decades somewhere in the 1500s when my ancestors didn't have such neat and tidy burials. They were simply laid upon vaults." He shrugged. "The masons are coming tomorrow to work again, and I must decide what to do about that section of the crypts."

"At—at one A.M.?" Chris asked weakly.

He smiled. "We're a late-night people."

"I don't believe you."

"*You* don't believe *me*? I catch you breaking into the gem salon, and *you* don't believe *me*? Christina, the palazzo is mine. I have a right to be wherever I choose within it."

"In the crypt?"

"It's my crypt!"

Chris let out a long breath. He had moved the flashlight again. She could see the full body relief on the stone where he sat. It was a man with carved stone boots, medieval leggings and a thin crown around his curling stone hair. His eyes were closed; his arms were reverently crossed over his chest. His facial structure was very similar to Marcus's. There was a thin silver spiderweb over his face, stretching to the sword he held against his form.

She found that she wasn't breathing very well. "Marcus . . . could we please get out of here?"

He paused, staring at her in the strange and macabre light. Then he sighed. "You're not going to tell me what you were doing, are you, Christina?" he asked her softly. A trembling sensation danced all along her spine at the sound of his voice, echoing slightly.

"I told you—"

"Yes, you dressed up all in black and went out scaling the walls. And wound up trapped—by the di Medici jewels." He stood, and she moved backward slightly, bumping her head against the arch again. He smiled grimly, but made no move to touch her. "You should have continued your pursuit of a di Medici husband. Wives do get the jewels, you know."

"Marcus, please."

"Ah, yes! Marcus, please! Good thing to say right now, isn't it?"

"I didn't even know where I was—or what these . . . things were."

He sighed. "Good heavens, Chris, what do you think one is going to find in the catacombs?" Still smiling sardonically, he reached for her. Chris couldn't help but allow a small gasp to escape, and he laughed. "I'm trying to help you. Watch out. Some of the tombs are low, and you can trip."

She had never really known just how warm his hand could be, until she felt his touch in the cold dampness of the catacombs. She felt her fingers curling tightly around his, and at that moment she would gladly have followed him anywhere, as long as it was out of the catacombs.

It seemed to take them forever to leave the tombs. Before they came to a floor-to-ceiling grate Marcus halted suddenly and trained his flashlight on the wall.

It was simple gray marble, with a number of brass plates. Chris realized that it was the "modern" section of the tombs and that the name on the last plate was Mario di Medici.

Chris felt as if an ominous silence was about to explode into something far worse.

Marcus started moving again. Now there were just walls and archways and the occasional squeak of a rat. In another moment her heart began to beat with relief. She could see light coming from the chapel, and the stairway that led to the main floor of the palazzo.

But Marcus stopped before they reached the stairway, turning to stare at her harshly.

"You told me the other night that Alfred had been murdered. He died of a heart attack, Christina. What were you talking about?"

"Nothing," she murmured quickly.

"Christina..." The pressure of his fingers increased on hers.

"Nothing! Nothing, I swear it," she babbled. "I told you, I lost my earring and—please, please, Marcus, let's get out of here. If I want the jewels I'll shoot for a di Medici husband, I swear it. Please, Marcus."

She was startled when he pulled his hand from hers, slipped an arm around her and bent to lift her into his arms. "You're shivering, Christina," he whispered to her.

She couldn't hide it; he was holding her very close. She could feel the strength and tension in the rippling muscles of his shoulders. He surely knew that she was terrified.

Suddenly she decided to tell him about the blackmail note, to enlist his aid—or taunt him into an admission that something was going on. Perhaps something in which he was involved. No! But if he *was* involved, wasn't she a fool to speak when she was in his arms, alarmingly at his mercy?

"Alfred was being blackmailed," she declared in a rush, attempting to pin his eyes with her own. "There was a blackmail note. I saw it. I *have* it."

His brows drew tightly together in a wary frown. "Where is this note?"

Chris reached into her waistband, but the note was gone. She closed her eyes with a sinking sensation. She must have lost it before plummeting through the trapdoor.

"I don't have it anymore. I swear it was there, Marcus. You have to believe me. You have to."

"You have to get your nose out of places where it doesn't belong, Christina," he whispered hoarsely, refusing to release her. He smiled. "You're still trembling."

"Marcus, let's go back and look for the note," she said, ignoring his comment.

"Chris!" he snapped, aggravated. "You're shaking like a leaf, and I'm not crawling around through spiderwebs all night to look for some figment of your imagination!"

"Marcus!"

"If there is such a thing, it will still be there later! Come on," he said more gently. "I'm getting you out of here."

She didn't reply. She held an arm about his neck and kept her gaze locked with his as he started up the steps. He carried her through the long marble hallway, past the entryway with its subdued chandelier, and down the hall to the kitchen, where he set her on the counter. He smiled a bit vaguely, dug a towel out of a drawer, soaked it with warm water and came back to her.

He gently began to clean her cheeks. "You're much prettier without the webbing about the face," he teased lightly.

He walked away and took a little bottle from a cabinet, shaking a pill into his hand. He poured her some water.

"Take this."

"What is it?" she asked suspiciously.

"Aspirin. It will help you to sleep tonight if you have aches and pains, or cold clammy dreams about dead contes and contessas," he teased.

Chris still wouldn't take the pill. He sighed with an effort at patience and pulled out the vial. "Look, Chris, they're all exactly alike! It's aspirin, I swear it! I wouldn't be trying to poison my entire family, would I?"

Chris realized that she was still nervous. And she wouldn't sleep without some kind of help. She dutifully swallowed the pill.

"Marcus, why wasn't Alfred buried here?"

"Alfred was not a di Medici, remember? Not that that would really have mattered; he was family. But he wanted to be interned at the church." He grimaced. "I can't say I'm fond of the idea of spending eternity in this place myself."

Chris smiled, but then she sobered. "Marcus, what's going on here?"

"I don't know what you're talking about."

But he did. She could tell.

"Are you protecting someone in your family?"

"If they need protection," he said dryly. "It would seem that they do, with a jewel thief in their midst, wouldn't you think?"

Chris fell silent. It was useless trying to talk to him. Tonight, at least. If she could get him alone again, far from the house, if she could get him to relax...

perhaps ply him with wine, she thought, holding back a laugh.

He left her to pull a pair of snifters from a cabinet. From another he took a bottle of French brandy. "I think you need a drink," he told her. He came back to her, standing right before her as he handed her a brandy.

"Should I? After that pill . . ."

He grinned indulgently. "I wouldn't advise emptying a wine barrel, but a few sips won't hurt you. You're as pale as the 'relations' I left behind," he told her, tilting her glass in her numbed fingers so that she was forced to drink.

She smiled wanly. "Contini *was* being blackmailed, you know."

Had she struck home? she wondered. His expression gave nothing away, but she remembered that several days before he had mentioned something about going through the books—and had snapped at her when she had asked about it. Had large sums of money been disappearing?

"He said he made out a new will," Chris said impulsively.

Marcus shrugged. He was so close to her that his chest was almost against hers, and his hips were wedged between her legs where they dangled down the counter. The warmth of his body was like the sun. Powerful. Searing. Undeniable.

He plucked the snifter from her hand and set it on the counter. She could only stare into his eyes, aware of what was coming and glad of it, eager for it.

He moved even closer. She felt the strength and warmth of his body as his arms came around her, holding her tightly, holding her close. His lips touched hers slowly, as if tonight he had decided to explore and savor sensation. His mouth moved lightly over hers, then drew away, and he looked at her again. His eyes held a heated sizzle, but also more. There was a tenderness in his gaze that was almost shattering.

As if he shared the attraction...and the caring, too.

Finding no resistance in her eyes, he swept his arms about her once again, and his lips touched hers with a greater passion, hungry, persuasive. He tasted of the brandy, and his scent was like a potent musk, reminding her that she was falling in love with him, that she was enchanted by the probing of his tongue, moving against her teeth, then finding her tongue and all the little crevices of her mouth. She ran her hands down his back, and shivered deliciously, convulsively as his hands ran along hers, before moving between them to caress her breasts. He found her nipples easily against the knit of her leotard top, grazing them to hardened peaks. An ache rose within her; she didn't want to lose him, not the scent, the taste or the touch of him. The wonder of being held and caressed beguiled her.

His lips drew slowly from hers. His whisper was gentle as his lips brushed her cheek. "Go to bed, Christina," he told her.

She lowered her eyes quickly from his. Her lips were moist from the kiss; her body still seemed to sizzle from the heat of his. She closed her eyes for a minute, trying to still the reeling sensation of wanting him.

She needed answers. She was supposed to be the seductress, yet she was getting so emotionally involved. She had to learn to control the sensations of her body and her heart!

He wanted her; she knew it. But she was going to have to learn to play her role with greater appeal—and far greater finesse—closing her soul against his power over it. He could be tender...very tender. And gentle. Yet she couldn't let that sway her....

She raised her eyes. His were very dark, hard and mysterious. "Go to bed," he repeated softly. He lifted her from the counter. "I've got to go out."

"Where?" she challenged him.

He placed his hands on his hips and cocked his head slightly. "If I'm harboring a jewel thief, I need to get rid of the evidence."

Chris lowered her eyes again, then raised them with a sweet smile. "Marcus . . . do you think we might get out of here . . . together . . . alone . . . for an evening?"

He stared at her for several seconds. "Yes, I think that we might."

"Tomorrow?"

"Yes. Now go to bed."

Chris kept smiling sweetly as she hurried out of the kitchen and through the entryway to the stairs. In her room, she locked the door carefully before running to the shower to wash away the last of the spiderwebs from her hair and body.

When she crawled into bed she was more confused than ever. Marcus just couldn't have been blackmailing Contini. But Marcus had been right there when Contini died, and he had been in the catacombs tonight. He had a flair for being in strange places. . . .

She was always throwing thinly veiled accusations his way—which he denied. She couldn't help but think that he was protecting someone. If only he would talk to her. If only she could trap him in some way.

It was difficult when you loved the man you were trying to trap. Loved him and distrusted him. And sometimes hated him.

Chris slept very restlessly.

And again she woke up in the night, certain that someone was in her room. But she didn't really feel that she was awake; perhaps she was only dreaming.

In her dream she opened her eyes carefully, keeping her lashes lowered.

It was Marcus. In a short robe, he was standing by her dresser. It seemed that he was going through her things.

She wanted to call to him, to stop him, to accuse him. But it was only a dream, and she couldn't say anything; she couldn't stop him or accuse him. She was too groggy to do so.

Chris blinked. Marcus wasn't there. It *had* been a dream. She rolled over and fell quickly back to sleep.

When she woke up in the morning she wasn't so sure that it had been a dream. She had been so tired! And she had taken the pill . . . and had the brandy.

Angrily Chris crawled out of bed and hurriedly washed. She was going to march straight downstairs, find Marcus and demand that he explain what he was up to.

She hurried down the stairs and through the hallway to the courtyard, but paused before exiting the inner terrace. There was another family argument going on.

Genovese was standing at the head of the table. Sophia was screaming something at him, and Tony was laughing. When Sophia turned on Marcus in anger he merely lifted a brow and shrugged, then said something very calmly.

Gina watched everyone silently, her eyes darting from her sons to Sophia to Genovese.

Chris decided she might as well make her presence known.

She walked out onto the patio, her skirt swinging, her smile cheerful. She pretended not to notice that a dead silence had followed her entry. She poured herself a cup of coffee, saying, *"Buongiorno."*

Marcus moved forward to crush out a cigarette; then he leaned back in his chair, watching her with a polite smile. "It is a good day for you, Christina. Genovese tells us that he has found Alfred's new will."

"Oh?" Chris tried to sip her coffee with nothing more than polite interest. Her heart was beating painfully.

"Yes. It seems that Alfred's funds have been distributed evenly. Half to you, half to the di Medicis—and Sophia, of course."

"Half!" Chris gasped.

"Oh, yes, and you're the executor. In charge of the pensions and so on. There are legacies for Genovese, Joe Conseli and Fredo Talio. Also a few other friends and servants and distant relatives."

"I . . . doubt if it's legal," Chris murmured uneasily. Dear God, they were all staring at her as if they would like to throttle her. Except for Tony and Marcus. Tony was amused. Marcus was . . . almost disinterested.

"Ah, what a pity!" Tony teased, catching his brother's eye. "Now she'll no longer need a di Medici husband."

Marcus shrugged. "Maybe she wants it all?"

Chris thought that he was smiling. The two of them were crazy.

Tony chuckled again. "We should think this one out, Marc. I would say that one of us might need a Tarleton wife."

Gina stood up and excused herself, then quickly left the table. Sophia followed suit, throwing her napkin on the table and muttering, "It's disgraceful!" She glared at Chris and walked away.

Genovese cleared his throat. He spoke in Italian to Marcus, but Chris understood his words: "What shall I do?"

"Take the will to Sal's office, please. He can handle it from there. Oh, take the launch. It will be quickest."

Genovese nodded and left, too. Chris gazed after him uneasily. Certainly Genovese couldn't wish her any harm; he had discovered the will and presented it. He could have just torn it to shreds. . . .

But something about him made her uneasy. He often appeared weasely and ageless, his eyes colorless. When he looked at Chris, he made her uncomfortable.

Marcus stood up abruptly. "I have things to do at my own office."

"Wait!" Chris cried. "I want to talk to you."

"It will have to wait. I'll be home early." He smiled slightly, and she wasn't sure if it was with mockery or not. "We'll be seeing each other all evening, remember?"

He started to leave the courtyard, heading in the direction of the steps to the via.

"Damn . . ." Chris began.

"Give up," Tony advised. He pushed back his own chair. "I'd best get to work myself." He kissed the top of her head. "Something's bothering him about the books. That's why he's so brusque. Don't let him bother you. I'll bring him home for lunch, I promise."

Tony left, too. Chris sat alone at the table for a while, then decided she might as well work off her aggravation and fear with some exercise.

She did. She went upstairs and worked out for a long while, trying not to wonder what the new developments meant. Marcus in her room at night . . . Alfred Contini leaving half his money to her. Well, if things had been left to her, she was damned well going to get into the galleries and find out what was going on with the books.

Chris glanced at her watch and saw that it was almost lunchtime. She showered quickly and dressed, determined to corner Marcus and find out what he had been doing in her room.

Just as she was brushing out her hair, she heard his voice from the grand entryway below. She stepped out onto the balcony and glanced down. He was talking to Genovese, but he seemed to sense her presence. He looked up at her expectantly.

"Stay there, Marcus, please!" Chris called.

He smiled, his eyes a dazzling fire. "I'm here."

Chris whirled from the balcony banister, moved toward the stairs with firm steps and started down.

But on the fourth step the floor suddenly gave away. The wood of the step groaned and shattered beneath her weight.

Chris fought valiantly for her balance, but her shoe was stuck in the cracked wood. She jerked at her foot and went catapulting down the rest of the stairs, a scream tearing from her throat.

She landed with a hard crash on her head. She stared upward. The chandelier danced like a trillion suns above her.

"Christina! Christina!" It was Marcus's voice that she heard, his arms that she felt around her. His eyes were fire, she decided. A blue blaze. But like the crystals of the chandelier, they began to dim.

Bit by bit the light faded, and then was gone completely. The pain in her head had been like a large black bird, spreading its wings over her eyes, over her mind, and she slipped silently from consciousness, murmuring, "Marcus . . ."

Chapter Seven

Even in the realm of her subconscious, it was dark.

Chris dreamed she was in the catacombs. The walls were dank and musty and she could hear a roar, as if the water of the canal surrounding the tunnel was rushing like a full sea in turmoil. All the archways were deep and darkly shadowed, yet she had no choice but to run from one to the next, toward the crypt.

She was being pursued.

She kept telling herself that her pursuer could not be Marcus, but when she turned in flight she saw him, tall, dark and as mysterious as the shadows, not running after her but maintaining a steady pace. He was stalking her. And she knew that when he passed from one archway to the next he could change, if he so chose. He could become St. Mark's great winged lion, or he could become a panther, as black and deadly as the night.

She kept running until she found herself in the crypt. She banged against the gate. Marcus was calling her, and she looked back. But in the darkness she couldn't tell which he had become, the winged lion or the panther. Was he trying to hurt her, or help her? She didn't know, so she forced her way through the gates. And then she remembered that all she would find at the end of the tunnel was the walled tomb where dozens of di Medicis lay together in the sleep of eternity. She wanted to turn back, but someone was pulling on her wrist. She stared at her hand, trying to scream. The stone reliefs from the tombs had become flesh, and those long-dead di Medicis wouldn't allow her to escape.

"Christina! Stop it! You will wrench the needle from your arm."

Her eyes flew open and came into immediate contact with hard blue ones. "Marcus!"

"Yes, of course," he murmured, and she realized that his large bronzed hands were on her shoulders, pressing her back against a pillow. A cotton-covered pillow.

"Where am I?"

"In the hospital. You've suffered a slight concussion. Not a bad one, but bad enough to keep you here a few days. But you're going to be all right. Or you will be, if you'll settle down."

Dazed, Chris sank back against her pillow. She gazed at her hand; it was bandaged, and a tube was feeding a colorless liquid into her veins. She turned to Marcus. He was in a blue-and-white striped, short-sleeved knit shirt and jeans; she could see the hard muscles of his bronzed arms, very dark against the stark white of the hospital sheets. His eyes were very blue—and fathomless. His features were drawn, his jaw very rigid.

Chris closed her eyes for a minute. The step had broken, and she had fallen. A step that a half dozen other people used daily had happened to fall apart when she stepped on it.

She had fallen through the step soon after Tony had laughingly informed her that she was rich—very soon after. *Too* soon after.

She felt a tender touch against her cheek and opened her eyes. Marcus was smiling. "You're really all right."

She lifted the tubed and bandaged hand. "Then what is this?"

"This is because you've been out of it a while. They will keep you here a few nights to observe you."

"I don't feel too bad." Chris moved and winced. She did have a headache.

"You'd feel worse if you tried to stand up right now," Marcus murmured. He was sitting beside her on the bed and appeared very comfortable. Chris was startled when someone moved beyond him. It was Tony, sitting in a chair. He came up to the other side of the bed and smiled before bending to brush her forehead with a kiss. "You have a bruise on the head, you know. A concussion."

"Tony, call the doctor. He wanted to know as soon as Chris came to," Marcus instructed.

Tony smiled encouragingly, tapped her nose playfully with a knuckle and left, calling to someone in the hallway.

Marcus leaned close to Chris, very tense. "You need to get out of Venice. I'm still not sure quite what you're up to, but this city does not seem to be healthy for you."

"What do you mean?" Chris said with a gasp, lowering her voice quickly as a stab of pain shot through her head. "Marcus! What are you talking about? Was this done to me on purpose?"

"No, of course not. That wooden stairway...it has always been a problem."

"Marcus, did you go back to the galleries? Did you find my earring? Did you—"

"Shush, Christina, you are not to be excited. Yes, I went back to the galleries. I got rid of your rope and your grappling hook. But..." He hesitated, and she felt his probing stare for long seconds. "I didn't find any earring. Nor a 'blackmail' note."

"You didn't find an earring, or the note...but Genovese did find a new will," Chris muttered bitterly, closing her eyes again.

"Yes, and it appears as if you did come out the heiress. Suspicious, isn't it? You come to Venice to charm the old man, he drops dead of a heart attack and voilà, the money is yours."

"I *am* suspicious!" she flared, staring at him furiously again. "And I'm the one in the hospital!"

He waved an arm in the air. "An accident of time and place."

"You don't believe that, Marcus di Medici. You know that Alfred was being blackmailed. Marcus, you know what's going on."

"Christina, you are being hysterical."

"I am not!" She closed her eyes immediately after her denial; her head had begun to ring like the bells of St. Mark's on Sunday. It was foolish to argue with him; she knew it. She opened her eyes and smiled at him sweetly. "Marcus... I need your help."

"My help?" he murmured sardonically. But he went no further, because the doctor entered and shooed both him and Tony out of the room. The doctor was a pleasant man with a heavy accent, who was ready to cheer on all Chris's attempts at Italian. Somehow they stumbled along together; he assured her that she looked fine, that she would be all right—and that she was lucky that she apparently knew how to break a fall. He promised to see her in the morning to release her.

When the doctor left, only Tony returned to the room. Chris lifted a brow and Tony smiled, taking a seat beside her on a chair, rather than intimately on the bed as Marcus had done. He picked up her hand, the one without the intravenous, which the doctor had promised would quickly be removed, and played idly with her fingers. He sighed. "What a week."

"Yes, it has been, hasn't it?" Chris murmured. "Tony, where did Marcus go?"

"To shoot the staircase, I think," Tony teased. "No, seriously, he had to get it fixed immediately. He wanted to talk to the doctor, and he said that he had a few things to take care of at the galleries. Why? Am I bad company?"

Chris smiled. "No, you're not. I just don't ever seem to be able to pin your brother down these days."

Tony's cheerful smile faded. "He has been a bit mysterious, even for Marcus. But don't worry about it. You'll be out of here soon enough."

"And then what?" Chris murmured, closing her eyes.

"Well, then you'll have to start learning all about the galleries. You're an owner now, you know."

Why? Chris wondered fleetingly. Why had Alfred done this to her? She didn't want the galleries, and she didn't want all these people hating her. All she wanted to do was find out what was going on—what *had* gone on so many years ago.

"Tony?" she said softly.

"What is it, Chris?"

"Do you . . . hate me because of Alfred's will?"

Tony was silent for a second; then he burst into laughter. "Good God, no! Why should I?"

"Because it should have gone to you . . . or to your family. Or to Sophia. I'm an outsider."

"Yes, and the most fascinating thing I've seen in years." Tony chuckled agreeably. "Chris, the di Medicis were never dependent on Alfred, despite my dear brother's constant harping about money. I like to think that both Marcus and I are brilliant businessmen."

"I think that someone does hate me," Chris said lightly. She expected Tony to deny her words immediately, but he didn't. He hesitated again.

"Maybe you should get out of Venice for a while, Chris," he murmured. "For a few days. See Rome, or tour Florence. Or go to the Riviera and get a nice tan."

"Tony, are you worried about me being in your house?" Chris demanded tensely.

"Don't be silly," he said, but she sensed that he was lying. Tony was worried, and if Tony was worried . . .

"Ah, Chris! Here comes the nurse with your dinner. Maybe I can charm her into bringing me a tray, too." His eyes twinkled as he cocked his head slightly. "Want to make any side bets?"

"Against you? Never," Chris murmured.

She was glad she hadn't bet against him, because the nurse did bring a second tray. During dinner Tony turned the conversation around to the galleries, trying to give her an education on various Renaissance painters. Chris realized that he could be charmingly stubborn when he chose; he wasn't going to talk about the will nor imply in the least that her mishap on the stairway could have been anything but an accident.

"What about your mother?" Chris asked in the middle of a discussion on Michelangelo.

"What about her?"

"She resents me."

Tony shrugged. "I don't think so. I think she's getting over it." He paused, then grimaced. "I think that Mother is falling in love again."

Chris gasped. "You're kidding!"

He shook his head. "Every Tuesday she goes to the church for parish work. And she's been staying out for dinner afterward. I think it has something to do with a retired banker named Umberto Cellini. I think he'd like to make it more serious. Perhaps she would, too. She's been a widow a long time."

Chris digested that bit of information slowly. "And what about Sophia? What will she do now?"

"Stay on, I guess. She really is a marvelous housekeeper—a great supervisor, I should say. But that will be up to Marcus. The palazzo is his, you know."

"And what about you?"

He laughed. "Don't worry about me. We have various properties, a number of which are mine. I don't have any younger-son syndromes, if that's what you mean."

"I didn't," Chris murmured. But did she? She didn't know what she thought about anything or anyone anymore. "It is curious that Alfred never married Sophia."

Tony shrugged. "No, it's really not so strange. You forget, Alfred was an old man—from the old Italy. I think he always thought himself a class above his mistress. But he must have loved her. He never left her. *C'est la vie!*" he added in French.

Tony stayed with her until eight o'clock; then he kissed her forehead and left, promising to see her in the morning.

Chris closed her eyes, trying to sleep, but it seemed impossible. Someone, she was convinced, had tried to kill her. Someone had tampered with the steps. She couldn't believe it was Tony; she couldn't believe it was Marcus....

She opened her eyes and almost screamed out loud. Genovese was standing half in and half out of the doorway, staring at her with his dark but colorless eyes.

"Signorina Tarleton, a thousand pardons!" He came quickly into the room, running his fingers over the brim of a worn fedora. "I didn't mean to startle you."

Chris tried very hard to smile. "That's all right, Genovese. Thank you for, uh, coming to see me."

He shook his head solemnly. His voice became a whisper. "I came to tell you that you must be careful, that you should get away from Venice immediately!"

Chris felt shivers race along her spine. "Why, Genovese, do you know something?" she demanded.

"Si..."

He stopped when he heard a slight sound at her doorway. Chris looked beyond him. Marcus was standing there.

Quiet, calm, straight and tall. He was in a dark vested suit, watching them both with shielded eyes. He moved into the room, passing Genovese with an absent smile and coming to Chris. He sat beside her on the bed and took her hand in his.

"How are you?"

"Fine. I'm quite certain."

His eyes moved to Genovese; his smile was polite, his gaze speculative. "It was good of you to come see Chris, Genovese."

"Yes, I just wished to see how she was." He bowed his head a little nervously. "I'm leaving now. *Buona sera*, Signorina Tarleton."

He was out of the room before Chris could respond. She stared at Marcus furiously. "Why is he afraid of you?"

"Afraid of me! He isn't—that I'm aware of."

"Well, it's curious, isn't it, that everyone is warning me to get away from Venice?"

Marcus seemed to start. He released her hand and paced nervously to the window, like a cat on the prowl. He lit a cigarette as he stared out into the night. "Perhaps you *should* leave Venice for a while, Christina."

"Why? Because you know that something's going on? You know that my father didn't murder yours—"

"I know nothing of the kind!" he proclaimed, turning to her in anger. He stalked to the door of her room. "Go to sleep, Chris. I'll come to get you in the morning."

Tears stung her eyes as she saw him walk out of the room. There seemed to be no one to turn to. She wanted to trust him so badly, yet she couldn't.

And she didn't want to sleep. She didn't want to dream about righteous winged lions and silent black panthers stalking through the catacombs.

Chris stayed awake, staring up at the corniced hospital ceiling for a long, long time. She determined then that she would not be frightened away. She would be careful, but she would get to the bottom of things. She would quit accosting Marcus and start trying to charm him again. The answers were somewhere....

The galleries, she had to get back to the galleries again. Her earring had to be there, along with the note. If she could just find the note...

Then she could prove to Marcus that everything she was saying was true. Except that...except that she already thought he believed her, no matter what he said. He *did* know that something was going on.

Chris let out a little sob. Marcus . . . Marcus was the worst of it all. Insanely, she was falling in love with him. Sometimes she hated him, and she was afraid to trust him. But she was falling in love with him.

Marcus . . . if she could just sway him to her side. If she could only get him to talk to her. . .

While Chris finally drifted into a restless sleep, Marcus paced the doctor's office below. Dante Rosellini was an old family friend, and Marcus trusted him, but he was still worried. He had already spoken to Dante—enough for his friend to know he felt there was a great deal wrong. But now this! These damn pills were going to derail his plans of making Christina sweetly, deliriously, *pliantly* tipsy.

His left hand was in his pocket as he moved about pensively; in his right he clutched a small container of white pills.

"Does she have to take these, Dante?"

Dante Rosellini frowned. "No, Marcus. She does not *have* to take them. They are only a mild tranquilizer...to take the edge away from things. But they are not necessary. Why?"

Marcus grimaced. "I was anxious to take her to dinner tomorrow . . . and to ply her with a little wine. She really is all right?"

Dante arched a knowing brow. "She is fine. I have kept her here purposely to assure it. And, Marcus, there is nothing wrong with you taking her to dinner. Nor with 'plying her with a little wine.' But if you intend to do so, then do not let her take the pills. But I don't understand this. I've never known you to have the need to coerce a woman to your will!"

"I have a need to protect this particular woman," Marcus responded quietly. "And I'm afraid I'll have to coerce her to do it."

"I'm not so sure I like this."

"I don't like it myself, Dante. Trust me. I have her very best interests at heart!"

Dante Rosellini shrugged and lifted his hands. He pushed his chair back and walked around to lean back on his desk, watching Marcus astutely. "What are you up to, my young friend?" He grinned suddenly. "I cannot believe that this is a new form of conquest for you."

Marcus sighed. "No . . . not exactly." He sighed. "I wish she would leave Italy, but she is not going to do that."

"*Mia bellisima?* My pretty little patient? You are worried. What is it that you suspect?"

"I don't know. I don't know where the truth lies anymore."

Dante Rosellini walked around his desk again and sat in his chair. "You blame her for your father's death—"

Marcus interrupted him with a grunt of impatience. "I never blamed a child—"

"But you do—in a way. From what you say, you are refusing to trust her. Open your eyes to the things around you. You came to me to tell me about the staircase. You do not even trust your family. I suggest you find your answers quickly."

"I plan to," Marcus said quietly. He shook the little bottle of pills. "I just want to keep her alive while I do so and discover what it is she really wants."

"I just wish I knew exactly what you were doing," Dante said seriously.

Marcus paused, then sighed, and fully explained himself. Dante stared at him, not sure whether to smile, or protest emphatically.

"It's a rash plan and very dramatic. And I'm going to pretend that you never told me about it."

"Do you see another, if she refuses to leave?"

The doctor sighed. "No. I hope it will be enough. Perhaps you should be making a few demands on your family."

Marcus laughed with little humor. "I can hardly see anyone admitting to blackmail or murder. Can you?"

"Perhaps not, perhaps not. Ah, well. Best wishes—and *salute*!"

"Thanks," Marcus said dryly. "*Arrivederci*, and oh, *per favore*, tell her that I will come at about five o'clock."

"Si," Dante murmured unhappily.

Marcus left the hospital and returned to the palazzo in the launch. As soon as he arrived he went to check the staircase. It had been fixed and completely checked for faults. It was now in excellent condition. The carpenter had told him that the only way the wood might have fallen in was if it had been purposely weakened.

The palazzo was quiet. It seemed as if it slept, along with its inhabitants. Marcus walked slowly up to his room, but he didn't turn on the light. Instead he slipped out onto the terrace and into Christina's room.

He sat on the bed, smiling sadly as he smoothed a hand over the cover. *"Amore mio,"* he murmured. "You came, and you changed everything. You changed me."

Changed him, yes. In many ways. He had never known fear like this before, because he was afraid for her. He had held her, kissed her, felt her sleek body grow fevered next to his. He knew the light scent of her French perfume in his sleep; it haunted his dreams. Her shape, supple, rhythmic, alive and lovely. Her eyes, as rich as honey, as tawny as those of the lioness. She was a challenge, a fighter—and a temptress, and he could all too easily be tempted. A touch, a glance, and he had wanted her. He had known that she would be a glimmering fire. Warm and sweet, a tempest. He could still feel the wonder of her breasts, filling his hands, taunting his senses along with the taste of her lips, her throat.

She hated him. She was drawn to him. If only they had met on a beach in France, or on a ski vacation in Switzerland.

But they hadn't. She was James Tarleton's daughter returned. And she had stirred up embers of the past that were setting a slow fuse to the present.

He stood abruptly, walking back out to the terrace. She was really going to hate him by tomorrow night, he thought dismally. But he really had no choice. He could prove nothing; he didn't even know what to suspect. And the only thing he could do until he trapped the attempted killer was protect her with all he had to give.

And somehow get her to keep her damn nose out of things. And find out what she knew—and what she had really come for.

The money? It was possible. Revenge? That was possible, too, if she believed her father had been horribly wronged.

And it was also possible that she was everything she seemed, everything that was haunting him, teasing him, taunting him....

She was trapping him in her silent web of beauty; he was falling more and more deeply in love with the daughter of a man who it still appeared to him could have been the only one to murder his father....

He sighed. Tomorrow night...

At four o'clock the next afternoon Marcus phoned the hospital. The nurse came on the line, and then the doctor.

"Marcus, she's gone," Dante told him unhappily.

"Gone! I told you to keep her there. Dear God, Dante, didn't you understand—"

"*Si, si!* But I wasn't here. She twisted the day staff around her finger. She planned to surprise everyone by getting back home by herself and all. She—she hasn't come home yet?"

"No, she's not at the palazzo," Marcus murmured uneasily. He found out that she had left several hours earlier, then hung up the phone.

For a long moment he stared down at the receiver, completely tense. He needed help. Right now he needed help badly. But it had come to a point where he didn't trust anyone. At least, he had warned himself not to trust anyone. Not even those who were his blood, people he loved.

Not even his brother.

But that, he decided firmly, was foolish. He knew Tony almost as well as he knew himself. He had to trust someone.

Suddenly he was furious with himself. How had he let his own mind become so narrow that he couldn't see the obvious? Tony *was* his brother. Marcus turned, shaking his head a little at his own foolishness. He was in trouble now, and his brother was the one to call on for help.

"Tony! Tony!"

His brother came running from the courtyard when he heard Marcus's call. "Tony, Chris left the hospital. Hours ago," Marcus told him.

Tony gazed at him worriedly. "Where do you think she went?"

"I don't know. Take the launch, please, and see if you can't find her on the canals or the streets. I'm going to the galleries."

Chris had had no problem whatsoever wheedling her way out of the hospital. She was, after all, she had reminded them sweetly, an adult and an American. Responsible for herself and her own welfare. And, of course, she was very, very sweet.

Neither did she have any problems getting to the galleries—or inside them. They were open today. There seemed to be tourists all around; Chris joined them for a while, wondering just what it was that she was looking for.

She eventually made her way over to the historical exhibit. She didn't see Joe, Fredo or anyone else that she knew. It was easy to be anonymous.

She walked around the figures, smiling as they went into action. They really were excellent. Lucrezia Borgia was the best; she had a voice and face that implied determination. She might have been a murderess, but she had also been a woman out to get what she wanted. Chris shrugged and walked on past her. Someone called out something in Italian, but Chris wasn't paying any attention. She kept following the circle, pausing as she saw that a costume had been laid out on a glass case, probably for the Catherine di Medici figure that was still missing.

Chris started as the lights suddenly went out. She realized then that the galleries were closing for the day. She must have heard the announcement earlier and simply not understood it.

She should hurry up and get out.

But should she? Apparently the guards hadn't seen her, or they wouldn't have turned out the lights. Now was the perfect time to do a little exploring, and she wouldn't even have to break in.

But how was she going to get out? Chris wondered. The alarm system would probably go off if she tried to get out through the door.

She shrugged, certain there would be a way. She could even go down the trapdoor if she had to, then ignore the tombs and race along the subterranean tunnel to the palazzo. Or, much easier, she could get on the phone and call Tony or Marcus to come get her.

Chris moved to the door and looked outside. Beyond the balcony she could see the last two guards in their medieval uniforms, chatting as they set the switch by the entry doors, looked around the place one last time—and exited.

She glanced back at the silent figures in the robotronics room. She shivered a bit, then slipped along the long hallway toward the gem salon. Marcus hadn't found the note or her earring, but she knew that they had been there. But then, she thought miserably, did she really know yet that she could trust Marcus?

Or did she just *want* to trust Marcus?

Chris went straight to the case with the di Medici jewels and carefully got down on the floor—avoiding the trapdoor, just in case someone was beneath her!—then searched studiously in the moonlight. Frustrated, she sat back. Marcus was right: there was no earring, and there was no note. She sighed. Someone had found them. Or else Marcus had found them himself and wasn't admitting it to her.

Chris started suddenly as she heard a door open below. She stood quickly, frowning, and walked silently back to the door. She couldn't see anyone—and there were no more sounds.

Quietly she walked to the balcony to look down to the courtyard. A soft gasp escaped her, and her heart began pounding wildly.

There was a figure in the courtyard, a tall figure clad in a long dark all-encompassing cloak.

Chris started to back away from the balcony just as the figure looked up. Its features were so shadowed that she couldn't see them at all. She sensed that the figure had seen her, though.

And she knew it when she saw the figure starting for the stairway. Chris emitted a little cry and started running down the hall. She slipped through a door, barely aware that she had reentered the robotronics exhibit. She dared a quick peek through the door, but could no longer see the cloaked figure. But then she heard a noise: the sound of a secretive footstep. It was coming from the gem salon, right next door. This room would be next. And it was almost certain that the cloaked form was carrying the knife that had glinted so lethally in the moonlight on the night Alfred had died.

Chris spun around desperately. She saw all the figures, silent in their poses. And then she saw the Catherine di Medici costume, lying on the case.

She ran to it, throwing the full old-fashioned skirts over her head and pulling them down quickly. Her own skirt and blouse were completely hidden. There was a headdress, too. Like horns with a veil. Chris threw it on, praying it was straight. She swept the veil across her cheek and over a shoulder. She pitched her purse far beneath the pedestal and jumped onto the circular stage with the other figures, finding a pose in a deep curtsy before a courtly gentleman with bloused trousers who was bowing deeply himself.

Her heart began to thunder again. She had been just in time. The door to the room opened, and the hooded figure entered.

Chris longed to look up, but she didn't dare. She listened as the figure walked around the room, coming closer to her, closer. Footsteps, slow, one after another. Coming closer still. Pausing, until she could feel her heart thunder and her blood run cold, the hair seeming to rise at her nape. . . .

And then the footsteps passed her by. Chris began to breathe more easily in relief, then froze once again in horror. At the doorway the cloaked figure was playing with the switches.

The lights came on. The figures began to move. All at once. Saying hello, introducing themselves.

The courtly fellow in the bloused trousers moved, slapping her in the face as he extended an arm.

Chris didn't allow herself to react. She prayed that her light Italian would be up to par for a few words. She allowed herself to blink once, remembering all the times she and Georgianne had posed as robots in Parisian boutiques to make extra money. It was just like mime: separated mechanical movements. A tilt here, a bend there, nothing smooth or flowing, a little slower than real life.

"Io sono Catherine di Medici," she murmured, deepening her curtsy to the "friend" who had slapped her with his own mechanical movement. It was all she could think of to say, and it didn't really matter, because all the other figures were talking, and the conversations were blending in the night. *"Io sono Catherine di Medici,"* she repeated. "*Mi piace Venezia.*" Softly, softly. Just enough that her lips moved, so she looked real . . .

The hooded figure flipped the switch, and the figures were still. Chris caught herself, posing in a deep curtsy once again. She wanted to look up so badly that she thought she would explode, but if she did, she could all too easily die. She waited, barely breathing.

And then she heard the figure turn away and pull the door shut.

Still Chris waited. Waited and waited. Finally, when she could bear her stance no longer, when her limbs were about to break, she moved. Carefully, very carefully. She stepped from the circular stage and silently crept to the door, wincing as the costume skirts rustled around her. She opened the door a crack, but could see nothing. She waited for a few more minutes, leaning against the wall, trying to breathe slowly. Then she peeked out the door again. No one. Silently she stepped out into the hallway and moved to the balcony. She could see nothing on the ground floor. She kept looking, hugging the balcony as she moved closer and closer to the stairway.

And then she heard a movement on the stairs. She looked quickly to her right, and the cloaked figure suddenly pointed a blinding flashlight into her face.

Chris screamed and spun around. The door to the gem salon was right behind her. She ran into the room, closing the door and leaning against it. She glanced around a little desperately, saw one of the jewel cases and ran to it, then dragged it back hurriedly and braced it against the door. Then she hurried to the di Medici case, crawled to the floor and searched for the hinge to the trapdoor. For several seconds, in which she began to pray fervently, the spring eluded her. Then at last it gave. Closing her eyes and praying again, she pitched her body downward.

She hit the hard stone and met total darkness, as she had known she would. And she tried very hard not to panic at knowing that everything she touched was part of the tombs—including the spiders that lived among the dead.

For several minutes she just sat, breathing hard and trying to muster her courage and sense of reason. Then she stood, silently apologizing to the long-dead di Medicis for crawling over them. She ducked her head, aware of the archways. If she could only find her way through the tombs and locate the hallway, she would begin to see light, the light from the chapel at the end of the tunnel.

It seemed to take forever to make her way around the first set of stone monuments. Then she began to pray that she was going in the right direction, and that she wouldn't panic and start running like an idiot until she killed herself by crashing headfirst into marble or stone.

In the end she did panic. At first she hadn't heard it: the soft sound of a footstep against stone. But finally she did. Footsteps, footsteps in the tombs, coming toward her.

Suddenly a flashlight sent a golden ray into the darkness, and Chris screamed, long, shrill and terrified.

"Good God! What are you doing down here again?"

Chris brought a hand to her eyes to shield them from the glare. "Marcus?" she whispered.

The light danced, and then he was next to her, holding her before she could fall.

"What are you doing?" he demanded. "Another lost earring? And just for kicks you decided to dress up like Catherine di Medici to find it this time?"

He was alive and real, warm and strong, and she was so glad to see him. But he was furious, and she was still terrified—and she wanted to tear his heart out.

"Damn it, Marcus! Someone was up there! Coming after me."

"And what the hell were you doing up there? You were supposed to be at the hospital, waiting for me!"

"Marcus! There was someone after me—"

"Yes! Probably the guards. People aren't supposed to be prowling around after the galleries have closed."

"Marcus, the guards don't wear dark cloaks."

Chris broke off. His arms were around her, and she was clinging tightly to him, glad of the strength of warm living muscle beneath her fingers. But then a chill touched her. Where had he come from? He could have been the figure; he would have known that she was down here.

No, no, no! Because he could kill her as easily here as he could have in the galleries. But suddenly she didn't want to say any more. Her heart was sure of Marcus's innocence, but her head told her to trust no one. If it had been Marcus . . .

She had to be charming and sweet. Had to convince him that she hadn't seen anything, didn't know anything . . .

"Uh . . . maybe it was one of the guards. Maybe I panicked."

Chris threw herself against his chest, her heart pounding. She pleaded in a muffled whisper, "Marcus, help me, get me out of here. *Per favore*, Marcus!"

His fingers wound into the hair at her nape, his touch almost rough as he tilted her head back, staring into her eyes. His were cynical and angry. Then his mouth ground down on hers, consuming her with a brutal kiss that softened almost instantly. Did he hate her? Or care for her? Was it possible that he had been a murderer—or was he her "winged lion" of justice, her only salvation?

None of it mattered when he kissed her, when his lips moved against hers with persuasion and hunger. His lips left hers to find her cheeks and throat, and then returned to consume her mouth once again, his tongue parrying deeply, as if desire could be assuaged in that single assault.

Chris went limp, weary and lost as she leaned against him, dismayed to know that she cared for him beyond all reason. Could she manipulate him with honeyed words? Could she seduce where her anger failed...? If she did, she would only be giving in to the demands of her heart.

"Please... Marcus," she whispered, clinging to his shoulders, allowing her fingers to roam over them.

"I don't think you should make an appearance upstairs as Catherine," he warned, and she felt his hands on her body as he helped her strip away the awkward headdress and costume. He started to toss them aside. Chris suddenly gasped, seeing something in the beam of the flashlight.

"What is—"

"Marcus!" It was barely a whisper. "Look! The cloak!"

He frowned and bent down next to a sculpted angel that stood sentinel over a tomb. He picked up a large swath of dark material.

"It is a cloak," he said curiously. "How did it get there?"

She wanted to scream and back away from him. Only two people were there: she and Marcus. But illogical as it was, she still couldn't believe that Marcus would harm her. She didn't want to believe it.

"I—I told you, the figure wore a cloak."

He held the material for several seconds, then dropped it. "Leave it and leave Catherine's gown. Let's see if we can get out of here without being seen."

His fingers were tight around hers as he led her quickly through the tunnels. Chris was glad to follow him blindly. But when they neared the other side and she could see the light from the chapel and the stairs to the palazzo, she hung back suddenly, swallowing fiercely and forcing herself to speak.

"Marcus, what were you doing down there?"

"Looking for you," he said bluntly. He pulled her into the light, staring at her critically, trying to brush away the few spiderwebs that still clung to her hair.

"But . . . why?"

"Why? Because you just got out of the hospital!" he said impatiently.

"What made you think of the galleries?"

"Instinct. Or maybe I'm coming to know you. I don't really know. What difference does it make?"

She evaded that question and asked another one. "Marcus, who has keys to the galleries?"

"Tony and myself. Alfred had one, but I don't know what became of it. Why?'

"It's obvious. Oh, never mind. Let's go up."

"Yes, let's go up. And you can go straight to your room and get dressed."

"Dressed? For what?"

He smiled suddenly. It was a little grim, his teeth very white against the copper of his features. "For something nice. We're going to go to dinner and spend the evening out. Away from the palazzo. As you wanted—away from everything."

Chris stared up at him. Slowly she nodded. She had to get him to talk to her. They would order wine; she would be as sweet and charming as possible. She would force him to admit that Alfred had been blackmailed because someone other than her father had murdered Mario di Medici.

"That would be wonderful," she said softly, smiling at him, then walking past him to the steps. Suddenly she turned back, watching him as he followed her. "Will you give me an hour? I really would like to dress up tonight."

"An hour is fine." He squeezed her hand, and they continued up the stairs.

"You found her!"

Tony was standing at the top of the stairs, smiling with relief. "Christina, I combed half of Venice."

Marcus's hand tightened around hers. "She was in the chapel. I told her one of us would wring her neck if she ever pulled such a disappearing act again."

Tony shrugged, trying to give Chris a glance that was reassuring, as if to say, "His bark is much worse than his bite."

But she couldn't be reassured. Not when Marcus wasn't telling Tony the truth.

Not Marcus, not Tony. It just couldn't be one of them. But Tony was right there at the top of the stairs, and it seemed that they didn't even trust each other....

"We're going to go out, Tony. Would you mind letting Sophia or Genovese know that we won't be here for dinner?"

"Not at all," Tony murmured. He touched Chris's cheek with his open palm. "I'm glad to see you safe and sound, *bella* Christi." He smiled at his brother. "I'll find the gorgon."

As Tony started down the hall, Chris turned to Marcus. "My purse!" she whispered. "It's back in the robotronics room—"

He caught both her hands. "I'll get it. And I'll be waiting for you in the entryway. One hour."

Chris nodded and headed away from him. She felt him following her. At her door she paused, staring at him.

He smiled. "I just wanted to see you get to your room."

She smiled and hurried inside.

"Use your lock," he told her curtly, and then he was gone.

Chris showered, shampooed and dried her hair, then dressed in the new black cocktail gown she'd purchased. She was nervous, excited, apprehensive and exhilarated. She was going to get away from the palazzo with Marcus. And somehow... somehow she would force him to get to the bottom of things.

Unless he was there himself...

No!

Chris gave herself a critical gaze in the mirror. The gown was dazzling, low-cut, sheer, with a V at her back. The skirt was fluted; it swirled with her every movement. Her hair was clean and swept around her shoulders in shining waves. She closed her eyes; she could and would be charming. She would disarm the man....

She would have to, she realized. Because the hooded figure would really be after her now.

Chris glanced at the old German clock on her dresser. Her hour was up. She exited her room and came to the balcony. Marcus was at the entryway; he looked up, saw her and smiled, a devilish fire in his eyes. He whistled softly, a low sound that warmed her from head to toe. She smiled dazzlingly in return and started down to him.

He was in black, too. Black tux, black vest. A stark-white shirt emphasized his dark looks, the indigo intrigue of his eyes, the hard lean strength of his frame. She had never seen him more handsome or compelling. More like a black panther than ever, sleek and cunning and at home with the night.

Chris took a deep breath as she reached him, and offered him another smile. He took her hand and slowly kissed it, his eyes touching hers. She would be all right, she promised herself. She was quite certain she knew the nature of her prey.

Chapter Eight

He had a hired gondola waiting for them by the steps. She raised her eyes in inquiry, aware that he usually preferred to use the family's own means of transportation.

He smiled and took her hand to help her into the boat. "It's our grand night out, remember?" he whispered softly, and she shot him a seductive look in return. His breath caught momentarily in his throat; she was stunning, all the more so in beautiful motion. In the arresting black gown she moved like the waves of the sea, like a soft cloud floating across the sky, lulling, beguiling. When she smiled at him, he felt as if strings inside him tautened, as if, should she beckon, he would follow her anywhere, through all the fires of hell and back again....

Ah, but I am the puppeteer, and she the dancer on the strings tonight, he reminded himself.

He kept smiling as he seated himself beside her. The scent of her perfume was subtle; it wafted around him like a woven chain of golden angel's hair.

The gondolier pushed away from the Palazzo di Medici.

Marcus reached beneath the seat and produced a chilled bottle and two frosted glasses. She laughed lazily, easily; her eyes were a brilliant burst of gold and green beneath the sensual heavy-lidded crescents of her deep-honey lashes.

"Wine, on a gondola?" she inquired.

"Asti spumante," he returned, handing her a glass and adding lightly, "It's the only way to see Venice, you know."

"Is it?"

"Of course." He entwined his elbow with hers, careful not to spill the sparkling liquid. He took a sip, watching her do the same. The gondola was cushioned, and he leaned back on one elbow, inviting her to follow suit. Her lashes lowered briefly; a small secretive smile curled her lips. When her lashes rose again her eyes were bright, like topaz in the night, and he knew that they were playing a game of cat and mouse, circling warily, and that there was a very dubious distinction between the role of cat and the role of mouse. She was out for something; she intended to play things her way and win. That was why she was with him. But tonight the round was going to go to him.

Still, there was no reason for her to realize that yet.

He leaned over and brushed her lips with a light kiss. She seemed perfectly relaxed, ready to purr at his touch. He kissed her again, dumping his champagne overboard as he did so.

"You're not drinking up," he told her softly. "We're out to forget everything, to watch the moon, to see Venezia as lovers might."

She allowed him to refill her glass, as he did his own. She cast her left elbow over a cushion, stretching her body luxuriously near his, idly playing with the lapel of his jacket. "Marcus, it would be much easier to enjoy the night if you would admit a few things."

"Such as?" He caught the fingers that teased his chest, uncurled them slowly and kissed her palm.

"Your glass is empty again," she told him, taking over the role of hostess.

"And so is yours."

"So it is . . ."

She poured more asti spumante for them both, stretching one arm over the side of the boat. He pretended not to notice as she dumped hers overboard.

"Marcus," she murmured, resting her head against his shoulder.

"Hmmm?"

"You know that Alfred was being blackmailed. Admit it."

"We're not here to talk about Alfred."

He ran his fingers through her hair, smoothing it from her face as the breeze lightly tossed it about. Her cheek felt as soft as a rose petal.

Another gondola passed. The young couple in it laughed and called out to them in Italian, and threw flowers on board. Chris laughed as she clutched the flowers. The moon played on the water; the lights on the palaces they passed added hues of sparkling crimson to the deepest blue. They passed St. Mark's Church, and she smiled up at the winged lion.

Her head still lay against his shoulder. "Marcus, you think someone in your family is involved in something, don't you?"

He ran his finger slowly over her lower lip. "I think you're involved in something."

"Me?"

"You do keep turning up in the strangest places. And you did say that you were after Alfred's money. *And* it seems that you managed to obtain it."

"Don't be absurd," she began, and then she laughed. "I told you why I was in the galleries—"

"Yes, you told me what you chose to."

"And you have told me nothing."

"But perhaps," he whispered softly, nuzzling her ear, "you will persuade me to do so. Ah, here's the restaurant."

Inside, they were led to a secluded booth, with the water before them. He sat beside her, slipping an arm around her shoulders. He explained all the items on the menu. When the antipasto came he teased her into feeding him olives, and his teeth lingered over her fingers, his tongue playing across their tips. In the black gown, her shoulders bared, her hair a cascade of tawny silk about them, she was very beautiful and very exotic. He had to remind himself that he didn't really trust her in the least, that she had airily proclaimed herself a huntress....

And that he knew damned well she was on the hunt right now.

He smiled. "More wine?"

"You've hardly touched yours."

"Oh, on the contrary! I've finished it."

"Let me pour you more."

"Ah, not without you!"

Her smile was a little weak, but she accepted more of the sparkling wine. How much had she consumed?

Quite a nice amount, he calculated, smiling as he watched her drain her glass along with him.

The rest should be very, very easy.

He teased her again, telling her that he divulged his deepest secrets when the vintage was right. She kept drinking to keep him drinking.

And he kept smiling, subtly amused. She was forgetting that he was an Italian—raised on wine.

Between the pasta and the scungilli he led her to the dance floor. She moved like a ripple of water, graceful, sensual. He allowed himself to inhale the fragrance of her hair and flesh, to savor the brush of her body against his.

By the time they finished dinner she was giggling delightedly at his stories. She leaned against him as they walked out and tripped over the dock, still laughing when he swept her into his arms to carry her onto the gondola. Her head was tilted back; her eyes met his. They were cat's eyes, topaz, sizzling with laughter, sensual as a purr, as the soft touch of her fingers against his cheek. He waved a hand at the gondolier and sank to the cushions, holding her, smiling as she trustingly curled her arms around his neck. He kissed her, long and deeply, his hands molding over her shoulders, enjoying the satiny feel of her arms, finding her breast in the shielding darkness, curving over it, loving the way it filled his hand.

And then he held her against him, shuddering, forcing himself to become remote. They were almost there.

The gondola rocked against the dock. "Come on," he whispered to her.

"Where are we?"

"An old church."

"Oh, you're going to buy it?"

He grunted, helping her from the gondola. She tripped again, laughing, smiling up at him. A twinge of guilt touched him; he was taking a very drastic measure. As she stared up at him, smiling with her wide topaz eyes, he reminded himself that though she might be as sweet as a kitten now, she had the claws of a tigress when she chose.

"Oh, Marcus! These steps . . . they're moving!"

"Don't worry, I'll help you."

"*Will* you help me, Marcus?"

"Of course."

They walked into the nave of the old building. She stared up, fascinated by the frescoes on the wall. He tugged at her arm. "Come on, the priest is waiting for us."

"Oh, we're going to get a tour!"

"Something like that."

He held her tightly as they walked up the aisle. The priest was there, along with his clerk and a cleaning lady.

"Oh, they're on the tour, too!"

"Yes. Listen to what he's saying."

Marcus glanced at the priest and nodded. The man began a monotonous chant in Latin.

"I don't understand him!" Chris whispered, and then she giggled.

"Just nod and say *si* when I tell you."

She did so. Then the priest served Mass. Chris tried to suppress a giggle when he came out with the chalice.

"Oh, Marcus! More wine! I really can't."

"Just a sip."

And then it was over. Done. The priest blessed them. All she had to do was sign a certificate.

"What is it?" Chris queried.

"Just a register. It says that . . . you've been a guest."

"Oh." She signed her name with a lovely flourish. "And now?"

"Now we're going home."

"Yes, I really think that I should. I'm so tired all of a sudden. . . ."

She practically collapsed in his arms. Marcus picked her up easily and paid the priest a very hefty sum for his evening's work.

He carried Christina out to the gondola and told the gondolier to return to the palazzo as quickly as possible.

At the steps he also paid that man very well. Then, hoisting her in his arms, he entered the main entry hall, where he heard voices from the courtyard. He hurried up the stairs.

In his room, he laid her on the bed. She was light and limber, floppy as he set her down. "Marcus . . ." she murmured, and she tried to sit up, throwing her arms over his shoulders.

"Shhh, you can sleep now, Christina."

She opened her eyes and smiled in a daze. "Hold me, Marcus. The boat is rocking."

He held her for a moment, then pressed her back to the bed. She brought her palm gently to his cheek. "You really are a nice guy, Marcus."

"Yes, I'm just charming," he muttered dryly. "Hold on. I'll be right back."

He slipped onto the terrace and into her bedroom, where he found one of her gowns. When he returned her eyes were closed, and she was curled up with a pillow. He tried to pull it away from her. She smiled and murmured something, pulling it closer. He sighed, then pulled off her shoes and stockings. She laughed and wiggled her toes. "Marcus, you're tickling me."

I'm tickling you! he thought, dismayed at the hot rush of desire that ravaged his body as his fingers touched the bare flesh of her thighs. "Sit up, Chris," he told her harshly. "You can't sleep in that thing."

He pulled her up, and she fell limply over his shoulders. He fumbled with the hooks at her back, then managed to pull the dress over her head. She fell back against him, her bare breasts crushed to his chest. He pushed her gently away and felt that fullness again, flesh that was soft, breasts that were firm and beautiful and shapely, rose peaked, and so tempting that he groaned. In the morning, she would hate him. If only she were screaming and yelling now . . .

"Marcus . . ." she whimpered softly.

He laid her back on the bed, closing his eyes and shuddering fiercely. He reached for her nightgown and opened his eyes. For a second he paused, breath drawn. She was stunning. Tanned and slim, with haunting dips and shadows; long, long limbs, sinewed, firm; a curving waist; a rounded bottom hidden by the thinnest wisp of lace.

He raised her again, fumbling with the white gown. Her breast brushed against his arm, and he muttered several soft curses in Italian. Finally he got the gown over her head and pulled over her torso.

But his nerves were shot. He quickly smoothed the gown down and pulled the covers over her. Then he walked to the terrace to allow the breeze to cool his burning flesh and painful desire.

At length he meticulously stripped off his own clothing and crawled into the bed beside her, keeping his distance. It was difficult. Her back was to him, but she kept inching over. Her derriere became a soft battering ram against his hips.

"Ummm . . . Marcus," she muttered. He gritted his teeth together, then turned to hold her, fitting his arm around her, his hand at the curve of her breast. He cursed himself a thousand times over. She was pliable. As soft and pliable as a kitten purring beside him.

He need only encourage her and she would turn to him....

Strange, he reflected in haunting agony, it didn't really bother him a bit that he had conned and coerced and deceitfully tricked her into marriage. It was the only way that he could stay beside her and protect her. But no matter what she did, he couldn't allow himself to take sexual advantage of her. No matter how much he wanted her. One day he would have her. But she would know all about it. Her heart and soul would be as willing as her supple sensual body.

Lying there seething, fuming, aching—screaming inside—he forced himself to plan for the morning. She was going to be in a rage, so it would be most effective for him to take the offense.

When she awoke he would be ready. Waiting, watching, poised for attack and as hard as rock.

And when morning came he *was* ready. He saw her awaken; he saw her confusion and her horror. And when her eyes met his with topaz fury and accusation, he smiled....

"Buongiorno. Buongiorno, amore mio," he drawled softly. Then he stalked slowly toward the bed and sat down beside her. His eyes were hard, his body tense, his voice taunting and implacable.

It was time to tell her—if she didn't remember—that the game had been played for real. The laughter was over, along with the cautious circling; she had to be made aware that his actions were in deadly earnest and that she couldn't fight him. Whatever he said or did, she would have to support him and be the perfect blushing bride.

Whatever her feelings were—and she looked as if she'd gladly strangle him at the moment.

She would have to bend to his will. Her life might very well depend upon it.

But inwardly he flinched at the cold fury and hatred that seemed to gleam from her eyes. He braced himself and continued to keep his voice cool and mocking. "What? Can she be angry? Dismayed? How so, my love? You wanted a di Medici man. You said so often enough. Well, you've gotten one. I could resist the temptation no longer. But perhaps you feel that you brought the wrong di Medici to the altar?"

He saw her fury increase and her muscles tighten, and he caught her wrists right before she could slap him.

"Why?" she demanded in a whisper that was violent and heated and incredulous...and very, very hurt.

He could not apologize, but neither could he remain so hard. *"Cara..."* Tenderness softened his voice, but he had to play the game out. "Why? Because it was your wish, of course." He touched her cheek, and again he felt the misery of his betrayal. *"Cara..."*

She jerked away from his touch, lowering her eyes. Well, Marcus asked himself dryly, what had he been expecting? He stood up impatiently.

"We have both known that something had to happen between us. Did you take me for a saint? I have only given you what you wished."

She didn't believe a word of what he was saying...and why should she, when it was all lies?

"Or perhaps," he said mockingly, "it was truly Tony whom you wished to captivate. He is the more malleable, is he not? But, alas! As you Americans are so fond of saying, You have made your own bed. Now you shall lie in it."

Why was he goading her so? Marcus wondered as one of the silk pillows came hurtling at him.

Because he couldn't explain things to her yet. And because he couldn't bear her hating him.

And because he wanted her so badly, because he had come to care with such a terrible obsession, and was so terribly worried about her. . . .

He forced out a dry laugh. "Another cliché, but you're truly beautiful when you're angry!" She was... So beautiful as she stared at him with such dismay, such fury—and such hatred.

"Why?" she raged again.

"Why? You were there, too, my love. Oh, I admit, we were neither of us completely lucid, but . . . that is the course of love, my sweet." He had to get out of there. Away from the reproach in her eyes.

And he had to announce their marriage.

He started to open the door. She was out of the bed, racing toward him. "Wait! What are you doing? We have to do something about this. Surely we can arrange an annulment—"

"An annulment?" He gripped her shoulders, his fingers tightening. "*Cara*, I am on my way downstairs to make the announcement to the family. If you have any sense, Christina, you will keep your mouth shut! You will give the appearance of a sheepish—embarrassed, perhaps—but very happy bride. For God's sake! Haven't you the sense to stay alive!"

Fleeting emotions passed through her eyes, but the strongest remained fury. Marcus tightened his jaw and bit his inner lip. He wanted to shake her. He wanted her to understand that he was trying with all his might to protect her.

But he couldn't explain.

Nor could he admit his own suspicions to her.

He closed his eyes quickly, then gave her a little shove and hurried from the room.

Chris felt as if she were drowning. Everything moved too quickly through her mind. Everything.

Everything that had happened since she had come to Venice.

She couldn't move. She could barely reason.

She was in shock.

She was Marcus di Medici's wife.

Chapter Nine

Chris stared at the door after Marcus had left, still stunned, still unable to believe what she had done. What *they* had done. And the one single question continued to ravage her pounding head: *Why?*

Shivering, she sank back down to sit on the bed, trying to gather her wits about her. Marcus had married her, and she was quite convinced that though he was attracted to her, he certainly wasn't in love with her. So . . . why?

Because he was protecting her? Or someone else?

Marcus couldn't have murdered his own father. He had only been twelve at the time. But neither, Chris believed with all her heart, could her father have killed anyone. Marcus had tricked her into marriage without loving her; he had gone down to make a pointed announcement to the others about their marriage. Again, *why*?

Because he wanted someone in his family to believe that Alfred Contini's money and holdings would all stay in the di Medici family?

Oh, God! It was all so confusing. And it was getting worse and worse, and now she was really terrified....

No, Marcus hadn't murdered his own father. But there was a blackmailer as well as a murderer running around. There had to be, because Contini must have been blackmailed into keeping quiet about the murder. And that blackmailer must have been the one to cause Alfred's death. A blackmailer capable of murder, too.

Chris had seen a cloaked figure on the night Contini died; that same cloaked figure had appeared in the galleries, hot in pursuit, only yesterday. And both times when she had seen the figure, she had seen Marcus immediately afterward. They had even found the cloak together....

At first she had assumed that the di Medicis were as wealthy as Contini. But from all the talk—including their own words—they were not. Marcus and Tony both claimed not to need Contini's money, yet both of them were always spending money as if it were water.

Oh, God! Chris thought again, the pain in her head and the tumult in her heart making her dizzy. She lay back on the bed, conflict raging inside her. If she could only remember more of the night! What had happened after they had come back to the palazzo? He had too much power over her, way too much power. And she didn't know if she could trust him or not....

There was a knock at the door. Chris started and bolted up quickly, so quickly that her head began to pound all over again. "Who is it?" she called out. Dear Lord! This was his room; she was in it, ostensibly living in it . . . now . . . with him. It was crazy. She felt like panicking, running . . . disappearing. Maybe she had pushed her luck too far; maybe she should just get away while she still could. She was being a fool, seduced into belief in a man who had just proved himself more dangerous than she had ever imagined.

"Christina! It is Sophia. Marcus said you wanted coffee. Let me in, please."

She needed coffee! Nice time for him to think so! When all the damage was done . . .

She took a deep breath and opened the door.

Sophia swept into the room, setting down a tray with a silver pot and a china cup and saucer. Without glancing at Chris she poured out black coffee and handed her the cup, then stared at her critically.

"So, he married you."

Chris raised the cup a little helplessly. What had he told her to be? A happy, if sheepish, bride?

"I had expected something between you," Sophia muttered. "It was most obvious . . . but this!" She shook her head as if disgusted, then murmured, "Well, *salute*, Christina. You've done quite well here, haven't you?"

"I thought I was doing quite well before I came here," Chris murmured dryly, but then she remembered that she was supposed to be a happy blushing bride and she stepped past Sophia to stare out the terrace door, wincing slightly as the sunlight seemed to rip into her eyes. "But, of course, nothing in my life has ever been like Marcus." That was true. Nothing and no one had ever touched her life as Marcus had.

"Hmmph!" Sophia muttered. "Yes, they are something, aren't they, the di Medici men? But don't count your blessings too soon, Christina. They are temperamental. They would be the kings of their castles. And they are as attractive to all women as they are to you. You must ask your mother-in-law one day. Life with a di Medici will not be all one glorious romp between the sheets."

Chris took a sip of her coffee; it was so hot it burned her throat. She choked, but was careful not to look at Sophia, not to give anything away.

"Mario and Gina di Medici had marital problems?" she asked innocently.

"Of course. Who would not?" Sophia supplied maliciously.

Chris tensed, suddenly determined to draw Sophia out. "Sophia, do you mean that they fought... frequently?"

"Constantly. But you will see for yourself. It will be worse for you. You're an American. And Marcus is an Italian man. Gina at least was Italian, too. But...it has been your choice."

"I don't believe you!" Chris charged. "Gina di Medici was very much in love with her husband from all that I hear!"

"Yes, yes, she loved him!" Sophia said impatiently. "That's half the problem, yes? To love so much... and feel so little in return! And so the fights. Row upon terrible row. Why, even on the day that your father murdered Mario—"

Sophia broke off suddenly, and Chris tried not to pounce on her. "My father did not murder Mario," she said flatly, then quickly added, "But you were about to tell me, Sophia—weren't you?—that even on the day that Mario died, he and Gina were involved in a marital battle."

"It is none of your concern!" Sophia snapped.

Chris smiled with what she hoped was naïveté. "It *is* my concern; I've just married Mario's son! And I must learn to keep him. Poor Gina! It must have been all the worse for her to lose her husband when they had been engaged in a marital spat! It must have made the pain all the worse."

"I'm sure it did," Sophia murmured, watching Chris curiously. Then it seemed she lost all patience with the conversation. She shrugged. "I am amazed that Marcus married you, yet he has, and so I wish you both luck. You will excuse me, please? Gina is going to church, and I wish to get her key to the galleries."

Chris frowned. "Gina's key?"

"I've told Marcus that I shall go in today and defer his appointments."

"I, uh, I thought only Tony and Marcus had keys to the galleries."

"No, no. Gina has one, too. Why?"

"Nothing, nothing," Chris murmured. Sophia swept her with another critical gaze, murmured that she looked like hell, and told her that she needed some rest if she intended to keep her husband for a week. Chris smiled and thanked her icily for the advice.

As soon as Sophia left Chris walked weakly back to the bed and sank down. She braced herself and swallowed her coffee, praying it would help.

Despite its heat, her teeth were chattering. Gina di Medici had a key to the galleries. Marcus had purposely lied to her about his mother. Gina and Mario had been fighting on the boat. Did Marcus think his mother had killed his father? Did he believe that this charade of a marriage would hold his mother at bay without incriminating her? Did he believe that, if Gina was behind things, she would no longer attempt to harm Chris if Chris were his wife? Or perhaps it was the money! If they all believed that the money was still in the family—through marriage—did Marcus think that she would be safe?

Oh, dear God, she had to get away from them all!

There was another tap on the door. Chris was as jumpy as a bruised boxer about to receive another right punch to the jaw. "Who—who is it?" she called.

There was no answer, only a scraping sound against the door. She jumped up to swing the door open. There was no one there, only a note lying on the floor. She picked it up.

Someone had worked very quickly. In large block letters were the English words: "A di Medici bride has a place awaiting her in the di Medici crypt."

Chris dropped the note, inhaling deeply. The night had been insane; the morning was becoming sheer lunacy. She had to get away and sort things out, had to find some way to make her head stop pounding. And dear God, she didn't want to see Marcus again. . . .

Chris set the note on his dresser and nervously hurried from his room along the terrace to her own. She was shaking so badly that she could barely dress, and as she dressed she started wondering how she had gotten into the white gown, and when she started thinking along that line she started shaking all over again.

Somehow she managed to pull on a corduroy skirt and knit blouse, and then she remembered that her purse must be back in Marcus's room. She slipped quickly back along the terrace, and nearly screamed with tension when the phone beside the bed, French Provincial like the clock on the dresser, started to ring.

She froze, certain that someone would catch it on an extension downstairs. But the shrill ringing continued until her nerves were at the breaking point. Chris grabbed the phone and practically screamed, "Hello!"

There was a long silence. And then a very soft, heavily accented voice spoke. "Christina . . ."

Her name was drawn out. Shivers, like icy rivulets, raced from her nape along her spine.

"Who is this?" she demanded. "What do you want?"

"I have what you want," the voice told her. "Information."

"Tell me what you're talking about!"

There was silence again, and then, "Can you pay? My price will be high, but my information will be worth it. I know who killed Mario di Medici."

"What?" Chris gasped. She realized with a sick feeling that she had the blackmailer on the phone. But he had information to sell to her, and at this point she was very willing to pay.

"Yes, yes! I'll pay," she promised. "Tell me—"

"Not on the phone. Go to St. Mark's. To the Basilica. Sit in a pew and I will find you."

"Wait—"

The phone went dead. Chris stared at it, hung up the receiver, then picked it up again hurriedly, wondering if there were any way she could get an Italian operator to know that she wanted to trace a call.

She shivered again. Had the call come from outside the palazzo? Or was it possible that it had come from within the palazzo itself?

She sighed with frustration. She would never be able to make an Italian operator understand what she wanted. If she tried, she could end up with the operator calling back several times and possibly wind up with someone else on the phone.

Chris hesitated for a second, wondering if she shouldn't tell Marcus about the call. In turmoil she reminded herself that she couldn't trust Marcus any more than anyone else at the palazzo.

Indeed, she could trust him far less! she thought bitterly. Her life was a legal tangle because of him; he had taken her out and married her....

No! She definitely couldn't trust him, and only moments ago she'd been desperately wanting to get away from him. She saw her purse on his dresser and grabbed it, then quietly opened the door and stepped out onto the balcony.

From the courtyard she could hear voices. She couldn't go that way. She hurried down to the landing, then out the main entryway, practically racing down the steps.

She could see a vaporetto coming, but it wouldn't stop for her, not on the di Medici steps. Anxiously she started looking for a gondola. It seemed forever before she saw one; she hailed it quickly. And for once in Venice she didn't see or appreciate a thing. All she could think about was reaching the Basilica. The gondolier spoke a smattering of English; he tried to point out the impressive palaces. He told her how those condemned to death had walked the Bridge of Sighs, but she barely heard him.

When they reached St. Mark's Square Chris shoved a wad of lire into his hands and stared up at the Basilica, then started hurrying across the Square. Pigeons soared and scattered all around her, but she ignored them, impatiently weaving her way through a crowd of tourists to walk up the steps into the church and enter the nave.

She didn't see the artwork or the tombs, or any of the soaring beauty of the Basilica. She stared straight ahead at the altar, then looked around nervously, searching for someone who might be looking for her. She slipped into one of the pews, knelt—and waited.

No one came. Tourists flocked around the artwork and the smaller altars that lined the sides. They lit candles; they knelt and prayed. Chris grew restless. She stood up herself and walked around. She lit a candle, unable to pray, or even think. Eventually she wound her way back to the pew where she had been seated.

Her heart began to pound. There was a note on the pew exactly where she had been sitting. She picked it up. "You were followed. Same time. Same place. Next week."

A bright flash of red at the rear of the Basilica suddenly caught her attention. Glancing up, Chris felt a chill settle over her. She saw a figure in a bright-red hooded cloak leaving the Basilica.

"Wait!" she called.

Priests and tourists turned to stare at her in shocked disapproval. Chris ignored them and started to run.

Outside the sunshine blinded her. She blinked furiously. The figure in red was gone.

Feeling sick and disappointed, Chris started down the steps. The Square seemed to be filled with dozens of tourists and hundreds of pigeons. Her headache returned a thousandfold.

She emitted a sharp expletive and started slowly across the Square, trying to scan the crowd for traces of red. Someone gripped her elbow and she spun around, a startled gasp escaping her. "Marcus!"

His fingers felt like talons, rough around her arm. His eyes were dark and churning, like the sea, and a pulse was beating in his throat at a furious rate.

"What in God's name are you doing?" he demanded harshly. "I go up after announcing my newly acquired state of marital bliss, only to discover that my blushing bride has disappeared! Just what do you think you're doing?"

She could feel his anger rushing over her like hot simmering waves. Instinctively she tried to shake free of his hold; he didn't even appear to notice.

"I, uh, I felt the need to go to church!" she retorted, forcing her chin up in a show of bravado. "Quite frankly. I was praying for a way to get away from you—oh!"

He gave her a shake that wrenched her arm roughly, and she paused quickly, wondering what would happen if she started to scream insanely in the Square. He smiled as if reading her mind.

"This is Italy, Christina. And I am an Italian. Don't expect much help against your legal husband here. I asked you: what are you doing?"

"How did you find me?"

"Quite simply. I asked among the gondoliers. Talk to me, Christina."

"Talk to you! Why?" she asked him a little hysterically. "You've already tricked me and put us both in a totally untenable position. What more can you do?"

He raised a brow politely. "Would you like to find out?"

No, she thought, swallowing nervously and lowering her lashes very quickly to hide her eyes. She knew damned well that she'd never win in a one-on-one confrontation. She had to change her approach with no qualms. Not after what he had done.

"No," she murmured out loud, wondering again how she could get away from him. She was going to have to trick him somehow. She would have to make him believe that she had entirely accepted the situation, then get to the police and the American embassy.

She raised her eyes to his, trying to appear very hurt, very lost and a little helpless. "Oh, Marcus! I'm just so confused and...miserable. Marcus, you know that Contini was murdered. You know that things are going on.... Marcus, we need the police."

He released her arm, but entwined her fingers tightly with his own and started walking back through the Square toward the boats in the canal. "Marcus!" Chris snapped.

He stopped, staring at her. "What?"

"Damn it, Marcus! Why did you...why did you pull last night? Why did you marry me?"

He blinked. A shield as effective as a cloud fell over his eyes. "Because I couldn't bear life without you one more second, *cara mia*," he said with a humorless smile. He started walking again.

"You're a liar, Marcus!" Chris snapped. His fingers tightened around hers; she felt the heat of his tension enveloping her like something tangible. Sensation rippled all along her body in a massive shudder, making her hot, making her weak. Where was he dragging her now? What was he going to expect of her? For a moment she hated herself. Hated her absolute weakness. No matter what happened, no matter how intelligent her thoughts, how aware her reason, he could touch her and he would have all the power. She would sizzle, she would tremble, unable to discern fear from the engulfing excitement that ravaged her when he was near.

She had to get away....

"Where are we going?" she asked him.

"Back to the palazzo—to act like newlyweds," he told her curtly.

Chris lowered her head, not trying to escape his hold. She had to make him trust her again....

He waved down a motor launch and rather roughly helped her aboard. When they were seated Chris slipped her fingers around his arm and rested her head against his chest, not daring to check his eyes for his reaction. He tensed for a moment, then eased, running his fingers lightly through her hair with a tenderness she had not expected. "Marcus," she murmured, "I'm so frightened."

"Don't be," he told her a little huskily. "I mean to protect you."

Protect her. Protect her. She had been called to St. Mark's. He had appeared. He was always appearing....

She shivered. Not Marcus, not Marcus...

Too soon, the launch reached the di Medici palazzo. Marcus helped her out and she continued to cling to him. "I don't understand what we're doing," she whispered to him, trustingly, she hoped.

He smiled down at her. Again she felt that there was tenderness in his eyes, in his touch.

"Is it truly so horrible to find yourself married to me, *cara*?"

Chris pressed her cheek against his chest. "No, Marcus." God help her, it was the truth.

His fingers moved gently over the top of her head. "Let's get back upstairs. Perhaps no one will realize that we've been gone."

Chris smiled. What was she going to do? Charm him? Disarm him? But they were slipping quietly back into the palazzo, quietly back up the stairs....

Quietly back into his room.

Marcus closed the door and leaned against it, staring at her. His eyes fell over her, touched hers. He grinned slowly, then started walking toward her. Chris tried not to tremble when he took her into his arms. The sensation of fire lapping all along her flesh washed over her. There was a roaring in her ears, and she felt a sweet, sweet dizziness. An ache inside her...

His lips touched hers gently, moist and warm. His tongue probed her teeth, delved beyond them. Chris held on to him, feeling engulfed. She closed her eyes and fought for strength.

She teased his nape with her fingers, returning his kiss. And then she drew away, smiling shyly.

"Marcus, will you give me a few minutes? I—I'd like to slip back to my room, to shower and change...and come back to you," she added huskily.

He watched her, neither smiling nor frowning. She couldn't read a thing in his indigo eyes, in his tense stance or rigid features.

"I'll wait for you," he said simply.

Chris nodded and turned to the terrace. Not until she was certain she was past his vision did she hurry.

And then she did so on tiptoe, rushing to the French doors from her room to the terrace, waiting as her heart pounded away and then biting down hard on her lower lip as she tried to silently open her door.

She slipped off her shoes and padded onto the balcony. His door was still closed. She tiptoed down the stairs, praying that no one would make an appearance in the entryway. Again she opened the main door slowly, barely breathing.

When she had closed it behind her she raced down the steps to the canal, waving frantically for a boat. One came to her, and as soon as she was seated she told the gondolier, *"Pronto! Polizia, per favore!"*

The gondolier looked at her as if she were a crazy foreigner, then shrugged and started down the canal. Way too slowly, Chris thought nervously. She should have held out for a motor launch. At this rate she was never going to reach a police station.

Finally the gondola pulled up to a square. Chris realized with dismay that she didn't even know where she was. She paid the man, asking him, *"Dove polizia, per favore?"*

He pointed around a corner. Chris thanked him, then started up the square to a narrow via, staring at the buildings carefully. She saw a sign and sighed. The man really had brought her to a police station.

Chris opened the door and walked in. The outside of the building had appeared ancient. Inside there were modern desks with typewriters, glass partitions and shrilling telephones. There was a man at the front desk in a uniform, and she went up to him.

"Per favore, parla inglese?"

The man set down his pencil and looked at her. He shook his head, smiled and asked her in Italian to wait a minute.

Chris nodded gratefully. She walked nervously around the small outer chamber. A second later a door opened and another man in uniform, an older man with a kindly smile, started out. Chris smiled with even greater relief and started hurrying toward him. But then she gasped, stopping dead in her tracks as Marcus stepped out from behind him.

"No!" she cried, stunned.

Marcus smiled. *"Cara!"* he cried in apparent relief. She didn't know exactly what he said to the fatherly police officer, except that it had to do with how horribly worried he had been and how relieved he was to see her, especially since her mind was still so fogged after the accident on the staircase, which had seemed to steal away all her reason.

The middle-aged policeman clucked in sympathy.

"No, no! You don't understand at all," Chris began, backing away from the pair. Marcus was still smiling, still calling her his beloved and sounding truly like a grieved husband; Chris could see his eyes, and there was an expression that she was coming to recognize all too easily.

He was furious with her. He also knew that he had her cornered, and he was very much enjoying the situation.

"Wait, sir, listen to me!" Chris pleaded to the officer; he shook his head blankly, and she realized that he didn't speak any English. She tried desperately to come up with some Italian; instead, she started babbling in interspersed French and English, convincing the officer if Marcus hadn't already, that she was definitely suffering from delusions.

Chris stared at them both in growing frustration, fury and fear. "Oh, never mind!" she cried, backing toward the door, then turning blindly to run. She reached for the door, then gasped as firm fingers grabbed her arm, jerking her back. She spun and found herself encircled by Marcus's arms, crushed tightly to him. He was still smiling, his touch upon her gentle; his voice was soft, the tone very solicitous.

But his words—spoken in English—quite bluntly belied his tone. "You've had it, Chris. You're caught, tied, cornered. I've given him our marriage certificate and the doctor's report on your concussion. Now, shape up, *amore mio*. Smile at me sweetly, or by all the saints, you will be able to charge me with abuse before the night is over."

He was serious. But she did feel cornered—too cornered to behave rationally.

She kicked him as hard as she could in the shin. He grunted slightly; she heard his teeth grate. His eyes narrowed to glittering ice but he didn't relax his hold one iota.

He turned to the police officer and said something in Italian. The man shook his head, then waved, glad that she was the di Medicis' business and not his. Marcus gripped her arm with no mercy, and half pushed, half dragged her back out into the waning sunshine and along the via.

He was walking so quickly and so angrily that she could barely keep up. To her dismay, she felt herself shivering. She had no idea where he was leading her or just how far his fury would take him.

And it was getting dark.

Chris tripped over a break in the tile of the walkway. "Marcus!" she gasped breathlessly. He didn't hesitate in his stride at all; he just gripped her more tightly, dragging her along.

"Marcus..." There was a plea in her voice. He stopped, but not out of courtesy. His features were so tightly drawn that she would gladly have sunk into the ground.

"Sorry, Christina," he snapped coldly. "No more tricks. If you have any sense whatsoever you'll just shut up."

He started walking again. She had no choice but to follow him, her anxiety growing by the minute. Her heart kept insisting that he could never hurt her, but her head kept saying that he was ready to wind powerful fingers around her throat and strangle her.

They soon reached the square. She saw that he had brought the motor launch. Seconds later she was being rather roughly lifted down to the rear seat. She started to rise, but he pressed her back. "I'm warning you, Christina. Don't push me."

The motor roared to life. Marcus obeyed the speed and traffic restrictions, but just barely. He didn't touch her; he kept his hand on the tiller, his profile implacable as he stared straight ahead.

Chris swallowed uneasily as she noted they weren't following canals that were even remotely familiar to her. She was even more horrified to realize after several speedy swerves and turns that they were on some kind of an open waterway.

"We're not going back to the palazzo," she observed, moistening her lips.

"No, we're not," he replied bluntly.

He increased his speed. They were slicing through the water, and the color of the sky was beginning to match that of the water. Chris felt a little ill, suddenly seized by panic.

"Marcus . . . ?" she murmured.

He faced her again, his countenance as dark as the water by night. "Don't even talk to me right now, Chris. I mean it. Do us both a favor and *don't talk to me*!"

She closed her eyes and miserably shut up. She opened her eyes again when she realized that the wretched speed of the launch was slowing.

They were coming to a dock, a regular boat dock. Chris realized that they had left Venice and reached the mainland. The motor idled while Marcus steered the boat into a berth. Then he jumped to the wood planking and reached a hand down to her. Chris hesitated, until he snapped out her name. She took his hand and allowed herself to be pulled up. He kept her hand and started walking, his strides uncomfortably long as he started down the dock to a parking lot. He knew where he was going; he led her straight to a bright-red Ferrari, pulled a set of keys from his pocket, opened the passenger door and practically shoved her in.

Chris considered bolting as he walked around the car, but he was too quick. She saw his face as he opened the driver's door and reconsidered immediately. If there was any sense of mercy left in him at all, any further aggravation from her would strip it away entirely.

The Ferrari roared into action with a fury that seemed to match that of its driver.

Chris buckled her seat belt, leaned back and closed her eyes again. They were on the road for several minutes before she found the nerve to open them. They had traveled at high speed for at least fifteen minutes before she dared to ask him where they were going.

"Adazzi," he answered briefly. He glanced her way, but his eyes were in shadow, and she didn't know if his temper was beginning to ease or not. "To the villa."

To the villa... Chris couldn't see anything at all. They had gone through one town, but now all she could see in the darkness was shadowed landscape.

Then Marcus cut his speed, and they took a sharp turn to the right. They were on a rutted road that ran past scattered buildings. They took a sharp left then, and the car began to climb. She saw light suddenly, and the car jerked to a stop before a walled whitewashed villa.

Marcus got out of the car. There was a wrought-iron gate in front, up a short pathway from the car. He opened the gate with a key, then turned back to Chris. "This is it, Chris. And there isn't anywhere to go. Believe me, this isn't a tourist town. You won't find a soul who speaks English. Get out!" he finished.

Chris took a deep breath and crossed her arms over her chest. "You must think I'm insane if you expect me to go anywhere with you when you treat me the way you do."

"I'm going to think that you're insane if you don't get out of that car now and quit making my life an absolute misery within the next few seconds," he snapped, his words carefully enunciated.

Her voice, to her absolute horror, was barely a whisper. "Marcus, I'm afraid."

"At the moment you have no reason to be. But if you're not out of that car..."

She slammed the door and walked with a rigid spine to the gate.

She followed him through a small but beautifully flowering garden to a porch, where he unlocked the front door of the small two-story building.

Taking a breath and hoping that her show of bravado was real, Chris followed him.

She was startled by the up-to-date flavor of the villa; modular sofas and chairs were grouped before a contemporary fireplace in a sunken pit. She could see that past a small dining room area, only a counter separated a bright white-and-yellow kitchen from the main room.

There was also a staircase leading to darkness above.

Chris stayed near the door, her back to it. Marcus strode into the room, throwing his keys down on the nearest sofa. He stripped off his tweed jacket, tossed it on top of the keys, pulled off his tie, threw it down, too, then walked around to sink down, leaning his head back and closing his eyes—totally ignoring Chris.

Chris stayed where she was. After a minute he rubbed his temple, then opened his eyes, turning around to stare at her with an uplifted brow.

Chris shook her head in exasperation. "All right, I give up. What are we doing here? Come to think of it, I give up entirely on the past twenty-four hours. What the hell are you doing?"

"What am I doing?" he repeated. He shook his head. "Damned if I know," he muttered, as if it were all her fault. Then she saw his lashes lower, his eyes narrowing once again, as if her question had rekindled his anger. "There is one thing I can tell you, Chris, and that's that we're going to be here until you choose to tell me what the hell is going on!"

"*Me!* You're the one who—"

"Sneaks around galleries with rope and grappling hooks? Disappears the morning after her marriage, then runs to the police station after very sweetly declaring that she needs a shower?" he taunted. Then he smiled. "There's a shower upstairs."

"I don't want a shower anymore."

"Oh, yes, you do."

"No, I—"

He stood up, still smiling. Chris moved away from the door, circling him to reach the stairs. "I haven't got anything with me," she muttered. "You chose to take off like this without warning—"

"You'll find everything you could need."

"Whose everything?" Chris heard herself query, feeling an absurd tug of jealousy. To her horror, he noted it.

"I'm thirty-three years old, Christina. And not a monk."

"If you think I'm going to—"

"Yes, I think you are." He smiled again. "My shin is still killing me."

"It should have been more than your shin," Chris muttered. Then she was suddenly furious. "You bastard! What you've done is totally illegal! You purposely fed me wine, you coerced me...you're crazy!"

"Yes, and tired and hungry. So—"

"Don't think you're going to touch me, Marcus," she said, praying it would come out as a warning, not a desperate plea.

"Quite frankly, I believe I've lost the desire," he stated disinterestedly. "But you are going to tell me exactly what you've been up to!"

The argument could go in circles forever. Chris realized that she felt gritty, exhausted and famished. Marcus had obviously sent someone up to the villa to prepare it for occupation; the light had been on. Hopefully there would be food here. And if she meekly melted into the woodwork, he might just leave her alone for the night, and by morning she could think of something.

Chris straightened her shoulders and started up the stairs.

"Light's to your right on the wall," he drawled to her.

"Thank you," she said briskly.

Chris found the hall light, then the bathroom. It was very modern, with a huge shower and sunken tub, and a wall-length closet. She opened the closet door and found soap, towels, toothbrushes, toothpaste and a feminine floor-length, terry-cloth robe.

"And I wonder who the hell it belongs to!" she muttered angrily, throwing it to the floor. She stepped into the shower and turned the water on hard—and started shivering again.

She still wasn't sure that she wasn't in the clutches of a maniac, and here she was worrying about his previous companions!

She closed her eyes, allowing the water to run over her face. She was in love with the maniac. No matter what he had done to her, she had to cling to the belief that it was because he cared....

Fool, she berated herself in silence. Then she hurried to scrub herself and get out of the shower, worried suddenly that he was going to burst through the door and either strangle her—or seduce her.

She was forgetting something very important. However ludicrous it seemed, she was legally married to him. He would never have staged such an elaborate scenario if he hadn't been certain of what he was doing.

Chris turned off the shower. She stepped out and dried herself, then picked up the robe that she had tossed on the floor. It wasn't a bad fit, but there were no buttons, only a sash. She hugged the robe around herself tightly, then belted it, took a long breath and walked back downstairs.

Marcus was in the kitchen. He didn't look up as she approached the counter, compelled to do so by the aroma of something cooking. There was a frying pan on the stove; oil was simmering there, with a touch of garlic and herbs. There was a bottle of unlabeled wine on the counter; Chris poured herself a glass, noticing a little uneasily that Marcus was chopping chicken pieces with a massive cleaver.

"Want to tell me what you were doing at the church?" he asked without looking up.

"Why? You won't believe me. Or you'll pretend not to."

He glanced up at her. "Humor me," he suggested. "And while you're at it, get a pan under the sink for the spinach."

Chris walked around the counter to get the pan. She didn't like being as close to him as she was. The kitchen was modern and convenient; it was also very small.

"Start talking, Chris. And now that you've got the pan, you might want to wash the spinach."

She turned on the water, thinking that if he hadn't been doing the majority of the cooking, and if she hadn't been starving from not having eaten all day, she would definitely have resented his tone.

"I was called," she said.

"Called?"

"Yes, I was called. I assume it was by the same person who was blackmailing Alfred. He told me to come to the church, that my father didn't murder yours, but that he knew who did."

"So why the hell didn't you tell me?" Marcus demanded in a low growl.

Chris hesitated. Maybe her evidence was slim, but it seemed sound to her. Gina and Mario had been fighting on the boat. According to Sophia, they'd always had marital problems. Crimes of passion were well-known throughout Italian history. And Gina had a key to the galleries, which Marcus had lied about. Why, if not to protect his mother?

There seemed to be only one thing to do: accuse Gina before Marcus and see what his reaction was.

"Because it's obvious," she murmured. "You think your mother killed your father. That's why you staged this—Marcus, no!" Chris screamed.

She had wanted a reaction. Had she drawn too much of one?

He had turned around in fury, the cleaver in his hand. Suddenly all she could see was the knife that had flashed in the galleries on the night Alfred Contini had died, and she panicked.

She instinctively jerked around, pulling the spinach pan with her. It flew up in the air, catching Marcus's temple. Not all that hard, but hard enough for him to know he'd been hit! And, of course, just as the pan grazed him, she realized that he hadn't been about to stab her. All he had been doing was holding the cleaver.

"Marcus, I didn't mean to..." Her voice trailed away.

But it was too late. He was staring at her with anger, as if he certainly didn't believe her.

"I am going to strangle you," he muttered, a little bewildered. And then she saw his lips compress until they were nothing but a grim line and he took a step toward her, reaching for her.

"Oh, no!" Chris said, gasping, and tried to barge past him. She felt his hand grasping for her arm. He missed, but his fingers caught the terry-cloth robe. She tried to keep running. The robe stayed in his hand, and her impetus sent her crashing to the floor half naked, the rest of her tangled in the robe.

"No!" she shrieked again as he straddled her, grabbing her wrists and pulling them over her head to keep her from wildly pummeling him. Chris closed her eyes and started babbling desperately. "Please, Marcus, I didn't mean to! I don't care what happened in the past. I don't care if you were blackmailing Alfred. I don't care what you're guilty of. I don't care who's guilty of anything. I don't care about any of it. I don't—"

She broke off. He hadn't moved; he hadn't said a word. She opened her eyes to see that he was staring at her with a curious light in his eyes and a bemused smile on his lips. She moistened her lips, then realized that she really was naked. His thighs were around her bare hips; her breasts were completely uncovered and heaving as she gasped for breath. The pressure he used on her wrists wasn't painful, nor did he seem furious anymore. He was a little amused, but not completely; there was an indigo glitter in his eyes, yet his features were very, very taut. "Chris, I didn't blackmail Alfred. Why would I?"

She hesitated. "Because he was sheltering the real murderer?" she whispered.

He laughed. "First you accuse my mother. But if I'm protecting my mother, why would I blackmail Alfred for doing the exact same thing?"

"I don't know," Chris murmured miserably. "I'm sorry...."

"Nor, Chris," he said quietly, "did I murder anyone. I'm not guilty of anything...except coercing you." He fell silent for a second, then took a long breath. "But, Chris, I do know that Alfred was being blackmailed."

"You do?" she whispered uneasily.

"Yes." He paused. "Large sums were going out of the company account for years. I never realized it before, because all of us were free to use that account when we needed it."

"You knew..." was all that Chris could think to whisper.

"I suspected, and then I knew."

She felt her flesh burn because his eyes were raking over her, and she felt as if they touched her with a slow unquenchable blaze.

"Did you really think I meant to attack you with a cleaver?" he demanded huskily.

"I—I panicked...."

"Perhaps," he murmured, smiling, "you should panic." He released her wrists and shifted his weight from hers, but she was still pinned to the floor. His hand coursed lightly down her arm where it was still caught in terry cloth, and then his palm was against her bare flesh, cradling her breast, teasing the nipple to a peak with slow sensual circles. She felt herself redden, and she closed her eyes with a shudder, willing her body not to arch to his touch. Yet her body ignored her will. His fingers moved over her ribs, caressed her hip, trailed down the little angle between her belly and her hip, and moved erotically over her inner thigh.

"I want you now, Chris," he murmured to her, a fever that defied denial in the husky timbre of his voice. She opened her eyes to see his above hers, probing, demanding. And then she closed her eyes again with a little sigh that caught in her throat as he kissed her, slowly, sensually, then commandingly. Chris rolled against him, glad of the hand that continued to sweetly torment her body, to touch her like a fire that promised to build and build and build....

His lips moved to the pulse at her throat, and then his dark head dipped low. He cupped one of her breasts in his hand and savored it with his mouth, taking the nipple between his teeth and raking it again and again with his tongue. Chris cried out softly, stunned by the shattering depth of the sensation. Yet while his mouth continued to lavish attention on her breast, his hand moved again, following the curve of her hip and moving along her thigh. His knee remained between hers, giving him the freedom to taunt and explore her flesh, and bring a rush of pleasure rippling through her as he sought her most intimate places with bold audacity.

Christina unknowingly raked her nails across his back, gasping out his name. He buried his head in the shadowed valley between her breasts, then brought his lips to hers once again. Finally his eyes met hers and she saw the question in them. Didn't he know he was assured of an answer? She couldn't give him one, not in words. She wrapped her arms around him, pressing her face against his shoulder, almost afraid of the depth of her need for him. "The . . . oil . . . is burning," she murmured.

"So am I," he chuckled hoarsely, but he unwound her arms from around his neck and rose. Chris closed her eyes. She heard his footsteps and the sound of a click as he turned off the stove. Then she felt his arms around her as he drew her to her feet, smiling at her as he lifted her. "I'll be damned if I'll take you for the first time on the floor when there's a wonderful bed upstairs," he told her.

She closed her eyes again, loving the feel of his body, the ripple of muscles, as he carried her up the stairs. He knew the way; he didn't turn on a light. There was a waning moon outside, and it cast enough of a glow so that they could see one another.

He didn't set her on the bed, though, but placed her on her feet, slipping his hands beneath the robe that still clung precariously to her shoulders so that it fell away from her, like an unveiling. She felt his eyes, hungry as they moved over her, and again she burned and shivered at the simple delight of his gaze. She wanted to touch him, but she didn't seem to be able to move. She stood with her eyes locked with his as he unbuttoned his cuffs and then the front of his shirt. He slipped off his shoes, kicking them aside, then tugged at his belt buckle. With the lithe movements she had come to expect from him, he shed his pants and briefs. Chris closed her eyes, shaking with her desire for him as he stepped forward and took her in his arms again. His body was flush against hers: hard thighs, muscled chest, throbbing arousal. And still he kissed her lingeringly, backing her toward the bed until she fell against it, welcoming him with a fever as he followed her down.

Now she was able to touch him. Her hands moved in a frenzy, stroking his face, kneading his shoulders, trailing down the long line of his back, her nails scraping over his buttocks, her fingers fascinated at his tight muscles. He whispered husky encouragement to her, Italian words that made no sense, yet made all the sense in the world. He nipped at her earlobe and at her neck, and again he moved to taste her flesh, her breasts and her belly, and all the while his hands soothed and ignited her, roaming where they would, eliciting sharp cries from her.

She was amazed and stunned and almost frighteningly aroused by his touch. He made love to her with no hesitation, giving no quarter, and she quickly lost control of all thought, consumed by the wonder of sensation, completely pliant to his will. She felt his fingers beneath her bottom, lifting her, and she felt a new burning between her thighs, deep and sensual, moist, as his intimate probing stroked her to a total frenzy where she heedlessly cried out his name, her head tossing, her hips arching with an urgency all their own. She begged him, and she didn't know what she was begging for. All she knew was that she wanted him, all of him, so badly that she was almost in tears.

He moved beside her, clutching her hand, bringing it to him. She swallowed, clutching him, caressing him, moaning softly, barely aware and yet thrilled that she had created the throbbing ardency of his passion, a little frightened and awed again at the ferocity of her feelings, at the absolute fever that controlled her. And yet his whisper was with her, the beautiful, encouraging cadence of his words.

He moved over her, spreading her thighs with the powerful force of his knees and his body. She saw his eyes, indigo in the night, laced with desire, and she clutched his shoulders before he could lower himself.

"Marcus . . . I . . ."

"Cara?" he whispered.

"I don't . . . know what I'm doing."

"Christina," he murmured, "you certainly do."

"No, I . . ."

He seemed to start. "The first time?" he queried with a ragged breath.

"I've spent a lot of time in school," she whispered lamely. "I've been involved...but never this involved."

The sound of his soft chuckle enveloped her all over again with warmth; he touched her face with a tenderness all the more gratifying because she could feel the leashed ferocity of his passion. He kissed her, and as his lips savored her, he thrust carefully, slowly into her, holding her body tightly to his own, absorbing the initial shock and immediately soothing her from it. There was pain, like the flash of a knife, but his strokes were slow and deep, and she was arching to receive them while her body still shuddered with both the shock and the growing wonder. The blaze began to build again, soaring like an indigo fire, and she gave herself up to its flames, kissing him, pressing against him, biting him lightly on his shoulders, grazing her hands again and again over his back, drawing delighted words from him when her fingers curved over his buttocks, inviting the total unleashing of his passion.

She had known since she had first seen him that he had promised this abandoned wonder, this absolute flaring passion. And now, as she writhed and cried and moaned, craving something ultimate, she knew the true extent of his promise. He lifted himself, thrusting deep...deep...deep...and it burst upon her, like shimmering light, totally shocking and magnificent, and she shuddered again and again in the aftermath, stunned by the shattering delight of complete sexual sensation.

For a long while she lay without moving, loath to allow the satisfied and drifting sensation to fade. A summer breeze swept through the windows, cooling them. Chris could feel his flesh, damp beside hers; in the pale light she could see his arm stretched across her midriff. She had never felt so close to a person before in her life; she had never been so content, and yet even as she tried hard to hold on tight to all that had been so wonderful, something within her began to withdraw. She'd always believed instinctively that she could trust him; now she believed so more than ever. But he was a di Medici; if he talked to her, he would still conceal his real feelings and his real thoughts. He had gone through quite a charade to keep her safe, and yet she still wasn't certain whether it had been done to protect her—or his family.

Lying in bed, feeling him, touching him, she realized very clearly that they were at opposite ends of the spectrum. She was a Tarleton. No charade could really turn her into a di Medici, not when James Tarleton was still considered to have been a murderer. And not when she had become a di Medici by dark and secretive means. She shivered suddenly, remembering Sophia's warnings about her future happiness . . . or lack thereof.

Well, it didn't really matter, Chris thought dismally. Sophia didn't know that Marcus had taken drastic measures merely because he didn't want another corpse on his hands.

He must have been thinking, too. He traced a finger idly between her breasts to her navel. Chris swallowed, not willing to deny him, but aware that she had to withdraw to salvage her emotions. She was glad that the room was dark.

Marcus sighed, as if sensing that he had lost her. He made no comment on their being together; he swung his feet over the side of the bed and found his pants. "Let's go downstairs and get something to eat," he said, and the suggestion sounded like an order. "And get everything straightened out that's happened from the very beginning." He picked up her robe and brought it to the bed, bending with a little smile on his lips before he kissed her briefly. "Belt it tightly, please. You're not going to get away with distracting me this time."

"Me!" Chris protested. She was glad of the robe, though, and quickly slipped back into it.

"Umm," he murmured, walking barefoot and bare chested to the door. He paused, looking back at her. Chris tied the robe, flushing beneath his scrutiny, even in the dim light.

"What?" she demanded at last, unnerved.

He shook his head. "You're a bit of an anachronism these days. For an American, that is."

"Oh?"

She saw the flash of his teeth in the moonlight. "Isn't it unusual for an American woman to actually come to her husband's bed untouched?"

Chris felt new color flood her features; he sounded mocking. She forced herself to walk smoothly across the room and past him on the way to the small hall and staircase. "I don't remember saying that I was actually 'untouched,'" she murmured coolly. "Nor, for that matter, are we really married."

He laughed, but she sensed no humor in the dry sound. "Oh, it was quite real. Trust me."

"But not intentional," Chris retorted, her face averted from his as she preceded him down the stairs. "It's another problem that's going to have to be worked out. Something you got us into and you're going to have to get us out of."

"Let's take things as they come, shall we?" he said impatiently, moving her out of his way so he could step into the kitchen and light the burner beneath the frying pan again.

She didn't respond, but just stared at him, wondering how they could be so close—and yet so distant.

He picked up the cleaver and started on the chicken again. When she still didn't move, he looked up at her impatiently.

"*Mi scusi*, darling, but for the moment you are my wife, Christina di Medici, and though I like to think we Italians have come a long way, it's not customary for the husband to be doing all the cooking. Especially after his wife just struck him with the spinach pan. Even if she did make amends rather nicely. Want to help?" The last was rather pointed. Annoyed, flushing again, Chris lowered her head and moved into the kitchen.

Fifteen minutes ago she had forgotten that anything in the world except the power of his pulsing body and her own. Yet he could talk to her as if he had barely as much as kissed her.

But he did intend to get to the bottom of things. To talk, to thrash it out. Wasn't that exactly what she wanted?

Yes, but . . .

She had wanted more. Some wild proclamation of love and devotion. Sweet words of adoration. A humble admission that, yes, he had tricked her into marriage, not only to protect her but because he had loved and needed her. . . .

Chris sighed and bent to pick up the spinach pan, thinking a little guiltily that she should ask him if he was okay. But then his hand smacked her derriere and she straightened instead to give him a nasty glance of outrage.

He laughed. "Come on. Let's get this show on the road. I'm starving. And," he added softly, pausing for a second to draw her body against his and span his hands around her waist as he whispered against her earlobe, "I'd very much like to get business out of the way for the evening. This opportunity is just too wonderful to waste."

For a minute Chris felt like hitting him over the head with the pan again, but she held dead still, closing her eyes and fighting for serenity instead.

She had no intention of denying her fascination for him or his desire for her.

Only of denying her love.

Chapter Ten

They ate at the kitchen counter, across from one another. Chris was glad, because as he listened to her, she had the feeling that he still doubted something about her, and the sensation was very irritating.

"So," he said, watching her as he sipped his wine, "you came to Venice only because the mime troupe came to Venice. You'd never called, written or sent a Christmas card because your family had shied away from the past. But you met Alfred and came right home with him."

Chris set down her fork, pushed her plate away and folded her arms on the counter with exasperation. "I knew a little about Alfred Contini, the di Medicis and the galleries. I was curious. Wouldn't you have been?"

He shrugged. "And right after you came to the palazzo, Alfred started hinting that he knew your father hadn't killed mine."

"Yes."

"He told you to meet him at the galleries. You went. You saw this figure in a cloak arguing with him. Then the figure pulls out a knife. Alfred starts running . . . and has his fatal heart attack."

"Yes."

"But you didn't bother to tell anyone about this cloaked figure at the time."

"I tried to talk to you!" Chris flared. "You didn't want to listen!"

He ignored her. "Anyway, in the gem salon, you saw what you thought to be a blackmail note. So you went through extravagant preparations and broke into the galleries."

"It wasn't at all extravagant or difficult," Chris retorted cuttingly, then she hesitated. "Until you hit the trapdoor."

"If you *were* being chased the second time, be damned glad that you knew about the trapdoor. Especially," he murmured softly, "after you'd crashed through the staircase."

"You don't think the staircase was an accident, do you?" Chris demanded.

"No," he admitted.

"And that's why you pulled the whole marriage thing?"

He shrugged. "It had crossed my mind before. It didn't seem that you would leave Venice—until after the wedding," he added dryly.

"I was . . . frightened."

"You idiot. You should have been frightened a long time ago," he snapped at her.

"Then you're admitting that my father didn't kill yours!" Chris exclaimed triumphantly.

"I'm not admitting anything except that Alfred was being blackmailed. And maybe that he was driven to his death by your cloaked figure. But tell me, what made you believe I might be a part of it all?"

Chris hesitated. "It seemed as if you were continually showing up exactly where things were happening! And it also seemed as if you needed money."

"I see," he murmured. "But apparently you think that Alfred was being blackmailed because of my father's death. I was twelve at the time. And if I had known something about my father's death, I would have shouted it down every street in Italy."

"Marcus, let's assume that my father didn't kill your father. But Alfred knew who did."

"You're not making any sense. Alfred was the one being blackmailed. Don't you think that could mean that Alfred was the one who killed him?"

Chris shook her head. "No, I think that Alfred was protecting someone else. Marcus, that has to be it. Because if the blackmailer has turned to me, and someone is trying to kill me, then it must be because the blackmailer has something to say about someone who isn't dead."

"All right, so we go over everyone on the boat that day," Marcus murmured. "Your father, my father. Our mothers. Alfred and Sophia. Genovese, Joe and Fredo. We've decided to leave ourselves out, right?" he queried a little sarcastically. "And Tony... he was too small to have killed my father."

"We probably need a motive," Chris murmured uneasily, looking down at her hands, then straight into his eyes. "Marcus, I know that your parents were fighting that day. And you lied to me about something. You told me that only you and Tony have keys to the galleries. Your mother has one, too."

He emitted an impatient oath that made her cringe a little. "I didn't tell you because you're dying to condemn my mother. And you're forgetting something."

"What?"

"My mother adored my father."

"Yes, but crimes of passion—"

"Get off it, Chris!"

"Fine!" she snapped angrily. "Let's hang my father, but God forbid we touch *your* precious noble family!"

He pushed back his chair and stood, taking his wineglass with him as he strode into the living room and sat on one of the modular sofas. "Why don't you quit with the attack and take a wider look at things?" he demanded coolly.

Chris began to pick up their dishes, scraping them distractedly and almost throwing them into the sink. "I am looking at things in a broad sense. You're not. And I don't believe a word you're saying, because you obviously think it's someone in your family or else you wouldn't have pulled this marriage bit."

"Leave the damn dishes alone!" Marcus muttered. "And come over here so we can get on with this."

"You walked away from me!"

He leaned back, closing his eyes and rubbing his temples. "Chris, we're not going to get anywhere arguing about this. Bring your wine over here."

She compressed her lips and stiffly complied with his suggestion, sitting primly on the edge of the sofa. He smiled and stretched out a hand, running his fingers over the tense muscles in her back. Chris despised her instant reaction to him; she remained straight, but longed to curl up against his bare shoulder.

"Ease up," he warned her softly.

"I saw the person in the cloak again today," Chris told him.

"Where? When?"

"Right before you grabbed me at St. Mark's Square. And whoever it was that called me left a note telling me that I had been followed." She hesitated briefly. "That's why I was so frightened today, Marcus. I had seen the figure—and then there you were.

And then that night when I went through the trapdoor . . . you were there, too, and so was the cloak."

His hand paused on her back. "Chris," he murmured, "there's another chute into the crypt."

"There is?" she demanded, startled. "Where?"

"Into the section where we really keep the family skeletons."

"But I thought that was completely walled off."

"So did I—until that night."

Chris shivered and took a long sip of her wine. "I got another note today, Marcus. One telling me that di Medici brides belong in the di Medici crypt."

"Damn it, Chris!" he exploded. "If you had told me about all of this I would have been in a much better position to trace what was going on! Have you still got all these notes?"

"The two from today," she murmured. "I never found the blackmail note."

"Well, give them to me in the morning. I want to get them to the police."

Chris nodded.

"What are we going to do now?"

He didn't answer right away. She sensed that he was smiling, and she turned to look at him. He *was* smiling, but he appeared tense, wired, and his eyes had a heavy-lidded glittering sizzle to them.

"Go to bed," he drawled softly in reply, causing her to flush and lower her lashes.

"Together?" she heard herself murmur stupidly.

He laughed. "It's what I had in mind." He reached up and plucked her wineglass from her fingers, drawing her into his arms. "Unless," he demanded a little tersely, "our conversation has given you an aversion to the idea."

She met his eyes, her own wide. "No," she said simply. It was enough; it satisfied him.

He stood, then walked around to check the door and turn off the lights. Chris rose herself, walking to the stairs ahead of him and pelting up them.

Tonight...tonight she was glad of the darkness. He was still new to her; the shattering excitement was still new to her. So new that she felt she needed the gentle cover of the night.

A little breathlessly she shed her robe and slipped naked beneath the covers, pulling them to her chin.

A few minutes later she saw his silhouette as he silently entered the room on his bare feet. She heard the rasp of his zipper and a soft thud as his pants fell to the floor.

She felt his naked flesh as he crawled in beside her. Her nerves seemed to dance with that simple pleasure, with anticipation.

But he didn't reach out for her right away. He propped himself on one elbow, and in the soft moonglow she could see his eyes and the small smile curving his lips. He did touch her then, placing his palm between her breasts, feeling the wild and erratic beat of her heart.

"It thunders like a frightened rabbit," he murmured lightly, and then his fingers curled and his palm closed over her breast, stroking. She moaned softly and moved against him, touching his chest, then running her hand down the length of his body, over his hips and toward his thigh. He leaned to kiss her lips, to trace them with his tongue, and then to brush light kisses over her cheek until he reached her ear, where he murmured softly, "If you wish something, *cara*, you must learn to reach out for it."

She hesitated just a second, feeling her heart skip a beat, then thunder again. Then she did reach for him, feeling hot flashes invade her body with sweeping delight at the passion she discovered. He moaned deeply, clutching her shoulders, caressing her breasts, brushing her knees apart to stroke her thighs and play between them.

"Oh," Chris whispered, burying her face against his neck, feeling on fire.

Suddenly his hands were raking through her hair, holding her head still, and his lips were on hers with a ravaging hunger. Chris shuddered with delight, then started at the smooth but shattering thrust of his body as he entered her. She welcomed him with a burning heat, crying out in wordless delight at his abrupt invasion, amazed at the pleasure of just feeling him inside her. She wrapped her legs tightly about him, absorbing the deep thrust, shuddering again and again as he filled her with wild rhythms and an exotic heat. This time she realized that, as sweetly primal as it was with him, it was more than sex. Her delight was in holding him, in feeling totally that he was hers. Perhaps that was also a primal feeling: holding, cherishing, nurturing the man that she loved. Being the woman that he needed. Feeling his hands and his lips as he moved, the moist heat of his kisses and his body. Wanting not only the glorious sensation of total release, but the gratitude of knowing that she, her breasts, her thighs, her hips, her flesh, her movements, were his and he was hers. She was his need, his desire, as much a part of him as he was of her. It was, for these moments, being totally possessed, while losing nothing. The reward was in being his woman...his wife.

She realized then, too, that it would always be different with him. Sudden hot passion at times, slow building delight at others. He was as unpredictable as a black panther. As sleek and wild as that cat of the night.

"*Cara,*" he murmured again, and he whispered things to her in Italian, things that urged and encouraged and abetted the running quicksilver in her blood, sending her thoughts spinning away on clouds, causing her body to tremble with fever and urgency. She was shuddering, writhing...exploding above the clouds, and shivering again with the wonderful possessive feelings and the warmth of him inside her. His warmth was with her still, even as he left her to roll to his side and pull her close.

Chris inhaled deeply and sighed with a contented little catch. His fingers moved idly, gently against her hair. She rested her head against the damp strength of his chest, wrinkling her nose slightly as the dark hair there tickled it. She wrapped her arm about his waist, happy as she felt his light kiss upon the top of her head.

She yawned and drifted quickly into a pleasant totally contented sleep.

Morning had broken when she opened her eyes again. The sun was streaming through the windows, and a variety of birds were carrying on a trilling cacophony.

Chris knew she was alone in the bed. The sheets beside her were cold. She gazed toward the window, and as she expected, Marcus was there leaning against the frame, staring out at the day as he sipped coffee. He was in a robe, the sun touching the gold medallion on his chest.

Today he didn't know that she had awakened; he wasn't waiting for her to open her eyes. She was able to study him for several seconds without facing the too-knowing indigo depths of his eyes.

A little chill crept through her at the sight of him. The sunlight seemed to make his reflections evident. His position was relaxed and thoughtful; his eyes were intense. Chris knew that he was thinking about the situation...or perhaps not thinking, but worrying. And Chris thought at that moment that his preoccupation stemmed from his own fears.

Because it was very probable that his mother or his brother was involved.

She closed her eyes quickly. Tony di Medici certainly hadn't killed his own father. But wasn't it possible that he could have been capable of blackmail? How, why? Because the di Medicis had expensive tastes. Because it might be very easy to stumble upon information that someone else would be willing to pay to have kept silent . . .

Not Tony, Chris thought painfully. Tony...who had been fun and caring. Tony, who had really welcomed her . . .

If not Tony, there was Gina di Medici. Had Gina been angry enough to kill her husband? Would Alfred Contini have paid a blackmailer to protect Gina?

"What are you thinking?"

Chris opened her eyes. She hadn't heard Marcus move, but he was standing beside the bed, smiling down at her with amusement easing some of the intensity in his eyes.

She blinked, hugging her pillow and smiling ruefully in return. "I was thinking about . . . our mystery," she told him.

He sat down, tracing a finger over her shoulder, offering her his coffee cup. Chris accepted, warmed by the intimacy of his action, watching his dark lashes shield his eyes and his thoughts.

"That wasn't the answer I was expecting," he teased her when he met her eyes again. "As a loving bride, you should have been thinking about our night together. You should have been wondering where I was . . . and longing to have me beside you again."

Chris smiled, lowering her gaze, a little flush coloring her cheeks. She took a sip of the hot coffee, keeping her eyes averted from his. Yes, I was thinking about you, too, she thought. But I've thought of you since I first saw you. I lay awake often wondering what it would be like....

And now I know, and I'm more hopelessly tangled within your web than ever. Body and soul, I need you and I want you, and God forbid you ever know how much, because it would be terrible to be so sadly pathetically vulnerable to a di Medici man.

"I, uh, can't help but worry..." she murmured as she sipped the coffee again.

He took the cup from her and set it down, then tugged at the pillow she was clutching to her breasts. Chris released it, meeting his eyes.

"We'll worry together...soon," he told her, and a hot vibrant shuddering took hold of her body as he swept his arms around her, rolling her against him. She felt the sleek hardness of his body, the implacable power and desire, and with a little sigh she gladly left all thought until later. Marcus would have it no other way.

Di Medici. At that moment she was Christina di Medici. His wife, lying in his arms, thrilling to his touch. She was madly in love with him, beneath his spell as she had never thought she could be. It didn't matter that her life might hang by a dangerous thread. When he touched her, when she burned and trembled and he moved like an all-consuming and demanding flame, she wanted nothing more than to give herself to that spiraling blue heat.

It was afternoon before they went downstairs.

Chris followed Marcus into the kitchen, where they prowled around the refrigerator and cabinets until they came up with a large stick of pepperoni, an assortment of cheeses and a thick loaf of Italian bread. They carried it all out to the sofa, placing the food between them. The inevitable bottle of wine was between them, too, and Chris stared at it warily as if it were a snake.

She believed now that Marcus would never really hurt her, but she had learned that he could be manipulative when he so chose, and she didn't want to be manipulated again. He wasn't being entirely honest with her; he didn't intend to tell her his thoughts or his feelings—and she wasn't about to be his puppet again, whether she was in love with him or not.

Marcus broke the bread and handed her a piece. "The first thing we have to realize here is that there are two people involved. The blackmailer and whoever the blackmailer is afraid of. Possibly the one who killed my father, assuming that your father didn't."

"The figure in the cloak," Chris murmured, taking a bite of her bread. She was famished again. Being with Marcus was like touching the moon. It was also pleasantly exhausting, and had a tremendous effect on her appetite.

He gazed at her briefly, his eyes opaque as they traveled over her. "Yes, the figure in the cloak. It seems to me that Alfred must have had the note from the blackmailer. He was showing it to our mystery figure and saying that he didn't feel like paying up anymore. If he wasn't going to pay up, the figure apparently decided that he should die. Am I making sense so far?"

"Perfectly," Chris agreed. "So, if we catch the blackmailer, we can catch the murderer. And both of them had to be on the boat the day that your father died. That means your mother, Sophia, Genovese, Joe or Fredo."

"Or one of us."

"The children?"

"Tony, you or I."

"I'd thought we'd decided that we were innocent."

He shrugged. "I think it's a fair decision. We have to let your mother out, too, because she isn't in Italy."

"That's big of you," Chris muttered dryly.

Her comment drew a sharp look, cold as the moon's blue gaze. "Your father still isn't exactly in the clear," he told her.

"But my father is dead," Chris replied coolly. "He isn't running around Italy, either. Unless you think his ghost is dressing up in a cloak to haunt me. Which seems unlikely, since he's my father."

"You're not amusing, Christina."

"And you don't want to face facts."

"Oh, stop it, Christina! We have no facts to face! You were so determined that you were the angel of righteousness that you didn't tell me anything when something could have been done. We have nothing—*nothing*—Christina."

"How could I tell you anything? You appeared everywhere there was trouble, and you didn't want to listen to a word I had to say! Then you seduced me into marriage. How far would you trust a man like that?" Chris demanded angrily.

He tossed one of the cheeses into her lap, rising with a swift movement to step behind her and catch her shoulders beneath his hands. He whispered heatedly in her ear.

"You are the cat burglar who breaks into galleries. Who makes sudden appearances to con old dying men out of their money. Perhaps you want the palazzo, too. You've gotten everything you wanted, haven't you?"

"No," Chris lied, wrenching herself from his touch. She met his dark gaze with a tawny fury glittering in her eyes. "I wanted Tony, remember?" she taunted.

"Ah, yes, sorry," he murmured, moving back around the sofa to pour wine into their glasses. "But you got me," he added softly.

"I don't have anything, and I don't want any wine."

"You've got me, *amore mio*—for the time being—and don't get any other ideas," he warned her lightly. "You might as well enjoy some wine, since it improves your disposition, and you're not going anywhere."

"I don't want my disposition improved!" Chris declared passionately. "Every time my disposition is good around you, I wind up in trouble. You have no sense of decency."

"What? I have a hell of a sense of decency! It's a pity you don't remember more about the night of our marriage."

"Oh...God!" Chris exploded in frustration. Then she threw the cheese back at him, taking him completely by surprise.

Somehow he caught the cheese. He looked at it for a second, then flew into a stream of colorful Italian curses. Chris froze for a second, certain he was going to tear her hair out, but then, as she watched him, she burst into nervous laughter instead.

He paused, looking at her as if nothing but violence was on his mind. Then he lowered his head, and when he looked up an almost imperceptible grin was tugging at the corners of his mouth.

"You should speak nothing but kindness to your husband, *cara*," he advised with a level edge. "Especially to the Italian husband you brutalized last evening."

"Brutalized?" Chris demanded.

He tossed the cheese to the floor and caught her face between his palms, sliding his fingers into her hair. "Absolutely."

Now she saw that he was smiling. But as he pulled her into his arms, hard against his chest, she knew his smile would always hold a hint of danger. "Would you want a brutal husband, *mia moglie*?" he queried softly.

She shook her head, lowering her eyes. His palm moved gently over her cheek, then shifted to caress her breast. "Nor do I care to feel the steel of your knives," he murmured.

She wasn't quite sure what he meant, only that for once she could sense some deep emotion simmering beneath his words. That touched her heart and reawoke all the feelings she had for him. Not for anything would she have reminded him that he had married her only to protect her, because he had known she faced a danger he had not wanted to admit.

When she looked up at him, he smiled, laughed and pulled her into his lap.

"These arguments are ridiculous," he said briskly.

"Yes, they are," Chris agreed, leaning against him and fingering the medallion on his chest. "So what are we going to do?" she asked a little breathlessly.

"Do?"

"Marcus... we've got to do something. We can't just let this go on and on."

He sighed. "No, we must find our blackmailer and our murderer before... before something else happens."

"So?"

He laughed. She heard the sound from his throat, from his chest. It touched her cheek and made her shiver.

"First," he told her, lifting her chin, "we complete our honeymoon. Just a few days, but that is something at least. No healthy Italian male would not do so. We'll go tomorrow to the Italian Riviera, to Portofino." He shrugged. "Maybe we'll go on into France, to Nice, or to Monte Carlo."

"And then?" Chris murmured.

"Then... we go back. In time we meet your blackmailer at St. Mark's."

She shivered slightly again. "Marcus..." she murmured, and then swallowed, not willing to create distance between them again. "Marcus, who do you think might have killed your father?"

She immediately felt the tension in his arms. "Not my mother . . . she was in love with him. Alfred, your father, Genovese . . . Joe, perhaps, or Fredo."

"Wouldn't it make more sense for Joe or Fredo to have blackmailed Alfred? Marcus, the di Medicis and Alfred had the money. Why blackmail someone with no money?"

"Yes, why blackmail someone with no money?" Marcus repeated. She felt his gaze on her and lifted her head, noticing something in his eyes.

"You're onto something!" Chris exclaimed.

He shook his head. "No, Christina. I was just thinking that you have the money now. Which is why, of course, the call came to you. You want the information. You desperately wish to clear your father." His arms tightened around her. "Christina, when we return to the palazzo, you must listen to me, do you understand? Blackmailers go to those they believe to be . . . vulnerable. Which means weak. You do nothing without me, do you understand? Unless you do wish to be brutalized?"

The soft threat in his voice caused her heart to take an erratic leap. "Marcus, we need to go to the police."

"I will go to the police. But I cannot prove that Alfred was murdered—or driven to his death—because he did die of a heart attack. The notes may help. I will take them to the police as soon as we return to Venice."

Would he? Chris wondered. Or was he still determined to catch someone himself? Someone he loved. Someone he could perhaps . . . dissuade from any further violence.

Chris didn't know. But she did believe with all her heart that he intended to let no harm come to her; she believed he would protect her with his own life.

But she wasn't sure of any of his motives.

Did it matter, as long as he cared for her and meant to shield her from all harm?

It might—if the murderer was more talented, more devious than Marcus thought.

"Do you know," he murmured to her suddenly, smoothing her hair from her forehead, "that your hands are always moving?"

She gazed at him a little suspiciously. He laughed. "No, I'm serious. It's your fingers, I think. I've noticed that when you're thinking about something or talking, your hands move. Like waves."

Chris started, then laughed. She placed her hand in the air, pulled her knuckles back taut, then straightened her fingers. "Is that what you mean?"

"Yes. Not so obviously, but that's the motion."

She smiled. "It's practice. Mime practice." she added softly, wondering a bit at the dark expression that touched his features. "It's a basic lesson," she continued. "Here." She sat up, smiling as she tugged his hand and brought it to the small coffee table before them. "Put your hand down, the palm flat. Now bend your fingers without allowing your palm to rise."

"I can't."

"Yes, you can! It just takes practice. That's how we 'build a wall.' See?" Chris proceeded to show him how the exercise helped to create the illusion of a flat surface. She smiled, but her smile faded quickly at his brooding disinterest.

"You are very good at what you do," he murmured.

Chris shrugged a little uneasily. "I hope I'm decent. I've studied under some of the very best."

"And you love it, too, don't you?"

"Yes." She smiled dryly. "It requires a very rigid physical discipline to keep your body in shape for the things it must do. You have to love mime to accept the discipline. But it's like anything else, really. Once you accustom yourself to the regime it becomes a little like breathing. As you noticed, I work my hands frequently without even realizing it."

He nodded, but again he seemed very distant. He had asked the questions as if he wanted answers, but it didn't seem as if he wanted to hear what she was saying.

Chris turned away from him, picking up her wine and sipping it quickly. She wondered if she would ever understand him, or feel that she knew him at all. Or that she could possess any part of him besides his sinewed body when she held him in a tight embrace. So many intimacies, and yet she didn't really know him at all. He was his own person....

A di Medici. And Sophia had warned her that di Medici men could bring a heartache to match all the ecstasy that could be found in their arms.

She felt his fingers trailing through her hair, and she turned to watch him. His expression was a curious one. He touched her as if she were something very special and unique; his fingers were gentle. And yet that wariness was there, as if he didn't understand much about her, either.

"Marcus?" she murmured.

"Yes?"

"Did I say something wrong?"

"No, Christina. What could you have said?"

"I don't know." She tried to grin. "Don't you like mimes?"

He shook his head evasively. "What would I dislike about a mime?"

"Then... it's me."

He shook his head again, smiling. "There is nothing I dislike about you at all." He laughed suddenly. "Except that you are stubborn and seem to have a passion for dangerous stunts. But at the moment—" he shrugged, and his gaze held a cobalt glitter "—you are perfect."

He pulled her back against him. Chris was content when he rested his chin against her hair and mentioned that they needed to shop for some clothing, since they couldn't wear robes to Monte Carlo.

Perfect, he thought again later as he lay in bed and waited for her. In so many ways. She had been born with her tawny beauty; her craft had perfected her movements and poise. She moved like a shimmering silver wave, her limbs long and sleek and graceful.

She appeared in the doorway, naked, hesitating. Now, in the semidarkness, her hair cascaded over her bare shoulders, rich tendrils of reflected copper and gold, enticing his touch. Her flesh was bathed by a soft glow; the moon cast its rays over the curves of her body and awoke his fantasies.

His heart pounded in his chest, and for a moment he was afraid, though not so much of the danger that awaited them because he was determined to solve things—and end them. That sheer determination and his simmering fury at the things that had been done made him confident that he could keep her safe and solve the riddles that had reached out to haunt them from the past.

But when the skein of mystery and confusion was unwound . . . what then?

He would never be able to hold her. Like an elusive nymph, she would escape his grasp. She was an American, proud and independent. He loved her for what she was but their cultures were different. The things, many of them intangible, that were an ingrained part of his life were worlds away from hers. The palazzo, art, the canals, religion . . . even language. He could speak hers fluently, but he thought in his own. And her profession . . .

She was an artist. A visual artist. Her graceful form was her canvas. The graceful, vibrant, sensual form that was totally wild and untamed in his arms. Her face, her smile, her wide, beguiling, topaz eyes. Onstage she entranced and delighted; only when he held her was she his completely.

He wouldn't want to change her, to hurt her, to take anything away from her. He did not want to claim the artist, only the woman. And though he could command and manipulate and hold her by strength alone, it would not be right, and it would not be enough. He didn't even understand what made her so uniquely special to him, only that she was.

And when she left the doorway, coming to him, naked, her steps as sensually slow as the supple ripple of her hips, he felt a shiver of need—and the fear of loss.

For a moment he felt something like paralysis constrict his throat and stop his breath. He couldn't reach out. Like the breeze, she could too easily elude his grasp.

Touch her, he commanded himself. Reach out; touch her. Feel the fullness of her breasts, the warmth of her skin. Touch her; hold her. Savor her caress.

Make her yours . . .

She came to him, sleek and slow. She slid between the sheets, and his hands moved to her hips, pulling her to him. He felt all the softness of her flesh, and the infinite warmth.

Fiercely, tenderly, he made her his.

Chapter Eleven

They took a small charter airline into Nice, and the two days that followed were the happiest Chris could remember. She lived on a passionate cloud, entranced by all the little things done by lovers, eager to forget everything but the moment.

They spent long hours on the beach, sipping tall cool drinks, playing in the water, returning to the sand. Chris would be ready to purr with contentment when he ran his fingers idly down her back beneath the sun, and she would know that he would suggest shortly they return to their room.

They had spent the first afternoon shopping. Chris had been a little bit staggered by the amount he had been willing to spend to supply them with a wardrobe for just a few days, and she had laughingly demanded to know if he was spending her inheritance or his own. He had shrugged and replied, "Both."

And then he had reminded her that they had agreed that there would be no future or no past for them during these days. They had agreed to forget everything and enjoy themselves.

It was ideal. Chris was a little glad to be back in France, and gratified to be the one who was totally comfortable with the language. Marcus was willing to sit back politely and watch her as she did the ordering in restaurants and the bartering in shops.

And for two days they didn't find a single thing to argue about. They combed the streets and shops, and drank espresso and wine at little cafés. They savored the sun and the delight of returning to their room whenever the urge struck, of bathing together, ordering up champagne and little trays filled with cheeses, meats and fruits, among them grapes, which, Chris laughingly learned, were a great deal of fun to feed to one another.

She was never quite sure what happened to stop their idyllic vacation so abruptly, only that it did end on their last night—at the casino in Monte Carlo.

The evening had started out the same as any other. He was in black tails that emphasized all the intrigue and darkness of his startling good looks. Chris had allowed him to splurge on a forest-green silk gown for her. It had jet beading at the shoulders and a low-cut neckline. She had decided that between them, they were beautiful, and the night was filled with easy laughter. He was close beside her as they gambled recklessly and successfully at the roulette wheel.

Then Chris felt a touch on her arm, and she heard her name called with surprise and enthusiasm. She turned to see that Georgianne was beside her, and that Tomas stood behind Georgianne.

"Christina!" Georgianne broke into a long and excited monologue in French, asking Chris what she was doing, and telling her what a wonderful time she and Tomas were having. Chris vaguely realized that Marcus was pulling in their chips and waiting behind her for an introduction and explanation.

Chris didn't know why, but there was already a stiff tension about him. Even when he wasn't touching her, she could feel it.

After she had greeted the tolerantly smiling Tomas, Chris turned back to Marcus. "Marcus, Georgianne and Tomas. We work together. We are all from the school in Paris, and went on tour together this summer. Georgianne, Tomas . . . Marcus di Medici."

He was very polite and courteous, and apparently very interested in the other two. When Tomas suggested that they leave the casino for somewhere quieter where they could talk, Marcus was ready to accept the suggestion.

While they waited for a taxi in front of the grand and glittering entrance to the casino, Georgianne demanded to know what Chris was up to. But as she spoke her eyes were on Marcus with open fascination and speculation; Georgianne was, above all things, a Parisienne. A soft lovely kitten—open and honest.

"I leave you in Venice with an old man; I find you in Monte Carlo with a young one!" Georgianne teased. "Is this a last fling before you return to Paris, or what?"

"It's a little vacation—" Chris began, but Marcus interrupted her smoothly, blandly.

"It's a honeymoon," he said, smiling.

Georgianne gasped and clapped her hands with pleasure. Tomas quietly congratulated them both.

Chris wanted to stamp on Marcus's foot, but his hands were on her shoulders, his fingers warningly tight. She gritted her teeth and smiled instead.

A taxi came, and they all climbed in. Georgianne kept switching from French to English as she asked Chris what she intended to do, had she informed Jacques yet of her marriage...and what of the school?

Chris stared hard at Marcus and replied that as yet, she had made no decisions.

They came to a small bar overlooking the Riviera and drinks were ordered all around. Tomas and Marcus began a conversation about the roads and sights between the Italian and French cities along the coast. Georgianne turned to Chris suddenly, switching instantly into hushed French.

"Christina! *Il est magnifique!*" She went on to comment on his striking eyes, his wonderful physique, his dark, intriguing, spellbinding looks. Her eyes sparkled as she congratulated Chris again, telling her in typical blunt good-natured fashion that it was somewhat amazing to see Chris up and walking, since it was most obvious that the man would be a demon in bed.

Chris listened with a flush warming her cheeks, and she urgently tried to shush Georgianne. Georgianne merely waved a hand in the air. "He is Italian, no? He does not understand me! Tell me, Christina! How romantic. A few weeks and voilà! You are married. He is wonderful, yes? A man. And what a man!" She laughed. "But Italian! How is that working with your American soul? Or does passion overwhelm all your American feminism and independence?"

"Georgianne—"

"Ah! Admit to me that he is wonderful and that at last you know the meaning of losing your heart."

"*Oui*, Georgianne! *S'il vous plaît*, sshhh!"

Marcus was across the table, ostensibly listening to Tomas's comments in English. But Chris kept catching his eyes on her. Along with the tension, she noticed a dry curve to his mouth, and she didn't know what he was thinking or feeling at all.

"You will not return to Paris," Georgianne said in French.

"Yes, I will," Chris retorted.

"And leave such a man behind? I wouldn't. He is too attractive to other women, and not a saint at all, I would assume."

"I have my life, too," Chris murmured unhappily. There was no way to explain the circumstances of her marriage. She glanced uneasily at Marcus again. She felt his eyes on her, burning her. Again she didn't know what he was thinking or feeling.

Except that this chance meeting—for all that he was being courteous and welcoming—had made him angry.

They spent several hours together, conversing in English. Tomas was fascinated by the galleries; Georgianne was knowledgeable about the art field, and discussed numerous painters with Marcus.

Both Tomas and Georgianne knew of The di Medici Galleries, and that they had opened a branch in Paris. Tomas gave Chris a wry grin and turned to his wife. "C'est la vie, eh? We are the Europeans, Chris the American. But here is our Christina . . . Contessa di Medici!"

Georgianne laughed, but Chris thought she would scream. She had felt as if she were on the edge of her chair all night.

Finally, the couples broke up for the evening, with Chris promising to get in touch with Georgianne soon and tell her what she had decided about work.

Marcus was silent when they entered a cab to take them back to their hotel in Nice. Withdrawn, brooding.

But when his eyes touched her, she felt their fire. Cold, icy fire from out of the shadows.

Chris kept silent, determined to show him that his unwarranted moods didn't affect her in the least.

But alone in their room, facing the shore, it was difficult. Marcus silently removed his jacket, cuff links and shirt. She felt his eyes on her all the while. Chris disappeared into the bathroom, donned a gown and then ignored him as she crawled into bed, now miserably tense herself, ready to jump at the slightest sound. But he didn't speak. He neatly hung up his clothes. She yawned and closed her eyes, pretending exhaustion. Then she was sorry she had closed her eyes because she couldn't hear him anymore, and she felt as if her nerves were screaming.

She felt his weight as he crawled in beside her, and his hand on her waist as he pulled her around. She opened her eyes. His were burning jet in the moonlight. A shiver of dismay streaked through her as he taunted in perfect French, "So, you have your life to lead and you're returning to Paris?"

What had she and Georgianne said? Chris wondered with growing alarm. He seemed so angry....

"You speak French," was all she could think to murmur uneasily.

"Mais oui," he murmured, a sharp edge to his low tone. "Venezia is in the north of Italy, contessa. And business often takes us to France, as well as Switzerland and Austria. If you choose to discuss me again, may I suggest that you don't do so in German? Perhaps I should also warn you that most Europeans study languages with far greater fervor than Americans. We share a continent, you see, with many neighbors."

He released her, smiled dryly and turned his back on her. "We'll return to the palazzo in the morning. We must solve the problems in your life—yes?—so that it may be returned to you."

Chris lay there, swallowing in pained and aching silence. She didn't understand quite what had happened, only that he had apparently tired of his own game. He had seduced her into his life; now he wanted her out of it.

She didn't sleep for a long while. She felt his weight beside her, his heat . . . but not his touch. She wanted to reach out to him, but hurt and confusion kept her still. And it felt so strange. She had grown so accustomed to being loved and held. . . .

She stared miserably out at the moon and listened to the waves pound lullingly against the sand. She felt like crying, but she couldn't. He might hear her.

She should never have come, she thought. Never have allowed him to seduce her into these days of drifting and never-ending pleasure. For Marcus it was a casual affair, just like any number with which he had probably entertained himself over the years. True, he had married her, but only to protect her. Their lovemaking was a fringe benefit, well deserved after such a sacrifice, she thought bitterly.

But neither bitterness nor anger could shake the pain. She had fallen in love with him.

It was probably natural that when she finally slept that night, she dreamed.

She was in the crypt again, running along the tunnel. Someone was behind her. Marcus? She didn't know. She only knew that she was frightened. She watched the archways, wondering if the shadow that pursued her would become a panther, black in the night, threatening to claw her to shreds.

But when she looked back she didn't see Marcus or a panther. And certainly not a winged lion of justice.

She was being pursued by a figure in a bright-red cloak.

And tonight she was carrying something. There was something in her hand. Something she knew she had to hide. Because if the figure in the cloak discovered what she had, she would be beaten and punished. . . .

Chris ducked behind a tomb. She reached a hand over the effigy of a long-dead di Medici and peeked over the edge. A spider crawled over her hand, and she inadvertently screamed. The figure in the cloak heard her, and she screamed again and again....

"Christina! Christina, shhh, shhhh, *amore mio*...."

Chris awoke to feel Marcus's arms around her, holding her, soothing her. She had broken into a cold sweat. Her gown clung to her damp flesh; her hair felt plastered to her brow. For several seconds her heart continued to pound.

"Christina... what is it?"

Her eyes at last focused on his. His features were tense and concerned. She swallowed nervously, remembering how he had rejected her. But the dream had frightened her badly, and she closed her eyes and rolled against his chest, burying her face against the dark mat of hair there.

"I dreamed that... the figure was after me in the tombs. That I had something that the figure wanted. Oh, Marcus..."

"Shhh, *amore mio*. It was only a dream. You will not be alone. Never alone. And there will be no reason for you to be in the catacombs." He held her close, soothing her until the trembling left her body and she began to cool off in the air-conditioning. Until she left behind the shadowy nightmare, and the fear drained from her body.

"Better?" he asked her.

She nodded.

"There is nothing to fear, Christina. I will be with you."

"I know."

He held her in silence for a while, and then she smiled, because she felt his palms moving over her body. He tugged at her gown impatiently. "Why have you worn this? Did you seek a barrier against me?" he teased.

She shook her head, meeting his eyes. "I don't think that a barrier could be erected against you," she whispered.

"You are right," he promised softly in return, and then she felt the touch of his lips against her bare flesh. Familiar heat and the sweet aphrodisiac of anticipation claimed her body, as did he. She could only be glad of the dream then, glad of the night hours that it gave them.

Because they did return to Venice, to the palazzo, in the morning.

Perhaps she could create no barriers against him, but Marcus was quite adept at building them against her.

He was remote during the entire trip back. Not until they entered the palazzo did he touch her again with more than absent consideration. And as they came into the entryway with its magnificent chandelier and Roman columns, she knew that his apparent affection for her was only for the benefit of others.

Genovese took their luggage. Sophia announced that there was coffee in the courtyard. Tony embraced Chris with his usual fervor. "You did take a di Medici husband after all!" he teased her. "Pity it wasn't me!" But he smiled at his brother, and Chris was convinced that the two cared deeply about one another.

She braced herself for her greeting from Gina di Medici, but to her uneasy surprise, Gina seemed to have quite accepted the situation. She smiled at Chris a little shyly, and then embraced her warmly. "I feared for a long time that my young tigers would never make me a grandmama. This was your home, and now it is your home again. Make it so fully, *mia figlia*."

My daughter. Did Gina mean it? Chris didn't know. She smiled, feeling a little ill.

"Alfred would have been pleased," Sophia murmured, and then they all moved to the courtyard. Joe and Fredo were going to stop by for coffee and to offer their congratulations, Gina told them.

The two men did come by. Marcus and Chris were toasted over and over again. Chris tried very hard to talk and laugh with enthusiasm about their honeymoon, but now that they were back at the palazzo life had become sinister again, and the distance Marcus had created between them seemed to have left her entirely alone in a pit of vipers.

Chris was glad when the discussion turned to business and Joe Conseli apologetically announced to Marcus that his presence at the galleries was urgently needed. Tony commented that she looked tired, and Chris was grateful that she could sheepishly admit that she was exhausted and retire.

Marcus glanced her way sharply. He told Joe, Fredo and Tony that he would be right with them as soon as he had seen his wife to their room.

When the door had closed behind them, he gripped her shoulders tightly. "Keep the door locked and go nowhere without me, do you understand?" She felt like an errant child with a schoolmaster, and heartily resented him.

"I'm not going anywhere," she murmured, slipping from his hold to wander across the room to where their luggage sat at the foot of the bed. But suddenly she was angry as well as frightened, and she wanted to hurt him, just as his brusque distance hurt her.

"If you want me, though, I'll be in my own room." She turned around, facing him blandly. "I think that playtime must be over, Marcus. We've come back to find a blackmailer and a murderer. Serious business," she said with a dry smile.

"What are you saying, Christina?" he demanded, his eyes narrowing tensely.

She shrugged negligently, but her lashes fell over her eyes. "I'm saying that the relationship ends here. Your mother said something that gave me quite a start. I, uh, wasn't exactly prepared for...the physical aspects of things." She moved around the bed, uneasily straightening the sheets. "Marcus, a divorce is going to be sticky enough. There could be other complications, which I...stupidly, I admit...didn't think about. But I'm afraid there's not much work around for pregnant mimes."

At that moment Chris didn't think there could be a greater danger in the world than Marcus di Medici. She felt his anger radiating from him like steamy heat waves off a hot sidewalk. She felt herself shivering inside, waiting, expecting a terrible explosion.

None came.

"Suit yourself," he said curtly.

Then he turned abruptly on his heel, exiting the room without another word. Chris let out a long ragged sigh and sank to the bed. And then she started to cry.

She didn't know how long she had been in the room when the phone started to ring. She waited, certain that someone would get it elsewhere in the house. But it continued to ring, and even before she picked it up, she was certain that it was the blackmailer.

"Hello?" she said breathlessly.

"Contessa di Medici, you must come now."

"Now...I can't come now."

"You must. You must come to St. Mark's. Now. There will not be another chance. I will be there. I will give you thirty minutes. If you do not come, you will never know. For all time, your father will be the murderer."

The line went dead.

She hung up the phone, then anxiously, feverishly, paced the room. Marcus had warned her not to leave, yet she didn't dare miss this opportunity. She gritted her teeth together, then hurried to the phone and called the galleries. She went through an operator, then a woman who didn't understand English or her attempts at Italian. Chris kept repeating that she was the Contessa di Medici and that she needed Marcus.

Finally Joe Conseli came on the phone. He asked her to wait a minute. When he returned to the line, he sounded very uncomfortable.

"Christina, I'm sorry. Marcus is on another line, long-distance to New York. It's very important. He can get back to you, but he asked me to say—"

"To say what?"

He cleared his throat. "That if you are calling merely because you have more complaints, you must simply wait until he can come home. Christina, I must go. He will see you later, yes?"

"Tell him..." Chris began furiously, then she paused. "Tell him not to bother!"

She slammed down the phone, then stared at it, swearing vehemently. Damn Marcus! And damn herself, she thought fleetingly, for creating the rift between them.

She gazed at the French Provincial clock on the dresser. She had already wasted ten minutes.

Still muttering out epithets about what Marcus could do with himself—and fighting the tears that stung her eyes—Chris grabbed her purse and made certain that she was leaving with an ample supply of lire. She stared at the phone one last time. "If you can't bother to speak to me, Marcus di Medici, don't you dare get angry over missing the grand finale!"

Chris was able to flag down a motor launch. They skimmed quickly over the canals to St. Mark's Square. She paid the driver and jumped anxiously to the ground, scanning the crowd even as she hurried through it. Tourists were everywhere. And so were the pigeons. They squawked and flapped their wings in frenzied flight as she ran anxiously through the flock.

She raced up the steps to the entrance of the church. For a moment the darkness blinded her; she allowed her eyes to adjust to the muted light. As always, people were everywhere, studying the statues, the graceful altars, the fascinating tombs. Chris kept studying the people around her. There was a tour group of Japanese gentlemen who smiled at her scrutiny, and bowed politely. Chris smiled absently in return. A number of old Italian women were praying in black widows' weeds; there was an American tour group near the main altar.

Chris sighed and walked to one of the pews. She sat, staring at the altar, waiting. No one came. She saw nothing out of the ordinary. Still she waited. And waited, and waited.

A full hour must have passed before she finally gave up. No one was going to approach her. She had come on another wild-goose chase.

Despondent and frustrated, Chris rose at last. She didn't see any of the magnificence of the Basilica as she walked back out to the Square, to the sunlight. She was so preoccupied with her own depression that she didn't even notice the activity on the Square at first. Only when she neared the dock, where she planned to catch a vaporetto, did she look up and notice the police cordons and the men in uniform running around, holding back the crowd, soothing a distraught woman.

There was a body on the Square, dripping wet, having been pulled from the canal. Chris made her way through the crowd. Police photographers were there; a coroner was bending over the body. Chris looked over the shoulder of a short woman in front of her, and she gasped sharply, almost screaming out loud at the terror that ripped through her.

The body on the ground was Genovese.

He was slightly blue, and there was a gaping red slit in his throat.

She did scream then, hysterically. A policeman came to her, gripping her. She tried to tell him that she was Christina di Medici, that Genovese was from her household. He tried to calm her down. Someone brought a flask of something; someone else started shouting orders.

And a blanket was drawn over the body.

Chris was seated by a pillar in the Square. The kindly officer placed another blanket over her shoulders while she sipped at some calming liquor. People were talking and talking and quizzing her; the only words she could understand were "di Medici." And all she could think was that Genovese had been killed. It was so obvious: Genovese had been the blackmailer. She had found the blackmailer.

But not the murderer. The murderer had managed to strike again.

At last, from her web of fear and horror, she heard a voice she knew. Deep, resonant, a little harsh and strained. He was talking to one of the officers, answering questions, then demanding impatiently, *"Dovè la mia moglie?"*

Chris looked up to see Marcus, his features tense, coming toward her. He slipped an arm around her, then continued to speak to the officer in quick Italian. The officer nodded, very courteous to Conte di Medici. Marcus led her away from the cordons, away from the police, away from the body. In minutes she was seated in the family launch and he was steering them away from the Square.

She wanted sympathy. Instead, he burst out with a furious spate of Italian that matched the roar of the launch's engine. Chris put up a hand and pleaded softly, "*Per favore*, Marcus . . ."

He stopped speaking. She felt his tension, his anger. "Marcus, I tried to call you—"

"It could have been you!" he thundered, and she went silent again, staring at the wooden floor of the boat. Seconds later they reached the palazzo. An anxious Tony met them in the entryway. Marcus spoke to him quickly, and Tony nodded. Marcus took Chris up the stairs, shutting the door abruptly behind him once they had entered his room. Chris walked to the bed, where she lay on her back, pressing her temples between her hands while she waited for his words.

"I am sending you away from Venice tomorrow," he told her coldly. "Until then, Christina, you will not leave this room. For your life, you will listen to me."

She didn't answer him.

"Christina!"

He was next to her, standing over her, and then he was sitting, shaking her shoulders.

"Yes! Yes, I understand!" she cried, and despite the dark fury in his eyes, she threw her arms around him. "Marcus," she whispered, "I tried to get you. . . . I tried. . . ."

For a moment he was stiff; she barely noticed. Then his arms wound tightly around her. "Don't you think I know that it was my fault?" he demanded gruffly. He unwound her arms from his neck and eased her back to the bed. He stared at her, and she couldn't understand the raging turmoil in his eyes.

He rose, securely locking the doors to the terrace. "I've got to go to the police station. You will lock yourself in, and you will not leave."

"Yes," Chris replied in a whisper. She forced herself to rise. He was still staring at her, a furious warning in his eyes again. "I'm locking it, I'm locking it," she promised.

"I'll make your travel arrangements," he said. "I'll be back as soon as I can."

Chris locked the door in his wake. She returned to the bed and lay there, terrified. She couldn't forget the color of Genovese's flesh, nor the red at his throat.

She remained in a daze on the bed until darkness fell and the shadows became too deep. Then she rose to turn on the lights. She showered, continually placing her face beneath the cool water. She dressed in one of her white gowns again and paced the room, longing for Marcus to return.

Genovese hadn't been the murderer. That left Gina, Fredo, Joe, Sophia—or Tony. People she lived with, ate with, laughed with . . .

There was a knock at the door. She froze, catching her breath. She inhaled again with shaky relief as she heard Marcus's voice, telling her that it was all right to open the door.

He brought a tray of wine and bread and steaming pasta. She hadn't realized how hungry she was; yet she couldn't eat because she kept feeling ill. Marcus told her that Genovese's throat had been slit, that the police had no real clues but that he had given them the notes she had received and told them everything.

Everyone in the house and at the galleries would be questioned. It was out of their hands.

Chris nodded. She kept drinking wine; it soothed away the raw edges of fear and pain. It stopped her from shaking.

At length Marcus told her irritably to go to bed and try to sleep. She crawled in, certain that she would never sleep. She didn't really want to, because she didn't want to dream about the catacombs again. And she didn't like closing her eyes anymore; when she closed her eyes, she saw Genovese's body on the Square.

Marcus didn't slide in beside her. She heard the shower running; she heard it stop. She saw him come out of the bathroom in his robe; she watched him as he walked to the French doors to stare out into the night. Time crept by. The numbness of the wine left her, and tension wound like a coil inside her. She slipped out of bed and walked to him, disregarding the ice in his eyes as he watched her. But when she reached him, she could go no farther. She stood before him, her lashes lowered, her heart sick.

"Marcus, my God," she whispered at last. "How can you do this to me? How can you remain so distant when . . ."

He lifted her chin with his forefinger, meeting her eyes. "When you are frightened?" he asked softly. "*Mia moglie*, there has been a murder. But between us, nothing has changed since this morning. I cannot allay your fears. It has been an eventful day. I have not had time to seek out a pharmacy nor would I have. You seemed rather adamant."

She tried to wrest her chin from his touch, but he would not release her. She lowered her lashes against him, almost closing her eyes. "I . . . don't care," she whispered at last. Still, he stood like a rock. "Marcus!" she cried, flinging herself against him. "Please, Marcus, for God's sake, hold me!"

His arms came around her at last. She felt his whisper against her cheek. "Christina, I cannot simply hold you. If I hold you, something else will follow."

"That's . . . what I want," she admitted, her voice muffled against his chest. With her head lowered she tugged at the buttons of her gown; then she shimmied the material from her shoulders and forced it to fall to the ground. Naked, she stepped into his arms, slipping her hands beneath the V of his robe, running the tip of her tongue over his chest. She felt the fierce pounding of his heart, the sharp intake of his breath.

His fingers tore into her hair, tilting her head back. *"Cara,"* he said bitterly, "are you aware that we might already have to face the consequences of our actions?"

"Yes," Chris whispered painfully.

"If so," he warned her heatedly, "you will not leave me. This is Italy, not the States. You will not take my child."

She couldn't tell him that she never wanted to leave him, that her greatest fear next to death was accepting the fact that he might not want her anymore.

"No," she said simply.

"It rests with you, *amore mio*," he told her.

"Yes."

At last he clasped her body to his. She felt the hardness of his desire, the force of his arms and his hips. She shuddered, sinking in sweetness to be held by him, to feel his power and need as he swept her into his arms.

And when he carried her to the bed he made love to her with a shattering ferocity, making her forget everything.

She wasn't afraid. Not at all. Not when he held her.

Chapter Twelve

Chris woke very slowly...puzzled. She had been dreaming, but not really dreaming.

It had been more like remembering, and the Chris she kept seeing was not an adult, but a child.

A child, running along the subterranean tunnels of the catacombs, clutching something in her hand—terrified that she might be caught with it. It was something pretty she had seen, something she had taken. And if anyone found out that she had taken it, her father would be angry. Furious. Everyone would be furious. And she kept running, because she was certain that someone was after her.

The dream—or the memory—faded. Chris blinked, then realized that her eyes had been open; the image had been so strong that it had been as clear as day in her mind.

She rolled over quickly to wake Marcus and tell him about the memory or dream, or whatever it had been. Maybe it would make sense to him.

But Marcus wasn't there. Her heart quickened a little as she remembered the night and her total surrender. But then, hadn't it been his surrender, too? Hadn't she had at least proved to herself that he could no more deny her than she could him? But what of the words she had whispered in desperation? What had he really been asking of her and what had she promised? What did he really want from her . . . ?

Her musings came to an abrupt end as she idly ran her fingers over the indigo silk where his body had been and came upon a sheet of notepaper with the di Medici crest at the top. It was brief and quite to the point.

Christina,

Had to go to the galleries. Closed for the day—police order—but had to give them names and addresses.

Don't leave the room. *Don't.* Teresa has been told to bring you coffee at eleven; lock the door after her. *Don't leave the room, capisce?* Unless you wish to learn all about temperamental and brutal Italians.

Marcus

Chris stared at the note resentfully. She was surprised he hadn't signed it Conte di Medici . . . or Marcus Rex.

She sighed, chewed nervously at her lower lip, then decided that he was right. She was safer behind locked doors.

But, she realized shortly, being safe was not quite the same as feeling sane. She showered and dressed, then nervously started pacing the room. Something was going to happen; she could feel it in the air. Or maybe that was just her imagination. Maybe she was certain that something was going to happen because the police were involved now. Knowing that the police were involved gave her a feeling of relief; it also allowed her mind to wander to her personal position.

Apparently Marcus no longer intended her to leave today. What did he intend? She started gnawing at a fingernail. She knew that he cared about her, but caring wasn't love. And to live with a di Medici, one would have to be loved by him. She couldn't endure to stay, wondering what he felt, certain that he sought out other women. He had married her to protect her; being Italian, or perhaps just being male, he was possessive. He wasn't about to let her leave with anything that was his, especially a child.

Chris picked up a pillow and slammed it across the room. She'd been so stupid! She should have thought of all this before ever becoming involved with him....

But really, it had all been so sudden....

And she didn't know if she had anything to worry about or not. It would take time to find out. But what should she do in the meantime? Keep going...like last night? Then she'd definitely have something to worry about.

She reminded herself that none of this would matter much until the mystery at the palazzo had been solved. Thank God her mother was safely playing ranch wife out in the American West. She'd be crazy if she knew that her daughter had married a di Medici—and fallen in love with him.

There was a tap at the door. Chris glanced at her watch. It was exactly eleven o'clock. Teresa called out that she had a tray; Chris opened the door, accepted the tray with a "*grazie,*" and locked the door once again. She took the tray to the bed and leaned against a pillow to gulp down her first cup of coffee, then slowly sip a second while inspecting the bowl of minestrone and the crescent sandwich she had been brought. Last night she had felt too sick to eat. This morning she was starving. She was also tense and bored. Eating proved to be a wonderful diversion.

But when she had eaten everything and finished the last of the coffee, she lay back, trying to analyze her dreams and memories about the catacombs. She really had remembered something. Something that she had apparently stolen as a child. Something pretty and fascinating. But what?

Hours passed. Chris worried about Marcus, about the police. About her personal commitment. Or had she made one? She didn't understand. She didn't understand him, or what he wanted, at all. He had been so angry after they had met Georgianne and Tomas, but she had been certain that he liked the couple.

She started as the phone began ringing. She almost answered it—but then remembered that yesterday Genovese had probably been murdered because she had answered a phone and agreed to meet him to pay for his information.

Finally it stopped.

Chris breathed a sigh of relief and went back to trying to untangle her dreams and the past again.

There was a tap at her door. Her stomach knotted. She didn't answer the door, and she didn't call out.

"Christina!"

It was Sophia, calling to her in annoyance. "Christina! Will you get the phone, please? It is Marcus."

"Oh!" she cried out, picking up the phone. but the line was dead; she had hesitated too long. She tried to get the galleries back, but the line was busy.

Cursing herself, Chris ran to her door and opened it. Sophia was halfway down the staircase.

"Sophia, excuse me. Marcus wasn't there anymore. Did he say what he wanted?"

"Yes," Sophia replied impatiently. "He wanted you to go to the galleries. To talk to the police or something, I believe." She shook her head uneasily. "Poor Genovese . . . all the years that he was with us . . ."

"Yes, poor Genovese," Chris murmured. Apparently Marcus had chosen not to tell the rest of the household what was going on. It appeared that Sophia considered Genovese the victim of a madman. "Sophia, I'm going to go to the galleries. If Marcus should call back, tell him I'm on my way."

Sophia nodded and started down the stairs again. She paused, looking back. "You'd better take a key. If they're up in the offices, they won't hear you."

"Oh," Chris murmured. "I don't have one."

Sophia waved a hand in the air. "I'll find Gina and get hers for you."

Chris thanked her and hurried into her room to find her purse. Sophia was in the entryway when she got downstairs, ready to hand Chris a set of keys. "You will need both. The top turns off the security, and the bottom removes the bolt, yes?"

"I understand. Thank you. By the way," Chris said, "where's Tony?"

"At the galleries with Marcus, I believe."

"Thanks again," Chris murmured. "And please, don't forget. If Marcus calls tell him I'm on my way."

Chris left the palazzo by way of the rear courtyard. She felt a little uneasy and didn't understand why. The sun was shining with a frenzy. The water in the canals danced with its brilliance. People were walking along, smiling, laughing, hurrying. But then, Genovese had been killed in bright daylight. And, she thought a little uneasily, the daylight wasn't going to last much longer. In another thirty minutes the sun would start to set. In another hour it would be dark.

She reached the square and looked up at the galleries. Black crepe still draped the columns. Up on the roof, the gargoyles seemed to stare back at her.

Chris ignored them and hurried up the steps to the doors. She banged on them for a minute, but got no response. Sophia, she decided wryly, had done her a favor by reminding her about the keys. Chris fooled with the alarm key first, hoping that she wouldn't set the sirens shrilling. She frowned as she played with the key to the dead bolt, wondering why something about Sophia's words had bothered her. She shrugged, unable to think of what it was that eluded her. Probably nothing important.

Chris allowed the doors to close behind her. Inside, away from the sunlight, it was already dark. Dark, and pleasantly cool. The galleries were air-conditioned, of course, but the marble and tiles were also cool, and it was a relief from the warmth outside.

"Marcus!" Chris called. Her voice echoed in the cavernous courtyard. Grimacing, she decided that she wouldn't call out again; she would just find him.

Where? she wondered with exasperation. She didn't know where his office was. She should probably have waited for him to call her back.

Chris started for the stairway to the second-level balcony. She was fairly certain there were no offices on the first floor; everything there was decorative, or set up for the convenience of the tourists and buyers.

She thought she heard something coming from the robotronics room. She started to call out, then remembered how her voice had echoed.

Chris hurried up the rest of the stairs, uneasily noting that it was growing darker and darker. She was anxious to get to Marcus and the police.

She burst into the historical room with his name on her lips. "Marcus?"

He wasn't there. No one was there. The figures all stared at her, frowning, smiling, their arms lifted in silent welcome, their faces macabre in the growing shadows of night. It almost seemed that their grins were evil.

They were just robotronics, Chris reminded herself. Material objects, run by computers manned by men. She started to turn around; it was obvious that Marcus wasn't there. But something caught her eye; a movement. Chris felt a rising terror as she turned back to the figures. Something was moving. One of the figures wasn't an inanimate object at all. It was a person, draped in a dark hooded cloak, a person who sliced the air with a touch of chilling laughter and jumped from the stage to the ground. Something glittered in the pale light that remained to fight the shadows of night. Something long and wickedly sharp. The blade of a razor-edged knife, raised high in the cloaked figure's hand.

"Christina."

She heard her name whispered; again the throaty laughter followed. It was too late to realize that she'd been an idiot.

She spun around to run.

Marcus waited impatiently, drumming his fingers on the front desk at the *stazione polizia*. How long had the damn phone been ringing at the palazzo? Five times, ten times? He kept waiting, trying to still a growing alarm. Where was everyone?

At last, at long last, there was an answer. *"Pronto."*

Madre?" Marcus queried.

"Si, si," Gina murmured.

"What took you so long to answer the phone? Where is everyone?"

"I don't know. I was out, Marcus. This is Tuesday, my day at church. And since Genovese will have his . . . service there, I wished to put in more time. Where are you?"

"I'm still at the police station. It's taking much longer than I thought it would." He hesitated for a moment. "Listen, Mama, I know this will hurt you, but they think that Genovese's death—and even Alfred's—stem from the time of Papa's death. You're going to have to answer some questions down here, too."

"What?" Gina inquired with a little gasp.

"I can't explain it all now. I will soon, I promise. I need you to do something for me, please. I can't understand why Christina did not answer the extension in the bedroom. Will you go and tell her I'm on the line?"

"Un momento."

Marcus waited impatiently again. It seemed that he sat at the desk forever, and the longer he waited, the greater his unease. At last he heard the line being picked up, and he started to breathe a sigh of relief. But then he heard his mother's voice again, and it felt as if a blaze of tension and fear raged down the length of his spine and beyond.

"Marcus, she isn't there. I can't find her."

"What?"

"I'm sorry, Marcus. I can't find her anywhere. Perhaps she decided to go shopping. Marcus, really, I did not approve of your marriage, but of course it was not my business. But you cannot treat a wife like a prisoner—"

"*Madre!* I've no wish to make her a prisoner, I wish to keep her alive! I've got to go. I've got to find her. If you do see her, *stay with her*!"

He dropped the phone, not even hanging it up properly. He was shouting to the police and to Tony, and rushing out the door. Suddenly, clearly, he knew who had murdered his father, driven Alfred to his death and slit Genovese's throat. The answer had been there all along. He simply hadn't seen it.

Dear God in heaven, if only he wasn't too late.

Chris burst from the historical room and raced along the balcony. She knew that she needed to reach the square and people. But when she reached the top of the stairway, she looked down to see Fredo Talio entering the double doors, dapper as a hit man in a pin-striped suit. He looked up at her; she saw his sallow features, his dark and somber eyes.

Fear washed through her heart in fresh waves. Fredo Talio... he was in league with the cloaked figure.

"Contessa di Medici..." he said, looking at her.

Chris screamed and tore away from the stairs.

"Christina, Christina..."

He kept calling to her, but she hardly heard him because she was facing the figure with the cloak. Her only escape would be through the trapdoor in the gem salon.

She flew for the door to the salon and ripped it open. The cloaked figure was right behind her. Chris raced for the case containing the di Medici jewels, followed by laughter. She chanced a glance back. The figure was by the door, a gloved hand on a rusted lever near the floor. Chris frowned, then gasped. The floor gave way beneath her—and she wasn't at the trapdoor.

Not the trapdoor she knew of, at any rate. Yet even as the floor gave way, she remembered that Marcus had mentioned another trapdoor, another chute....

Her body was plummeting downward, sliding, falling along a dark passageway. She slammed against the ground and was met by a fierce cold—and a musty scent of salt and decay. Desperately she tried to get her bearings in the darkness. She had to be in the catacombs. Somewhere in the subterranean tunnels.

Chris rolled, reaching up carefully to assure herself that she wouldn't crack her head against an arch. The cold here was startling, the stench of decay almost nauseating. Where was she? She had to find out; the catacombs could be like a maze, like a trap from which there was no escape....

She stuck her hand out, bracing herself to find a tomb or an effigy. She touched a ledge. Marble, and very, very cold. She tried to rise to follow the ledge.

She was startled by a fierce thud from behind her, from where she had lain just a second ago. And then every nerve within her seemed to scream in silent agonized panic as she heard the laughter again. Soft throaty laughter. A light blazed in her face; she threw her hands up to her eyes, but she was blinded. Instinctively she backed away from the light. She bumped into another ledge; she reached behind her to steady herself, and she touched something dry and brittle and wispy. She glanced down—and started to scream.

It was a centuries-old corpse. The hair remained about the skeletal head; the toothless jaw of the skull seemed to mock her scream. The bones were dressed in decaying silk.

For aeons it seemed that she screamed; only the sound of that cruel laughter brought her horror to a halt. She was desperate to survive; some inner sense told her that the skeleton belonged to the world of the dead. The skeleton could not hurt her.

The danger to her life came from the living figure who wielded the flashlight.

Chris vaulted over the marble ledge that held the corpse. The cavern was filled with ledges, and bejeweled and bedecked skeletons. She had to use them, to stay behind them, until she could discover the way out....

Poised to spring, Chris stared at the hooded figure, which was rising now. The figure, too, had taken the secret way down, knowing full well where it would lead.

Chris narrowed her eyes, trying to see beyond the blinding light. But it seemed that the game of disguise was over. As Chris watched warily, ready to vault again at a second's notice, the figure pulled back the hood and allowed the cloak to drop to the floor.

"Sophia!" Chris said. She should have known. The *key*. It was Tuesday. Tuesday—when Gina di Medici was *always* out.

"*Si*, *bella* Christi. Sophia," she said nonchalantly. She laughed again. "You are stunned, yes? But then, you were so anxious to blame poor Gina. Poor, long-suffering Gina! Twenty-one years ago I did her a favor... and she never had the sense to appreciate it."

"I don't understand," Chris said slowly. She didn't understand, and at the moment she wasn't sure that she cared. But she had to play for time. Time to find a way out. As terrified as she was in the dank and macabre tomb, she still refused to believe that this could be the end. Perhaps no one believed that they could die... until the moment came.

She had to believe! She had to believe and fight. Marcus! He would come home; he would find her gone. He would search for her—relentlessly—until he found her. Dear God! He had to. He had to search for her. She loved him; he had to love her....

Sophia shrugged pleasantly, as if they had met at a sidewalk café. "Perhaps I'm doing you a favor, too. Life, *cara*, is not sweet with the di Medici men. I warned you about that. But you are a little fool, hopelessly in love with Marcus. He's so much like Mario. And you see, I knew Mario very well."

"You...knew Mario...very well?" Chris breathed.

"Yes, but of course," Sophia murmured. "They all thought it was over the stupid statuette! We were on the ketch that day because they were trying to decide what to do about its disappearance, but the arguments . . . they had nothing to do with it." She smiled like a friend, like one woman expecting understanding from another. "You know how Marcus is . . . the attraction. I had been with Alfred for several years, but then, by chance, Mario and I were thrown together at the strangest times."

"You had an affair with him," Chris said.

"Yes. An affair. Wild and chaotic and as passionate as heaven! But Mario was in love with his little mouse of a wife. And I liked my life with Alfred. I never had money . . . I cherished his." She paused. "Mario wanted to tell them both about the affair. Gina would have forgiven him. Alfred would have thrown me out. Your father and Mario did get into a fight that day, over the statuette. I was on deck when it happened. They struck each other several times, then made up like little boys. When James went back into the cabin I determined to talk to Mario again." Sophia smiled again, very nicely. "You were out on deck . . . you don't remember?"

Chris shook her head. She didn't remember any of it; she couldn't believe that she had been there and had erased it all from her mind. She also wanted Sophia to keep talking.

Sophia sighed. "I thought that you had seen it all, that someday you would remember. I believe James thought you knew something too, something dangerous. That is why he left Venice."

"I don't remember anything," Chris whispered, moistening her dry lips. "What happened?"

Sophia leaned against one of the ledges, heedless of the corpse lying on it. The flashlight hung easily from one hand, her knife from the other.

"Ah, yes! You should get to die at peace, shouldn't you? All mysteries solved here, among a host of di Medici brides. Very dramatic, don't you think? I'm getting ahead of myself. I tried to reason with Mario, but he was set upon confession. We began to struggle. Alfred came out then. Poor Alfred! He thought that Mario was trying to hurt me. He came into it and pulled Mario from me, throwing him against the mast. He just struck it . . . wrong. His neck was broken, you see."

Sophia ran a hand along the marble slab of an open tomb, pausing. "Poor, poor Alfred! Such a good man. He was horrified. I had to convince him that he might lose his life for murder if he did not toss Mario overboard."

Chris tried to speak as conversationally as Sophia while hiding her desperation as she looked for a way out. She could see nothing, just stone walls, shadows and corpses covered with spiderwebs and decay. But there had to be a way out! Sophia had taken it on another night, the night Chris and Marcus had found the cloak in the tunnels. . . .

"What about Genovese?" Chris asked. "Did he . . . see what happened?"

"Yes, yes he did. And he did quite well for a number of years because of it. But then he became too greedy. When it seemed that you would have money, he was willing to sell the truth."

"But why did you kill Alfred?" Chris demanded.

"Alfred no longer wished to pay. He wanted to confess the whole thing. He spent his lifetime worrying about your father and you. Then you reappeared, and he was an old fool. I knew he was meeting you to tell you the truth. I couldn't let him do that. But . . . I did not have to kill Alfred. He very conveniently dropped dead for me."

Chris began to breathe very quickly. She had seen something. A crack in the wall, an uneven place where it appeared that the stone might move. If she could keep Sophia talking just a minute longer...

"You know the palazzo very well," she murmured.

"Yes. When I started working for Mario di Medici—Conte di Medici!—I was very young, and very beautiful. I had dreams.... I loved the palazzo. I dreamed of being a di Medici bride, you see. I hated Mario for being a fool. He denied me everything. But he died... and I remained in his palazzo. I learned it all. The history, the architecture. But, Christina, you became the di Medici bride. You are the one with the right to remain here forever and ever."

"Sophia..."

"I'm sorry, Christina. Your time has run out. It has been drifting away since you came. You see, I was always terrified that you would remember. You should have left it alone."

She started walking toward Chris, very smoothly, as if she knew every slab and every skeleton so well that she didn't even need to look around. Chris leaped over another slab, putting distance between them. She was younger, she reminded herself. Far more agile. She had a chance. Perhaps she was even the stronger of the two of them.

But Sophia had the knife.

"Fredo! Fredo Talio!" Chris exclaimed, causing Sophia to halt. "He was downstairs at the galleries. Is he in this with you?"

Sophia frowned. "No, of course not. He was at the galleries?"

"Yes, yes he was. He saw both of us. He heard me screaming."

"So?" Sophia queried, quite pleased with herself. "He will have seen you... and a mysterious figure in a cloak. Nothing more."

"Sophia! How long do you think you can keep this up? Death after death . . . you will be caught."

"No, *cara* Christi, there is no proof. Genovese is gone. Alfred is gone. And you . . . you will stay. Here with those lucky wives who came before you!"

Was Sophia insane, or just deadly? Chris didn't know, nor did it matter. Chris knew that she would have to pass Sophia to reach the break in the wall. But Sophia was coming toward her again. Chris instinctively set her hands upon a slab, ready to move, seeking a weapon, any weapon, to use against the other woman. Her fingers grasped bone and rotting silk; she couldn't even let herself think about what she was doing. She threw her skeletal club at Sophia, catching the older woman off guard. As Sophia gasped and stumbled back, stunned, the flashlight fell to the floor; shadows careened and danced. Chris leaped over the slab and raced for the break in the wall, her only hope.

She could barely see the wall. The dank mustiness of the ages clung to her like a shroud. She passed slab after slab of granite and marble, veering from the blank grins of skeletons, half sobbing, half listening for the woman who would surely pursue her again.

Then the shadowed wall before her seemed to move. It *did* move. It was as if the skeletons had come to life, as if a host of di Medicis had risen to embrace and restrain her.

They were reaching for her; shadows were reaching for her. She started to scream.

"Christina!"

The arms that wound around her were living and real, not just bone, but flesh and blood and muscle and warmth. The di Medici who held her was not a remnant of a forgotten past, but vital and strong and secure.

"Marcus!"

"Are you all right?"

"Yes."

"Tony, take Chris . . ."

"Chris, come on." A second set of arms swept around her. She saw Tony's smile, reassuring against the shadows and darkness and death. But Marcus was gone.

"Tony, wait. Sophia is there. She's got a knife."

"Marcus will be all right," Tony assured her. "The police are right behind us."

They were; the wall was moving again. Several men—alive and well and purposeful—were moving in. Lights were flooding the tomb. Chris shivered, not so much frightened as she was sad, touched by all those bygone lives, frayed silks, rotted furs, the mockery of elegance.

"I don't see Marcus!" she said with sudden alarm.

"There must be another exit," Tony muttered. "Come on, I'm supposed to get you out."

"Marcus—"

"Will be careful. He's a grown man."

"She killed Genovese."

"Marcus will be wary. Chris, come on."

She couldn't fight him; he had a lot of his brother's tenacity. And she did want very, very badly to leave the subterranean caverns of darkness and death behind.

There was another exit; Marcus knew there had to be when he could find no trace of Sophia. There was a marble slab on the floor, slightly askew, and as he moved it, he marveled at the woman's strength. It was heavy, but once it was shifted he saw a flight of slippery well-worn steps leading downward.

They led to a narrow walkway, one beneath the water level, but where the walkway ended another flight of steps began, leading upward. They, too, were well-worn. In days of political upheaval they would have been a wonderful escape route.

Just as they were now. Dank and slimy and worn smooth, they still provided an escape.

When he reached the top he was on a small via facing a bridge.

On the bridge he saw her, her hooded cloak on again. She stared back and saw him, then started to run.

Marcus started over the bridge. She rounded an alley. For a moment he lost her, and then he saw her again, on the next bridge. "Sophia!"

He heard a shrill whistle; the police were behind him now. Sophia heard the whistle, too, and saw that men were coming from either end of the bridge. She hopped up to the wide carved stone railing and jumped.

Marcus hurried to the bridge and vaulted over. The water was cool as his body sliced through it, as he kicked his way cleanly to the surface. There was no sign of her. He dived again. It was dark, very dark. The lights of the city glittered on the surface, but did not come into the canal.

He jackknifed his way downward again, reaching out. His hand found fabric, and he tugged at it. He managed to grasp her chin, to raise them both to the surface. He hauled her to the nearest dock; an officer was there to pull her out, to help him.

She lay there, swaddled in her cloak. Marcus, panting and gasping, dragged himself over to her. Her eyes opened, and she smiled. He saw that she still had her knife, and he wondered why she hadn't used it on him.

She reached out to touch his chin. "Never you, Marcus. Never you," she said gently in Italian. "You are . . . his son."

She smiled again, a little weakly. Her hand fell to her side. She shuddered a little, and then her eyes closed. Stunned, Marcus tugged the cloak away, certain that she couldn't have drowned.

He paused, lifting his hand away. A crimson splotch was running quickly over her side. Sticky. She had either taken her own life with her knife as a final escape, or else she had inadvertently stabbed herself when she hit the water. He would never know.

He rose, dripping wet, weighted down with the sorrow and anger of it all. So many people whom he had loved so dearly had been broken and destroyed because of warped passions he wasn't sure he would ever understand. His father, dead. James Tarleton's life ruined in a haze of suspicion. Alfred . . . Genovese . . . and Sophia.

But his mother was innocent. And Christina was alive. He shook himself furiously. He would never allow the past to darken the present again.

The officer began to speak to him, telling him that it would all have to be sorted out for the official reports. Marcus already knew that, but tonight he wanted to go home and try to salvage the present.

He needed to hold Christina, to cherish her—and convince her that they could start anew, with all skeletons cleared from the closet, the specters of their youth laid to rest.

Gina di Medici, appearing very lost, stunned—and anxious with worry about Marcus—was still trying to understand the whole story.

But she wasn't alone. Chris met Umberto that night. He was a middle-aged banker, quiet, reassuring, supportive and as confused as Gina.

They were gathered at the courtyard table, as they had so often been before.

Neither Tony nor Chris was helping much. They both broke into explanations at different times.

"You see, Gina," Chris tried again, taking a huge sip of espresso laced with sambuca, "I knew my father couldn't have murdered Mario. He was too gentle and honest."

"And your father," Tony reminded her. He grimaced at his mother. "So she suspected us."

"Oh!" Gina cried out, hurt and incredulous as her eyes found Chris. "You thought that I would have killed my own husband!"

Chris wanted to crawl beneath the table. "Not really," she lied. "I—I didn't know who to suspect . . . or who to trust."

Gina looked blankly at Tony. "I still don't understand. Why would Sophia have done this? She and Mario were friends, and Alfred and Mario were the best of friends."

"It was really an accident," Chris said. "A fight that got out of hand." She wasn't going to tell Gina now that the husband she had adored had been having an affair. Not when Mario had been so determined to straighten things out with his wife that he had lost his life because of it.

Gina shook her head. She held tightly to Umberto's hand. "For twenty-one years I lived with the people who had killed Mario. They stayed in his house.... They were my family. Christina, I did you a great wrong. And I did a greater wrong to your father and your mother."

"You couldn't have known, Gina," Chris said.

"Of course not," Tony assured his mother, rumpling Chris's hair. "Only a daughter could be so completely guided by blind faith."

"Daughters, wives, brothers . . . and lovers."

The assertion came from the rear of the courtyard. They all started, turning around. Marcus was standing there, his hair wet and as dark as jet, plastered against his forehead. Little pools of water were forming at his feet; his face appeared strained and weary.

"Marcus!" Chris knew that her glad cry was repeated around the table. She didn't think; she jumped up, knocking over her chair to run into his arms. He was soaked through and through, but she didn't care; she barely noticed. All she needed or wanted was the way that he held her in return, his hand slipping about her waist, his kiss touching the top of her head, his chin nuzzling a little absently over her forehead.

Tony was on his feet behind Chris.

"Sophia . . . ?" he asked his brother.

"Is dead," Marcus said briefly. He squeezed Chris's hand, then walked past her to kneel by his mother and take her hand. "Are you all right?" he asked her quietly.

She smiled at him. "Now that I see you, yes. I'm not sure that I understand completely, nor that I want to. It hurts to have it all come to the surface again, but not so badly. I am sorry for them all. Get off your knees. It is a humble position, one in which I am not accustomed to finding you. You need dry clothing."

Marcus grimaced and rose. Umberto handed him a drink, which Marcus accepted gratefully.

"I have a bit of a surprise for you all," Gina murmured, smiling at Marcus, then at Umberto. "Perhaps this is not the night for such news, but since we are all making confessions...Umberto and I are going to be married."

"What?" Tony gasped, then laughed. *"Mamma mia! Salute!"*

Umberto was flushing. "You are pleased?" he asked Gina's sons.

"Enormously," Marcus informed him, grinning broadly at last as he gave the older man a handshake. He kissed his mother, then Tony kissed her, too. Chris hung back a little awkwardly. Gina noticed her over Tony's shoulder, smiled and stretched out her arms.

"*Figlia mia*, come here!" she commanded. Chris stepped forward, and Gina rose, giving her a warm hug. "You are my daughter now, yes? With no bitterness of suspicion between us."

Chris hugged her and wished her congratulations, but could say nothing else. Gina drew back suspiciously. She gazed from Marcus to Chris. "This marriage between you, it was real, yes?"

Chris couldn't see Marcus; she knew only that he was behind her. And he wasn't answering.

Neither could Chris.

Tony stepped in cheerfully to save them both for the moment. "Of course, Mama. Has Marcus ever done anything by half measures?"

"No, that's true," Gina admitted. She began bustling about the table, collecting the glasses. "Then we must have another drink—to a new future!"

"To the future!" Tony declared. The drinks were passed around. Chris downed hers quickly, wincing at the strong taste of the sambuca.

Marcus set his glass down with a little click against the table. "If you will excuse me, I am soaked. Mama, I couldn't be happier. Christina . . ." He reached out a hand to her. She took it. He glanced at his brother. "In the morning . . ."

"Yes," Tony agreed. "In the morning."

His mother was frowning in confusion. "We see the police and really end it all," Tony told her. He shook off his seriousness and grinned at Marcus and Chris. "*Buona notte.*"

Chris found that she was shivering again as Marcus led the way silently, pulling her along with distance-eating footsteps. The night had been a violent one, weakening, shattering.

But it wasn't going to end. It was showdown time on a different level. She could feel it in the heat and power of his grasp on her hand.

He closed and locked the door behind him when they reached his room. Chris stepped ahead of him and stood silently, waiting, staring out the French doors into the star-speckled night.

She heard him behind her, stripping off his sodden clothing. "You're a mess," he told her. "Spiderwebs and all."

She didn't respond; she walked a little closer to the window. "What happened, Marcus?"

"I don't care to discuss what happened," he said, but he wasn't curt. "Tomorrow there will be time to talk again. Come here, Christina."

She started. His wet jacket, shirt, shoes and socks were on the floor in a heap. He was standing in his damp pants only; his bare chest was glistening copper. She had never seen his eyes appear so deeply blue, so penetrating. His hands were on his hips. She knew again that there would be no way out; tonight all things between them would be said.

She was terribly nervous, but she walked over to face him. He smiled, brushing at her hair. "I'm wet, but you're filthy."

He started undoing the buttons of her blouse. She felt herself tremble beneath his touch.

"What are you doing?" she asked, ignoring the obvious in her state of agitation.

"Taking your clothes off, so we can take a shower."

"We . . ." she murmured.

"Yes, we. You and I. The two of us," he said with an amused grin.

He kept at it, sliding the blouse from her shoulders. Chris reached out and touched his cheek, drawing his eyes to hers. "Marcus . . . ?"

He sighed, catching her hand and holding it between his own. "I had wanted to seduce you again before getting to this . . ." he whispered. He dropped her hand, and pulled her against him, crushing her into his embrace. His left arm was around her; his right hand coursed over her chin and her throat. "I am in love with you, Christina," he told her, almost harshly. "I tricked you, seduced you, kidnapped you . . . because I thought I had to. Chris, I can't ever tell her, but until today I couldn't, in my heart, clear my own mother. I am very aware that you are an American. I am aware of your work, and I know that I cannot take that away from you."

Chris smiled, incredulous, awed, beautifully delightfully dizzy. "Tell me again, please," she whispered.

"I understand about your work, but—"

"No, no, no. Say I love you. In English and in Italian. And in any other way you know how."

He pulled her closer, whispering against her ear. "I love you. *Ti voglio bene. Je t'aime. Ti amo.* I love you, *Te quiero.*"

She caught his face between her palms and pressed her lips to his hungrily, adoringly, savoring the warmth, the heated dampness, the surging strength of his desire.

He broke away. "You have to listen to me, Christina."

"Yes," she murmured, her topaz eyes huge. She would listen to him, but nothing that he could say could matter much at this moment. The stars had invaded the room; nothing could mar this moment, because he loved her.

Loved her. Loved . . . her.

"I could not tolerate your being gone," he was saying. "I am trying very hard. . . . I had thought that if you wished to keep your position we could move to Paris, for the time at least. We need to be away from the palazzo. I cannot give it up, though. It is my heritage. Still, we are opening galleries in the States, and perhaps we will both discover that is where we will wish to live. Christina, it will not always be easy. But I can swear that I respect—and adore—you for all that you do. You will maintain your profession. We will—"

"Compromise?" she supplied breathlessly.

"Yes."

"Yes, oh yes!" she cried, flinging herself against him again, half laughing, half sobbing. "Oh, Marcus! I didn't come here with the intention of trapping a di Medici husband, truly I didn't. But I've got one now, and Marcus, I'd fight heaven or hell to keep him."

"Tell me that you love me," he commanded her.

"I love you."

"In Italian . . . and any other way you know."

"Ti voglio bene . . . mio marito," Chris whispered. *"Je t'aime, je t'adore. . . ."*

She caught at his belt buckle, and shuddered at the heated ripple of his muscles in response. "I'll tell you in 'mime,'" she promised him, "in the very best language of all. I'm very, very good with my hands. . . ."

"The best . . ." he agreed.

Moments later they had stripped one another, and moments after that they were in the shower. Water, hot and delicious, skimmed over their naked bodies, and they joined again and again, expert lovers, yet tonight given something new, something very precious. Spoken love, given, received, tenderly cherished.

Shadows receded; brilliance touched their lives.

Beneath a cascade of tumbling water he took her into his arms. His kiss deepened, heated and wet. Her body slid along his, her kisses savoring his flesh, finding him, taking him, loving him, until he pulled her from the shower, forgetting all about towels, and laid her on the bed, tender and fierce, fevered, demanding and delighting. He ravaged her length with his palms, with the taunting dampness of his tongue. His intimate kisses sent her soaring to the stars, which seemed in easy reach, showering them with ecstasy. When he entered her, she embraced him, adoring his body with her own, shuddering with the force of his passion.

And she knew that nothing in life would ever be so sweet as loving him, and being loved by him.

It was late when they slept that night, having shared all the details of the past—and their dreams for the future. Very late, almost dawn. And some mechanism in Chris's mind warned her that she shouldn't be dreaming; it was all over.

But she *was* dreaming. Dreaming about the catacombs. There was something in her hand, and she was running because she had to hide the treasure she carried. Someone meant to take it from her; she would be severely punished if they knew she had it.

There was an angel near the wall, an elaborate angel that overlooked a carved marble tomb. Behind the angel was a little niche where a treasure could be secreted.

In her dream Chris saw the child reaching up and slipping her treasure into the little niche.... She could hear a voice, a woman's voice. Irate. Calling her...

She awoke with a start, bolting up in bed.

Beside her Marcus was instantly alert. *"Cara..."* His arms came around her, and she was deeply touched, because she knew that he thought she was frightened, that she could not forget the night among the dead.

Chris turned to him excitedly. "Marcus! The statuette! I know where it is. It's down in the catacombs behind an angel. Oh, Marcus! I'm certain of it!"

He frowned, and she knew then that he was worrying about her mind.

"Christina..."

"Please, Marcus! Please, I have to see if it's there!"

He sighed and threw his legs over the side of the bed. "All right, we'll go."

Chris threw herself joyfully after him, hugging him fiercely in her excitement, giving him a quick wet kiss.

"Mind putting on a robe?" he suggested dryly.

"Marcus!" she retorted, but her enthusiasm was too great to be contained. She hurriedly slipped into her gown and robe, and was at the door while he was still tying his belt. She started down the stairs.

"Wait, I'll get Tony and a flashlight," he called.

Chris impatiently tapped her toes against the floor. Marcus reemerged on the landing with Tony and two huge flashlights.

Tony was rubbing his eyes. He smiled at Chris. "Are you going to make a habit of such emergencies?" he asked her.

"No!" She laughed. "Just tonight. Please, come on!"

She led the way; the catacombs held no more fear for her. They trailed behind, continually warning her to wait. Chris couldn't. She burst through the gates and wound her way heedlessly through the tombs.

The angel was right beneath the trapdoor. Chris winced a little as she stuck her hand into the niche; she didn't know what else might be there. But her fingers met marble, beautiful pink-streaked marble. She lifted out the statuette.

It was labeled at the base in Italian, but she knew the words. "Daylight—tomb relief for Dante di Medici."

Chris handed the statuette to Marcus. He looked at it, then he looked at Tony.

"They were right," Tony murmured, fingering the marble.

"Yes," Marcus agreed.

"About what?" Chris demanded.

Marcus shrugged. "I believe it was very definitely done by Michelangelo. He had a style that could not be copied, not even by his students. We will find out."

"What does it mean?" Chris asked anxiously.

Tony laughed. "It means that if we weren't all filthy rich already, we'd be filthy rich all over again." He sobered, touching her hair, smiling. "It means, Chris, that a really marvelous piece of art will be given back to the people."

Chris gazed at Marcus. He smiled, too, slipping an arm around her. "It will go on display, Chris. We will probably give it to the government. Which means, of course, that we won't be 'filthy rich' all over again, but then, we don't really need to be, you know. What do you say?"

"I say that I'd like to give it to the government," she told him. "I . . . couldn't really remember, not until tonight. But, Marcus, I didn't steal it. Not at first. I saw it . . . in Sophia's room. I went in to touch it, and she came back. I hid with it, and then, of course, when she knew it was missing, I couldn't put it back. Everyone was so furious . . ."

"That you ran," Marcus finished matter-of-factly. "Chris, the statuette did not cause what happened. Sophia, Alfred—even my father—caused their own problems."

"I know," she told him.

She looked around them, then pulled her robe closer about her. "I think I'm ready to leave the tombs for a long, long time," she told them.

Marcus and Tony exchanged wry glances. They started back down the tunnel.

"Marcus?" Chris asked.

"Yes?"

"If I'm really going to be the Contessa di Medici, do you think I might do a few things with this place?"

"Oh, no! She's going to start changing furniture!" Tony moaned good-naturedly.

"Such as?" Marcus asked.

"Tony, take a pill," Chris remonstrated before replying to Marcus. "I'd really like to give those relatives of yours in the other section a *decent* burial. Like seal them all in, you know?"

Marcus and Tony both started laughing.

"I think we could manage that," Marcus promised her. They reached the stairway leading to the ground floor. He turned around to kiss her.

Tony turned to say something, then paused, closing his mouth with a shrug. He continued up the stairs.

They were man and wife, he thought. Had been for a while now. He hoped they had sense enough to go to their room before getting too carried away.

But this was Venice.

And that was love.

Amore.

Epilogue

Ummm . . . she knew exactly where she was.

At the Palazzo di Medici in Venice. Her home. Marcus's home.

Marcus . . .

She opened her eyes slowly.

The first thing she saw was her own hand, lying beside her face on the silk-covered pillow. Her long fingers appeared very delicate there. Her nails, with their polish of soft bronze, seemed fragile against the deep indigo of the sheets.

Indigo . . .

Christina opened her eyes wider. Without twisting her head, she further surveyed the room. Soft Oriental rugs lay pleasingly against a polished cream Venetian tile floor. The walls were papered in a subdued gold that lightened the effect of the deep indigo draperies and mahogany furniture. Across a breezy distance, highlighted by the morning dazzle of the sun streaming through French doors, was a large Queen

Anne dresser, its only ornament a French Provincial clock.

A year had passed since she had first awakened in this room. A year of learning, of laughter, of love. There had been any number of fights. Marcus was a temperamental man, passionate, intense. She hadn't expected every minute to be congenial bliss.

But never once in that time, through laughter, anger or tears, had she doubted his love. Nor his honesty, or his never ending belief in her. They'd spent the year in Paris so that she could teach; he'd accompanied the troupe on their summer tour. In a few days' time they would leave for New York. Marcus would be opening the new gallery; she would be taking a position at a college for the performing arts.

And next summer they would come back to the palazzo. When, she wasn't sure. Chris felt rather strongly that their child should be born on American soil; Marcus was quick to remind her that *she* herself had been born in Venice.

She smiled. She would convince him. And if not, well she *had* been born in Venice....

A shiver suddenly ran along the length of her spine. He was in the room. She knew it. She always knew when he was near. When she opened her eyes once more and turned, she would find him leisurely leaning against the frame of the French doors. But there would be nothing truly leisurely about him. He would be watching, waiting, a little impatient, perhaps. He tended to be the earlier riser.

She knew that he tried to be patient, but he was fond of waking her. Chris smiled. She didn't mind. He had a nice way of doing it. Fingers caressing her back, slowly, sensually. A whisper against her ear. A kiss...

But today...today she had known he would be at the doors. It was an anniversary. Their first. And there was a touch of the romantic about Marcus. He was, after all, a Venetian. And a di Medici.

There was a slight movement in the room. A whisper of sound in the air. He *was* watching her, Christina knew. Watching her, and waiting.

She smiled. *She* could suddenly bear the waiting no longer. He was there, and the force of his presence caused her to open her eyes and turn . . . and meet his smoldering indigo stare.

He was leaning against the doors, as she had suspected, dressed in a caramel velour robe. The V neck of the haphazardly belted garment bared the breadth of his chest with its profusion of crisp dark hair. A gold St. Christopher's medallion seemed to emphasize the masculinity of copper flesh and muscle.

His legs, too, were bare beneath the knee-length hem of the robe. Long sinewy calves, covered seductively with short black hair, gave way to bare feet.

"Buongiorno. Buongiorno, amore mio."

Chris stretched luxuriously and smiled, reaching out her arms to him. *"Buongiorno, mio marito, amore mio."*

He stalked slowly toward the bed. She met the striking sizzle of his eyes and embraced him with a sudden fever.

Over his shoulder she could see the brilliance of the Venetian sun flooding in. She closed her eyes, smiling with contentment. She still wasn't sure if she had married a great lion of justice, or a panther, as dark and intriguing as the night.

But she knew him very well now; she knew he would always be there for her, and that he had *always* been there for her. Willing to do anything for her, face anything for her. Fierce or tender, lion or panther . . .

It didn't really matter; he was, perhaps, a bit of both.

And she loved him for that.

"Happy anniversary, Chris," he told her softly. "I love you."

She laughed delightedly, slipping her arms around his shoulders. *"Salute*, Marcus. *Ti voglio molto bene."*

He caught her hands, laughing in turn. "I like your silent language best. Tell me all about it in mime."

"Ummmm . . ." she murmured, and gladly complied.